4445 0996

W9-AGY-794

Praise for the novels of

NAKED DRAGON

"Blair's first story in her new Works Like Magick series introduces wonderfully magical dragon men. The adjustments the hero must make to fit into this modern world are delightfully handled, and the main characters' interactions with each other and those around them make for a fun and enjoyable escape from reality." —*Romantic Times*

"FIVE STARS! Forget the vampires and demons, give me the dragons! Full of suspense, humor, and romance, this novel is sure to please any paranormal or fantasy fan . . . Annette Blair is one in a billion!" —*Huntress Book Reviews*

"Filled with fun, sex, and romance—with some suspense thrown in for good measure—fans of Blair's previous work will rejoice at seeing her start a new series." —*Romance Junkies*

"With whimsical and delightful supporting characters both magical . . . and non-magical . . . *Naked Dragon* is pure fun . . . Annette Blair has crafted an original and entertaining tale of love and redemption." —*Sacramento Book Review*

NEVER BEEN WITCHED

"A superb tale . . . Whimsical but heart wrenching . . . Magician Annette Blair provides a terrific finish to an entertaining saga." —*Alternative Worlds*

"A perfect ending to a witchy trilogy. Annette Blair's writing is pure magic! Highly recommended!" —*Huntress Book Reviews*

"A wonderful tale of love, understanding, and forgiveness, told with passion and humor. The reader will be captivated from the first page and will find it difficult to put this enchanting story down . . . [*Never Been Witched* includes] a good amount of hilarity and eroticism tossed in as only Ms. Blair can do." —*Fresh Fiction*

WITHDRAWN

BEAVERTON CITY LIBRARY
BEAVERTON, OR 97005
MEMBER OF WASHINGTON COUNTY
COOPERATIVE LIBRARY SERVICES

"The last of Annette Blair's witch trilogy is definitely, in this reviewer's opinion, the greatest . . . There is mayhem and humor . . . in this very sexy and highly entertaining story . . . Wow!"
—*Reader to Reader Reviews*

"A wonderful conclusion to a funny and enjoyable series."
—*Romance Junkies*

"I simply could not put this book down . . . Fast, intense, and suck[s] the reader in with a vengeance . . . The sweet paranormal touches, humorous language, and snappy dialogue are superb . . . This book rocked the house! Grade: A+"
—*Penelope's Romance Reviews*

"I highly recommend this series . . . to anyone who loves magic, humor, and romance mixed together with delightful characters guaranteed to keep you entertained and charmed!"
—*Fallen Angel Reviews*

GONE WITH THE WITCH

"A spellbinding story that totally knocked my socks off!"
—*Huntress Book Reviews*

"Wonderful characters, a riveting story line, and a sensuous undercurrent are just a few of the things that made this such a phenomenal story."
—*Romance Junkies*

"This story tugged at the heart . . . A definite addition to my keeper shelf."
—*Fresh Fiction*

"Annette Blair's second contribution to her triplet trilogy should come with oven mitts as it is hot, hot, hot . . . This is one road trip you do not want to miss!"
—*Reader to Reader Reviews*

SEX AND THE PSYCHIC WITCH

"Sassy, sexy, and sizzling!"
—*Reader to Reader Reviews*

"Ms. Blair's humor and wit is evident in many ways . . . A delight [that] will bring chuckles."
—*Romance Reviews Today*

"A sexy, hilarious, romantic tale with fun characters, snappy writing, and some super-spooky moments." —*Fresh Fiction*

"More hot scenes . . . spine chills . . . outrageous stunts . . . A witchy climax that will warm your very soul. I can hardly wait until the next Cartwright triplet spins her spell. Out-Freaking-Standing!" —*Huntress Book Reviews*

THE SCOT, THE WITCH AND THE WARDROBE

"Sassy dialogue, rich sexual tension, and plenty of laughs make this an immensely satisfying return to Blair's world of witchcraft." —*Publishers Weekly*

"Snappy dialogue can't disguise the characters' true insecurities, giving depth to Blair's otherwise breezy, lighthearted tale." —*Booklist*

MY FAVORITE WITCH

"Annette Blair will make your blood sizzle with this magical tale . . . A terrific way to start the new year!" —*Huntress Book Reviews*

"This warmhearted story is a delight, filled with highly appealing characters sure to touch your heart. The magic in the air spotlights the humor that's intrinsic to the story. A definite charmer!" —*Romantic Times*

THE KITCHEN WITCH

"A fun and sexy romp." —*Booklist*

"Magic. *The Kitchen Witch* sizzles. Ms. Blair's writing is as smooth as a fine Kentucky bourbon. Sexy, fun, top-notch entertainment." —*Romance Reader at Heart*

"Bewitching! Full of charm, humor, sensuality . . . An easy-reading, reader-pleasing story that makes you feel good all over." —*Reader to Reader Reviews*

Berkley Sensation Titles by Annette Blair

THE KITCHEN WITCH
MY FAVORITE WITCH
THE SCOT, THE WITCH AND THE WARDROBE

SEX AND THE PSYCHIC WITCH
GONE WITH THE WITCH
NEVER BEEN WITCHED

NAKED DRAGON
BEDEVILED ANGEL

Berkley Prime Crime Titles by Annette Blair

A VEILED DECEPTION
LARCENY AND LACE
DEATH BY DIAMONDS

Bedeviled
ANGEL

A Works Like Magick Novel

ANNETTE BLAIR

BERKLEY SENSATION, NEW YORK

THE BERKLEY PUBLISHING GROUP
Published by the Penguin Group
Penguin Group (USA) Inc.
375 Hudson Street, New York, New York 10014, USA
Penguin Group (Canada), 90 Eglinton Avenue East, Suite 700, Toronto, Ontario M4P 2Y3, Canada
(a division of Pearson Penguin Canada Inc.)
Penguin Books Ltd., 80 Strand, London WC2R 0RL, England
Penguin Group Ireland, 25 St. Stephen's Green, Dublin 2, Ireland (a division of Penguin Books Ltd.)
Penguin Group (Australia), 250 Camberwell Road, Camberwell, Victoria 3124, Australia
(a division of Pearson Australia Group Pty. Ltd.)
Penguin Books India Pvt. Ltd., 11 Community Centre, Panchsheel Park, New Delhi—110 017, India
Penguin Group (NZ), 67 Apollo Drive, Rosedale, North Shore 0632, New Zealand
(a division of Pearson New Zealand Ltd.)
Penguin Books (South Africa) (Pty.) Ltd., 24 Sturdee Avenue, Rosebank, Johannesburg 2196,
South Africa

Penguin Books Ltd., Registered Offices: 80 Strand, London WC2R 0RL, England

This is a work of fiction. Names, characters, places, and incidents either are the product of the author's imagination or are used fictitiously, and any resemblance to actual persons, living or dead, business establishments, events, or locales is entirely coincidental. The publisher does not have any control over and does not assume any responsibility for author or third-party websites or their content.

BEDEVILED ANGEL

A Berkley Sensation Book / published by arrangement with the author

PRINTING HISTORY
Berkley Sensation mass-market edition / August 2010

Copyright © 2010 by Annette Blair.
Excerpt from *Vampire Dragon* by Annette Blair copyright © by Annette Blair.
Excerpt from *Cruel Enchantment* by Anya Bast copyright © by Anya Bast.
Cover art by Arn0.
Cover design by Rita Frangie.
Interior text design by Laura K. Corless.

All rights reserved.
No part of this book may be reproduced, scanned, or distributed in any printed or electronic form
without permission. Please do not participate in or encourage piracy of copyrighted materials in
violation of the author's rights. Purchase only authorized editions.
For information, address: The Berkley Publishing Group,
a division of Penguin Group (USA) Inc.,
375 Hudson Street, New York, New York 10014.

ISBN: 978-0-425-23597-3

BERKLEY® SENSATION
Berkley Sensation Books are published by The Berkley Publishing Group,
a division of Penguin Group (USA) Inc.,
375 Hudson Street, New York, New York 10014.
BERKLEY® SENSATION and the "B" design are trademarks of Penguin Group (USA) Inc.

PRINTED IN THE UNITED STATES OF AMERICA

10 9 8 7 6 5 4 3 2 1

If you purchased this book without a cover, you should be aware that this book is stolen property. It
was reported as "unsold and destroyed" to the publisher, and neither the author nor the publisher has
received any payment for this "stripped book."

This book is dedicated with love and respect:

To my daughter Robbie-Lynn
for having the brilliance to marry her Kenyan.
To my son-in-law Peter,
who enriches our family in every way.
To Ann and Esther, smart, delightful young women,
granddaughters of my heart.
You make me proud.
And last but definitely not least, to our little Laura,
Cute, cuddly, smart as a button,
A toddler cyclone, often on wheels,
Who keeps us in stitches,
And everyone else running in circles.
Nuggles,
Gigi.

And to Tina and Sean's Connor.
You didn't stay long, but you brought love.
So much love.

ONE

"How could you die at a time like this?" Guardian angel fourth class Chance Godricson rushed toward the new arrivals, his many-colored dream robe flowing behind him. "Mountain climbing? Really? With your responsibilities?"

The newly deceased Fitzpatricks stepped back as Chance's anger vibrated the rainbow dome of pre-Everlasting.

The aurora borealis had nothing on eternity.

Minion angels in pastel robes materialized and propelled Chance away from the distressed couple, a firm hand on each of his wrists.

Chance struggled against his wardens while the Fitz-patricks were led away.

The angel Angus—Chance's friend and fellow prankster—appeared, shaking his head, his bushy white beard making Chance want to scratch his own clean-shaven face, though he resisted temptation, as all angels *should*.

Angus gave an empathetic sigh, scratched his fuzzy chin, then firmed his spine and his expression. "You have no purpose in this sector, my friend. Even if you belonged here, the Fitzpatricks were not yours to protect, much less to chide."

Chance fisted his hands. "But Queisha Saint-Denis *is* my responsibility, and she's the surrogate who carried their six-year-old twins. As Mr. Fitzpatrick insisted, and put in his will, Queisha becomes the twins' legal guardian at their death. She doesn't know it yet, but the couple's angry family does, and they hate it."

"Ach, now, Chance—"

"Don't shush me," Chance said with a tug against his wardens. "This couple's death will spell trouble for Queisha in ways even I can't imagine."

Angus folded his wings, which meant that he believed he had everything under control. "Queisha has always yearned for the twins she carried, Chance. Maybe they're exactly what she needs."

"The girls, yes. The complications they'll bring with them, no. You don't understand, Angus. On earth, the Fitzpatricks are at this moment considered *missing, not dead*, therefore their will has no power. It's a gray area for all concerned. They died in a remote location where their bodies might not be found for weeks or months. *If ever.* A vague enough situation to bring the twins' guardianship up for question. Who will get them for the interim? Who will control their fortune? What happens to someone as sensitive as Queisha when she learns . . . all of it?"

Angus's unibrow undulated like a fuzzy white caterpillar on the prowl. "I agree that this complicates the issue, but you've already been told by Raphael that you spend too much time looking to Queisha's welfare when others in your care need your attention."

Chance's wings bristled of their own accord, so he drew them against his body. "Queisha's troubles are more urgent than the rest of my charges' put together. And you know it!"

"Granted, Queisha has issues," Angus said, "for good reason, fears that have caused complications. Crivvens, her solutions have erected obstacles, but there's a limit to your role as her guardian. Her free will is her own, not yours, and not to be toyed with. You cannot protect her from life, Chance." Angus made a motion to dismiss the pastel-robed guards.

The minions disappeared while Chance rubbed his wrists, from habit, not pain—pain did not exist here, but the memory of it did.

When Chance looked up, Angus, too, had vanished, and Chance found himself standing beside a precipice from which earth sat bared to his view, a brink, razor sharp in its implications, earth's beauty mesmerizing but frightening in its pull.

From here, more than from anywhere else in the unending splendor of Everlasting, the earthen plane loomed: visible, vulnerable, and open.

Dangerously open.

Chance stepped from the allure of temptation.

Temptation? In Everlasting?

Of course not. A test, more like, and from the highest levels of angeldom. The archangels. Gabriel and Raphael.

He ran a hand through his hair. Everything he yearned for appeared so near, yet hovered light-years away. If the scene he watched at this moment—Queisha dancing with a tuxedoed hat rack—had a sound, it would seduce with promise . . . a tune as simple as the offer of an apple.

His heart pulsed at the sight of Queisha, sweeter than any fruit . . . *life giving* . . . as once had been said of the apple.

Chance stepped closer to the precipice so as to see her more clearly, so close that her vulnerability tugged at him in the same way it had nicked his heart and proved that organ's existence on the day she lived and he died.

He watched her make life count, her gown flaring, its skirt ending in colored points as she participated in *Dancing with the Stars*, alone, more or less, in the safety of her home.

Agoraphobia: an abnormal fear of being in public places or situations or places outside a familiar environment. If only she could leave the malady entirely behind her.

Chance found Angus beside him, again, also observing Queisha. "Angus, she'll consider her fears validated when she discovers that the twins' parents have died. Her road to recovery will grow longer, rather than shorter."

Angus nodded. "Aye, and who could blame her for faltering in her recovery after what she's survived?"

His friend's resolute stance worried Chance. "Are you here to warn me away from her again?"

Angus obviously caught the disapproving nuance of his own body language so he relaxed, clasped his hands behind his back, and turned from the precipice. "I hear that Gabriel and Raphael are thinking about washing their hands of you."

"Glad tidings," Chance said, going for glib. "So what message did they send?"

Angus toed the outline of a star in the pearlescent angel dust beneath their sparkling, leg-laced high-tops before renewing eye contact. "Gabriel and Raphael, *it is said*, believe that you reside too much in your heart, not here in Everlasting, but on the earthen plane . . . with Queisha."

"That's not much of an accusation," Chance countered. "Queisha's more angelic than I am. More than you, too, given your habit of listening at archangels' keyholes."

Angus coughed to avoid a direct response. "I will, unfortunately, grant that we're both more worldly than the girl."

Chance relaxed, relief washing over him. At least someone understood. "So you see my problem?"

"I see it better than you do, I believe. You're besotted by a mortal."

"No . . . No," Chance repeated. "No, I'm empathetic, like any guardian angel worth his wings."

Angus smoothed his beard. "Ach, and that's the problem. To your neglected charges, you are *not* worth your wings."

Chance kept the subject of their discourse—his unruly wings—from snapping in offense. "That's a harsh opinion."

"It's not an opinion, but a judgment."

"A judgment?" Chance straightened as understanding dawned. "Only the triumvirate can pass judgment."

Remaining silent—unusual for Angus—the Scot's rusty brows rose.

"The triumvirate? You mean that Raphael and Gabriel

called Michael—a bold move—and convened a Tribunal to discuss *my* behavior? That *cannot* be good."

Angus raised a facetious brow. "No bloody kidding!"

"Michael *is* the enforcer," Chance said, pulling his attention from Queisha. "How long will he observe me?"

"Michael has already finished observing you." Angus sighed. "You hear nothing we say. You belong to earth and to *her* even now. You focus on no one but her."

"That's not true." The heat of denial plagued Chance.

Angus shook his head. "What do you find so special about her?"

"She never feels sorry for herself. I like that."

"You like a lot about her," Angus said. "Someday, do me a favor: look back at this moment and remember, please, that I am a better friend than you think."

Before Chance understood his friend's intent, the Scot went shoulder to shoulder with him and shoved him off the precipice.

Shock and surprise shot through Chance, until anticipation sparked through him like fireworks on the Fourth as a whoosh of air filled his lungs.

TWO

Her capacious home spotless and ready for company, Queisha Saint-Denis's heart sped at the sound of her doorbell playing "Witchy Woman" in her visitor's honor.

"Fluff your fox stole and straighten that shirtwaist, Mrs. McGillicudy," Queisha told her foyer hat rack, straightening creamy pearls and smoothing a partridge hat feather on her way to the front door.

"Vivica, you look magickal, as does Isis," she said of Vivica's Savannah cat as she opened the door. "I'm so glad you called and said you were coming this way. I've been meaning to ask you about finding me a cook."

Vivica Quinlan, owner of Works Like Magick, Salem's premier employment agency, frowned. "How have you been managing without one?"

"Delivered takeout, actually, but according to my doctor, my nutritional standards leave something to be desired. Fact is I can't cook for beans. Speaking of which, I eat my food at room temp since the great kidney bean explosion of 2009. Not that I'm a dimwit, but did you know that boiled eggs also explode in the microwave? And that if you warm food in the can, you can create your own lightning?"

As they embraced, Queisha wallowed in the rare touch, a heart beating against her own. Physical contact always pierced deep, but she never let it show, hiding her emotions like an English palace guard.

She took her guest's light cotton leopard cloak—a match to her Savannah cat's fur—and spread it over Mrs. McGillicudy's shoulders.

"This spot overlooking Salem Cove is probably the best piece of property in Marblehead. The lilac bushes set against the plum and rose Victorian house looked absolutely striking from the boat."

Queisha indicated a painting of her home in the hallway leading to the French parlor where she and Vivica sat for a minute. "Aunt Helen had good taste. Twenty-three rooms and sixteen kinds of lilacs—which normally bloom in May, but start late and stay till mid-June given the cooling sea breezes. Of course, I don't use *every* room, but I have taken to teaching myself billiards of late."

Vivica lowered her lashes. "I know you made excellent use of the medical suite when I set you up as a surrogate a few years ago."

"I know. I moved in just in time to use it, didn't I?"

"Speaking of the twins," Vivica said.

"Were we?" Queisha's psychic radar went on high alert.

"Well, I was, and since I was your go-between, I still get regular reports on the girls . . . in the event you have any questions."

"Funny you should bring them up." Queisha shivered and rubbed her arms. "I woke up panicked about them the other night, as if they needed me."

Vivica released an unsteady breath. "You're in a co-coon of sorts here, aren't you? An insular world of your own making?"

Queisha wondered what that had to do with anything. "Life gave me cranberries so I added sugar." She shrugged.

"In honor of the Massachusetts cranberry bog?"

"We didn't have cranberry bogs in Los Angeles. I wanna see one someday."

"So have you considered getting treated for the agoraphobia?"

"My birth mother's sister had it and never left this house. For the longest time, I thought I had to deal with the cards dealt me. But a few years after the twins were born—on their birthday, mind you—I did exactly that. I called a psychologist. She sees me here three times a week. I decided life was too short not to make the most of it." She'd once gotten close enough to dead to know that firsthand.

"So are you more flexible, now?" Vivica asked. "Are you able to leave the house?"

"I'm not cured by any means, but I can go out to my yellow-brick patio now without crying, getting the cold sweats, vomiting, or passing out at the thought."

"I call that progress."

"It is. And look, I'm much less obsessive." Queisha pointed to her purple-and-lime layered outfit. "Swing dress over capris, so out of style they're in again, all because I wanted to match this old Hermès scarf." Queisha waved the bright fashion statement. "Sassy, hey?"

"I think you're an amazing woman, Queisha."

"A scaredy-cat who's trying to get over her fear of leaving the house? I hardly think so."

Vivica frowned. "But look at all you've attained."

"Attained? I ended up here by accident. I had a good adoptive mother, but after she died, I screwed up, my adoptive father threw me out, and I became a ward of the state. Then my biological aunt left me this house and her fortune, because someone told her I had the same fear of leaving home that she did." Queisha shivered. "Yes, I'm more flexible. But don't ask me to be a surrogate again."

"Why not? You were considered a perfect candidate."

"Probably because the agoraphobia hadn't been diagnosed yet. And I didn't anticipate the pain of giving up my babies. When I miscarried at sixteen, I figured fate took a hand. But giving a baby away? Again? No, thanks."

"Why did you agree to be a surrogate the first time?"

"I'd been given a second chance. The man who saved my life, and died because he did, told me to live for both of us. The opportunity to create life seemed the perfect way to thank him and make a childless couple happy."

"Interesting."

"Is that all you've got to say, Viv? No talking me into some crazy scheme?"

"I'm not here to ask you to be a surrogate."

Queisha folded her arms and tilted her head. "Which isn't to say that you don't have a scheme."

Vivica firmed her lips, rose, and wandered toward the kitchen. "When I get you a cook he or she will definitely like this. Your home is quite the legacy. It seems as though you have an angel on your shoulder."

"Make the cook a she, please, and I don't believe in angels." Queisha glanced out the window. *Talk about being evasive; Vivica was aces at it.* "I have an angel fountain though." Queisha turned back to her guest. "Anyway, would you like to have your tea on the water porch overlooking the Cove? On the yellow-brick patio overlooking the rose garden? Or in the widow's walk tower overlooking everything?"

"Oh, the tower, please. Isis and I love standing above the world, don't we, sweetie?" Vivica stroked her knee-high cat.

"The higher the better for me," Queisha said, thinking of the eternity she'd spent trapped at the bottom of the world. Vivica picked up a silver tray with a matching tea service, lady cakes, blue Wedgwood dishes, navy linen napkins, and pewter flatware. "Everything is gorgeous."

"Everything belonged to Aunt Helen." A ghostly presence who was probably watching them right now.

Vivica followed her to the elevator.

"My aunt had elevators put in for her bad knees. I utilize them to get places faster and keep my tea warm. Today, we're having Lively Lemongrass Peach tea. Tomorrow, Hibiscus Paradise." Queisha winked. "I fell in love with my aunt's tea cupboard. We would have been kindred spirits, I think. She never left this house, they say, like they'll be saying about me, someday, without knowing the truth."

Queisha didn't usually reveal so much about herself, but her sense of impending change, and Vivica's hidden agenda, seemed to call for plain speaking.

The white tower room was centered by a round tea table. Its floor-length, red-and-white-striped tablecloth matched the padded seats beneath the tall, Gothic windows overlooking the widow's walk.

Victorian dolls she'd made herself occupied two of the white rattan chairs at the table.

Since she didn't live in the greater world, Queisha didn't conform to it. She expanded her small corner and made it work for her. Life had to have some perks, though one of these days, she hoped to get in a car and drive away, if only for a while. The handmade characters with which she surrounded herself kept her company and kept her happy: dolls, hat racks, and life-sized soft-sculpted characters.

Vivica sipped her tea. "This is wonderful. So, do you want your new cook to live in?"

Queisha put down her cake. "I want someone with a sense of whimsy."

"Not a problem, sweetie. You charm the frills off your hat racks. You could open a shop in Salem with your fanciful creations. They're marvelous, by the way."

Queisha beamed despite herself. "Maybe someday I will." She believed in sending positive vibes into the universe, though her hands trembled in her lap.

Vivica reached over and patted her arm. "You can do it, kiddo. What are you offering your cook for wages?"

"You tell me, Ms. Businesswoman. I want to use your payroll services, too."

Vivica took notes. "Are we advertising that you want a cook who'll work days, with the possibility of eventually living in?"

"Yes, perfect." Queisha set down her teacup and went out to the widow's walk. "Come and take a look at Salem through my telescope."

"Yikes! You're not afraid to be up so high?"

"My phobia has to do with panic attacks, not heights."

Queisha adjusted the telescope. "The psychologist says I'm so afraid of having a panic attack, I panic and bring one on, but there you go. Staying home used to seem like the safest plan, until lately, but I'm sick of talking about me. Is that your bodyguard, getting pelted by hail in the boat at my dock? Looks like the storm is hovering only over him."

"It is. He's some kind of bad weather magnet. He's also like a human lightning rod. He says it has something to do with his Dragonelli heritage."

"Dragonelli? That's a name."

"Yes, Jaydun Dragonelli."

"He's *très* cute, or haven't you noticed?" Queisha winked.

"Eye candy." Vivica elbowed her. "I've noticed."

"So you hired *him* to watch your body?"

"Right, and I watch his." Vivica laughed.

Queisha raised a brow. "Do tell."

Vivica got a convenient case of the hiccups. "Oh no," she said almost on a wail. "Not now! Ex-excuse me, sweetie, but someone else needs my help. I'll be in touch."

"Someone *else*? Why? Do *I* need your help?" An edgy worry tripped Queisha's heart. Frankly, Viv's reaction evoked that peculiar nightmarish angst she'd had over the twins the other night.

"Don't worry," Vivica said running down the wide curved staircase, Isis loping at her side.

Watching from the top of the sweeping stairs, ignoring the flutter in her psychic center, Queisha half expected the owner of Works Like Magick to leave a glass slipper behind.

THREE

*Chance landed in a tall, narrow box, like a stand-*ing casket, with painful debris raining down on him, things like hammers and baseballs, reminding him that, here, pain did exist. "What the hellish bad dream is this place?" he muttered. "Probably *not* a confessional. What would I have to confess? I'm an angel."

"Aye and angels are nondenominational."

"Angus?" Chance whispered. "What are *you* doing here anyway?"

"Taking my punishment for knocking you down here."

"Serves you right." Chance reached out and touched walls on both sides. "What have you gotten us into?"

"Ach, stop your blatherin', it's probably just a closet."

"I meant in the grander scheme. Now how can we both fit in so small a space without stumbling over each other? Our wings alone should—"

"Hoot, man, I'm a cherub fluttering above your head, small as a middlin' fairy seasick enough to puke and a mite worried I will."

"*You're* worried?" Chance imagined the worst. "Hover in the far corner, will you? A cherub, heh?"

"Raphael himself turned me, and all for doing you a favor."

Chance frowned. "You got Raphael transfiguration-mad? We're in for it."

"No Everlasting kidding."

Chance considered the situation. "Raphael's the messenger angel, so we're supposed to find meaning in this, I take it."

Angus burped. "It means we're up for a punishment worse than my bollocking need to spew."

"Do not, I repeat, do not sp—" The wall Chance leaned on turned into a door that opened, and he landed on his ass. That's when he finally saw Angus, a bearded cherub tearing through a window screen to fly outside and into the bushes.

Before he could stand, Chance had to push a perforated tennis racket down his ankle and off his foot. When he did, he saw several wing feathers on the floor beside him, two in rose signifying his loss of patience and one in copper at his momentary lapse of faith.

Angus returned, having lost his pallor.

Chance indicated their surroundings. "Figures you'd bring us to an Irish pub and billiard parlor."

The mini winged Scot gave his friend a teeny little California highway salute, but then he looked around. "Methinks we're not in Everlasting anymore."

"How angelic of you—*not*," said the woman who'd released them, her hand still on the closet doorknob. "By all means, feel free to ignore me. I'm Vivica Quinlan. Hic. In case you care."

Chance gave her his attention since she had an ocelot at her side.

"What the—hic—are the two of you doing?" this Vivica asked. "I've never had a magickal supernatural ancient land in a client's home before. Hic. This could get stic—hic—sticky. What are you?" she asked, looking Chance over, "an angel in drag?"

"This is a *man's* robe," Chance said, highly insulted.

"Pardon me if I doubt you. Hic. But I believe I have one like it."

"It's a Technicolor dream coat. Don't you read the bible?"

"The Fake Angel bible? No. Hic. But it is rather amazing the way it shimmers and swirls into different colors."

"Not amazing, *angelic*. You should see my wings."

"Give us a peek then," she said.

"You're mocking me." But he spread them just to shock her.

"Yeesh, put those away before someone sees you." The woman looked behind her to make sure they were still alone.

Chance folded his wings.

"I mean, I *know* you're an angel," she said, "but what's your friend, here, besides screwed?"

"I resent that," Angus snapped, folding his tiny arms. "I'm a cherub."

Vivica tilted her head. "Never saw one who needed a shave."

"I need a cigar, too. Guess the old urges come rushing back when you touch down on earth."

Chance shoved the debris back into the closet and shut the door. "I'm Chance Godricson and this is Angus. He's been given a time-out, Everlasting style."

Angus folded his small arms. "How is it that she can see us?"

Vivica turned toward Angus. "I'm here to welcome the latest chameleon—hic—of the universe to breach the veil between the planes." She eyed Chance. "That's you, Crayola."

"Name-calling," Chance muttered. "I *must* be back on earth."

"You are, and I knew you were an angel before I found you because of this kickass case of the heavenly hiccups. Angels tend to do that to a witch, though I'm not sure why."

"Consider it a karmic handshake that travels badly," Chance said. "It's how I know that you and I do the same work, helping others. You from down here, us from above, most of the time," he added, checking the place out.

Vivica took a deep breath. "Fortunately for me, those hiccups are starting to clear up."

"I'm glad this is a pub and not a church," Chance said. "I was the kind of altar boy who put salt in the sacramental wine and glued a squeaky mouse to Sister Superior's pew."

"So you're a rascal angel. I call that whimsy." Vivica crossed her arms and leaned against the billiard table. "Can you cook?"

"Hades no!"

"Shush. Whisper, will you? Queisha will hear you."

"Queisha Saint-Denis? Is this her house?" Chance took a look around, recognizing several rooms. "Angus, we came straight here. I can't wait to see her. Vivica, where is she?"

Hands on her hips, Vivica's expression skewered him in place. "You need a plan," she said. "You can't just tell someone you're an angel. Besides, Queisha doesn't believe in angels."

Angus snorted.

Chance gave their greeter a double take, and she, he thought, tried to hide a smirk. "Why are you here, exactly?" she asked him.

Chance crossed his arms. "What's it to you?"

"We do the same work—remember the karmic handshake? I'm a highly evolved witch with the power of centuries behind me, a hereditary high priestess, actually, and I'm here for Queisha because life is about to test her to her cheeky limits. It might even wring the whimsy right out of her."

"No blessed kidding," Chance said. "Like because her twins are on their way from Switzerland?"

Vivica's spine went ramrod straight. "How do you know?"

"I had a face-to-face with their parents." Chance pointed upward.

Vivica paled visibly. "They're *not* just missing? They're dead?"

"Hello?" Queisha called from a distance. "Vivica, is that you?"

Vivica jumped at the sound of her hostess's voice, Chance's heart raced, and Angus caught his breath.

"Whatever you do, don't lie or you're outta here," the cherub whispered before he vanished.

"It's me, Queisha," Vivica called going to the bottom of the stairs. "Stay there, I'll bring some of that hibiscus tea up after I take Isis outside for a bit. I never left. I settled everything on my cell phone from down here."

"Oh . . . goody. I'm glad you can stay. I love having company."

"Blighted blessings," Chance whispered like a prayer. "She has no idea what she's in for. There's company . . . and there's company that'll knock her on her fine backside."

FOUR

"God only knows what we're in for," Chance whispered as Angus reappeared.

"Ach, and what does it matter. She's not the boss of us."

Chance cleared his throat. "Which she? Queisha, the *she* upstairs, who might fall apart when she learns her twins are orphans? Or the bossy *she* headed our way?" He indicated Vivica, who saw and heard them as she returned from the base of the stairs. "Or God, the She of Life?"

Vivica stopped in her tracks. "God is a woman? Excellent! Not that I didn't suspect. Anyway, listen, we don't have much time before I have to go back upstairs. Chance, as far as our mutual purpose is concerned, I'm the *she* you'll be listening to, because Queisha is about to need us, and badly. To start with, can you do something with your wings so as not to frighten her?"

"I should be able to compress them and slip them into

the muscle in my back—well, sacs that pass for muscle—not that I've ever tried it, but here goes."

Chance concentrated and found himself suddenly able to move his arms and elbows in a new easy way, and he appreciated the range of possibilities with this new freedom of movement. "Hey, whaddya know? It works. It itches like I've been rolling naked in angel dust, but it works."

Vivica raised a brow, and Angus raised two.

Chance went for an angelic look. "I only tried it once. The stuff gets in the darndest places."

Vivica shook her head and made a follow-me motion with her hand. "We're going out through the water porch, so Queisha can't see us from the widow's walk. I'm sending you back to Works Like Magick, my employment agency, where Jaydun, my assistant, will supply you with a wardrobe appropriate to carrying out your assignment."

"But, I'm Queisha's guardian angel. She *is* my assignment."

"On that we agree. She needs everything you likely suppose she does with two additions: one is an employee she's looking to hire, so supplying him/you will cover our backsides, and the other is someone that she doesn't yet know she needs."

Chance stopped. "What, or should I say *who* doesn't she know she needs?"

"A co-guardian for the twins—that's you—so she doesn't freak over the unexpected responsibility of their care, given her lack of experience. Let her think you were assigned."

"Assigned by whom?" Chance asked. "A cherub with a head as big as his body?"

"Bollocks. Thanks, my former friend."

Chance noted that Vivica looked anywhere but at Angus. "You could have been assigned by a lawyer as an advocate for the girls, or even by someone in the twins' family. Since you really are a bona fide guardian, you won't be lying."

Chance placed his hands on his hips. "I'm the twins' guardian angel, because I'm Queisha's. Does that count?" Shades of Hades, the bossy woman made an annoying kind of sense. "And what kind of employee do I need to become to cover our backsides, I shudder to ask?"

"As I said, I run an employment agency, so Queisha asked me to find her a cook. That's the position you'll have to fill."

Chance choked. "Are you mad, woman?"

"Not mad. Shrewd. We can't have outsiders in the house with you dropping feathers all over the place." She nudged one with a red high heel. "Or with Chatty Cherub here zinging in and out."

"Oh, she won't see Angus," Chance said.

Vivica barked a laugh. "Well you talking to air doesn't look sane to the casual observer, either. Queisha doesn't need any distractions while we help her come to grips with caring for the children she carried."

Chance rubbed his chin. "And with deciding their futures."

"I hate to agree with the boss lady," Angus said. "But she's right."

"I know she is, bless her," Chance said, "and by that, I mean, *damn it*. Since I didn't exactly plan this, I suppose Queisha's lucky Vivica's here to set us straight."

"I'll take that as a compliment." Vivica led them to

the yard where she opened her cell phone. A man on Queisha's central dock raised his phone to his ear and turned toward them. With a nod, he hung up and leapt their way.

Yes, he definitely leapt. With the speed of a bullet train and the grace of a . . . dragon? Chance blinked to clear his vision.

"Chance," Vivica said, "this is Jaydun, my bodyguard. Jaydun, Chance is a new client."

"A dragon?" Chance said. "Your bodyguard is a dragon?"

"Why not? Queisha's bodyguard is an angel," Vivica said. "I forgot that magickal supernaturals can sometimes see each other for who they really are, earth suits notwithstanding."

"Magickal? Me?" Chance shook his head. "I don't think so. Jaydun, do you know that you have a small coffee-colored dragon sitting on your shoulder?"

Chance reared back when the dragon twitched, parted sleepy lids, and revealed eyes the color of violets lit from within.

Jaydun chuckled. "Old Koko would rather catch a ride, though he flies like a kite. We've learned that miniaturizing our elders conserves their life force and allows them to travel here."

"That makes an odd kind of sense," Chance said. "Where did you come from?"

"The Island of Stars, parallel plane, home to a legion of dragons in danger of dying out. Andra, our sorceress, sends us, and when we get here, Vivica mainstreams us, don't you, Boss?"

Vivica gave a half nod. "Jaydun works for me. His

brother, Bastian, owns a local bed-and-breakfast. There are others due at any time."

Chance looked from one to the other. "Did my arrival wreck the process?"

"Not at all," Jaydun said. "We can only travel the planes when it's safe. Long story. We'll talk on the way to Salem, shall we?"

Koko took flight and settled on Vivica's shoulder to nuzzle her neck and hum satisfactorily.

Vivica winked. "He likes me."

Jaydun frowned. "Too much, if you ask me."   ⋅

Vivica smothered a giggle. "I can stand a little affectionate magick in my life."

Chance thought Jaydun looked jealous of Koko.

"I like you, too," said a little redheaded fellow, dressed in green, riding between Koko's neck and wings, clinging to a stub horn like a saddle horn, an addition to the magickal company that Chance hadn't noticed until now. "Not a leprechaun?"

"Yep. Paddy claims he's a dragon rider. Not sure where in the transition and tumble through the ether we picked *him* up, but he arrived with us."

"Basically," Vivica said, "Jaydun, Koko, and Paddy are my assistants, or my posse, if you will."

Vivica's cat meowed loudly. "Oh," Vivica said. "And Isis, too, plays a crucial role. Nearly forgot you, sweetie, and you're key to keeping our work from being detected, aren't you?"

Chance fisted his hands. "Magick. All magick. I'm not, you know. I am *not* magick! I'll fail Queisha because of it, won't I? I have no idea what to do to help her, other than the tasks you assigned, Vivica. Angus didn't exactly give me time to think it through before he knocked me down here."

"Bollocks. I resent that."

Chance gave the crusty Scot a withering look. "Like the archangels resent it, you bearded cherub."

Angus ignored his friend with a raised chin, fluttered over to shake Paddy's hand, "Irish myth to dead Scot," he said, then he flew in Koko's face for a good look, and got his beard singed.

Chance barked a laugh. "Serves you right."

Angus scattered chin embers with his small hand. "I just wanted a wee look."

"Ask next time," Paddy suggested. "Koko can be reasonable, more or less."

Vivica looked from the magickals to the angelics. "Don't worry, Chance, you don't need magick, you need love. Trust your instincts; they'll take you far. Now, Jaydun, take Chance to Works Like Magick and give him a business casual wardrobe, something befitting a court-appointed guardian who might have traveled a great distance to get here."

Might have, Chance thought with an impatience that made his temple throb. "Clothes hardly seem important at a time like this."

"You think *our* fearful Queisha will open her home to a Technicolor-dream-coat-wearing trick-or-treater in June?" Vivica asked facetiously. "By the way, do angels wear tighty whities or boxers under their lively rainbow robes?"

Chance looked down and saw himself from Queisha's point of view. "Gotcha."

"Good, go dress like a human."

She turned to her assistant. "Jaydun, the limo picked up the twins at Logan Airport about an hour ago, and they should be waiting for you by the time you get to the office. Supply Chance with all of the state-of-the-art technology that might be utilized by a worldly executive and a crash course on how to use it all. Set his netbook computer up with a printer and on-the-spot cooking lessons, the ones with the printable grocery lists. Bring him and the girls back here as soon as you can. I don't want Queisha asking why my rare visit is lasting so long."

Chance eyed the supposed acclimator. "You *are* going to tell Queisha that the girls are coming, right?"

"And give her time to have a panic attack?"

"I can see that I'm going to be really good at this." Chance rubbed the back of his neck. He sure hadn't missed stress or headaches in Everlasting. "I forgot, probably because I'm about to have a panic attack, myself."

Angus's wing flutter grew swift. He looked up. "Bollocks! A call back to Everlasting, probably to find out what being down here is going to cost us." The cherub saluted and disappeared.

Meanwhile, Jaydun was walking the shore tugging the boat by its line toward the public dock on the far side of Queisha's property, to a public right-of-way hidden by a row of mature lilac bushes.

Chance sat in the boat, stomach growling. "I suddenly understand Angus's jonesing for that cigar. I haven't had a craving in years but—" He inhaled deeply, salivating at the scents teasing him. "I want a hamburger, or lobster, or . . . Chinese food?"

"That's the chop suey sandwiches from the Willows." Vivica's eyes twinkled. "Earth's a good place to get *all* kinds of pent-up desires slaked."

The concept caught Chance by surprise. He hadn't

considered a resurgence of his physical needs. "I take it your dragons and leprechauns make you an expert on what someone would want on earth compared to . . ."

"A parallel, if distant, plane? Yes. Works Like Magick is a discreet employment agency for those who are more—or less—than human. I acclimate the chameleons of the universe, like you, with birth certificates, Social Security numbers, driver's licenses, and such, and teach you to live and work here. You'll seem like one of us. I'll seem like one of you."

Chance chuckled. "I am one of you. I haven't been dead that long."

"Dead? But you're an angel?"

"Righteous, eh? During orientation, God said she never has enough angels, so she recruits new ones daily."

Vivica looked him up and down. "That makes sense, but there must be so many of you."

"We're identified by groups. There's the Solitaries—they died alone, probably in their beds. If you died in a war, you might be a Boar Warrior or a member of a World War Unit. The Nine-Eleven Brigade speaks for itself."

"And you?" Vivica asked.

"Angus and I are with the Casualty Corps, though we died in different casualties. As for me, a helicopter delivering renovation supplies to the roof of a high-rise malfunctioned on landing, slid down the side of the building, and hit a gas main. Cascading explosions caused the building to fold in on itself. I was in the basement mall at the time. Eight years ago, Los Angeles."

"I am sorry. Jaydun, add to his computer software package lessons on world events and trends for the last eight years."

To Chance, it had seemed an eternity since he met Queisha in that mall, not that she would have recognized him the next day if he'd survived. "It's relative, how long someone is dead," he said, "and I'm back, aren't I?" *For however long the triumvirate will let me stay.*

FIVE

Queisha entered the tower from the widow's walk as Vivica returned upstairs. "Is everything okay with you, Vivica? Did you help whoever needed you?"

"I believe that I have everything in hand." Vivica poured them each a bracing cup of tea. "Did you say that you enjoy having company?"

Queisha perked up. "I love company. I've always wanted a house full of people. Noise. Laughter. Chaos. And I'm sick of waiting for that kind of blessing to come *to* me. Maybe that's why I started therapy."

"Well, no more waiting. Prepare to be blessed."

Queisha knocked over her cup, the resultant tea stain growing apace with her alarm.

She blotted the mess with a napkin, wishing she could fade her disquiet as easily. "How many people are coming? Who are they? Do I know them?" Okay, so she talked a good talk, except that she'd always imagined her house filled with people with whom she was acquainted. Not strangers!

Vivica winked. "It's a surprise. A big surprise."

Queisha remembered another big surprise and her adoptive father's words to her as a result, his last words to her ever: *You're a disappointment, girl. This would kill your mother, if she weren't already dead.*

Queisha clasped her hands to stop them from trembling, but not before Vivica noticed, led her to the window seat, and sat beside her. "Are you about to have a panic attack? Or are you just excited?"

"I'll disappoint you—them. Everyone."

Vivica's confusion called for clarification.

"I mean, I'm probably not up to entertaining. I have no experience."

"I never said you had to do it alone." Vivica patted her hand.

Queisha rested her head against the cushions and pinched the top of her nose. "You'll stay then?"

"I'll come often, and when you need me, call, but you'll have a great helper. You'll see. Not to worry. It's all arranged."

No relief was to be found in Queisha's palpitating heart or cold sweats. "A helper. One helper, but not you?" Why was she letting Vivica dictate her life? Well, because if Viv stood for anything, it was being supportive, though having a stranger around to let down did *not* sound helpful.

Queisha stood to pace while the tower room seemed to shrink and sway around her.

Vivica acted as if she'd done something grand, and Queisha hated to disappoint her. So she raised her chin and tried for a look of approval. "A house full, you implied." *Here being the saving grace.* "I need to change. Dress for company, you know." She grabbed Vivica's hand and pulled her down the hall, while those few sips of spiced tea did an Irish jig in her belly.

Queisha narrowed her choices to two dresses, holding one in front of her, then the other. "I can't decide. White or turquoise?"

"With your rich bronze skin, they'd both look awesome, but the retro Dior in turquoise looks quite festive."

Vivica received a call that made Queisha's raw nerves do that psychic flip again. When she exited her dressing room, Vivica beamed. "Haven't I seen you on the cover of *Vogue*?"

Queisha tried to ignore her shaky legs. "You know, Viv, you can stay as long as our guests do."

"No, they're your guests, not mine. Let's go watch for them from the widow's walk. They're nearly here."

As if she were going crazy, Queisha paced the widow's walk around the tower at least a dozen times until Vivica's white stretch limo pulled into her driveway, Jaydun behind the wheel. He went around and opened the front passenger door. Queisha froze and gripped the railing, her heart beating double time when a gorgeous, wide-shouldered Greek god who needed a shave stepped out. In pricey charcoal slacks, a turquoise shirt, and a basket weave tie that pulled the colors together, he made her remember what one missed when in solitary confinement, however self-imposed.

Their eyes met, and he faltered in his step as her right hand slipped from the railing, hard, and burned her palm with the scrape. As if seeing her wince, and understanding why, he closed his own right fist, and her pain dissipated.

Like a wooden soldier, he moved forward, breaking the filament connecting their fixated stares, as if telling himself to put one foot in front of the other.

Queisha took a forced breath with the same determination. In, out. In, out. In some nebulous way, she knew she'd been waiting for him, maybe for years. But not only him. She sensed the presence of more specific guests— guests whose hearts beat in time with hers.

At the knowledge, her panic attack symptoms dissolved, and the remedy, the warm, soothing honey of anticipation slithered through her veins.

Jaydun leaned into the backseat forever. Did someone refuse to leave the car? Who would remain in a backseat so long? Then it hit her—the whole beehive, not just the honey: little people. Strapped in their car seats. A host of metaphorical bees buzzed louder. A good buzz. Celebratory.

Queisha feared her curious heart would pump from her chest before she found out for sure. Then Jaydun lifted a little girl from the backseat, then another. Identical dark-haired girls.

Twins. Nearly seven years old, but small for their age. Petite. No wonder they still needed car seats.

Holding back the sob rising from a deeply hidden place, Queisha tasted blood on her lip before she realized she'd bit through the skin.

The girls looked up at her, and she felt the pull. Their gazes held a thrumming song of invisible yearning that entwined with hers and beat apace with her heart. She knew it as well as she knew she'd carried them.

In sync, each reached for the other's hand, but they separated for the Greek god, who stepped between them and closed his hands around theirs, one on each side. Lucky girls. Lucky hunk.

The girls would be seven in a few weeks, but someone forgot to tell them that six was a magickal age. They wore burgundy-and-tan-plaid school uniforms and no expressions, a good impression of the Stepford twins.

Without taking her gaze from the sight of them, Queisha bumped Vivica's shoulder. "Lace and Skye."

Vivica slipped an arm around her waist.

"They woke me for a reason the other night." Like a sleepwalker, Queisha went down the stairs feeling awkward, backward, and out of her element. But joyful, and already mourning the moment they must leave her.

Being alone would never be good again.

At the bottom, she touched Vivica's hand. "I'm afraid I'm going to be sick."

"Panic-attack sick?"

"Excited sick." She should remember not to get attached, but it was already too late. "I never hoped . . . Are they staying overnight?"

Vivica took her by the arms, gently enough for Queisha to get a worry knot in the pit of her belly. "Sweetie, their parents went missing during a mountain-climbing expedition on Tuesday."

"The night I woke afraid they needed me."

"Probably because the Fitzpatricks named you the girls' primary guardian if something happened to them. The man you saw—I'll introduce you after you meet the girls—is their temporary co-guardian, given these particular circumstances. He's here to help until their parents are found. You have final say in their care, but he might advise you or offer options you hadn't considered. If a permanent arrangement has to be decided on, that decision will likely be yours."

"Likely? Permanent? You mean if their parents die? The poor babies. How do I console them? How much do they know? They're going to hate getting stuck with me when they want their parents."

"They've come from a Swiss boarding school, Queisha. They might not know their parents very well."

Queisha straightened. "What? I didn't give them life to see them locked away. I know how that feels and I can hardly bear the thought of it." *Happy. Be happy*, she told herself. *Be yourself. Whimsy is good. Kids like to giggle. We can all change into play clothes and . . .*

All? She stopped walking so Vivica walked into her.

Queisha turned on her heel. "The co-guardian? He's not staying *here*?"

"He has to, sweetie."

"How can I be my playful self and get to know the girls with a stranger watching?"

"He won't always be watching. Three meals a day requires time and attention."

"Say what?" Queisha's chin went down with her brows and her frown. "Does not compute."

"Chance agreed to be your cook while he's here."

"His name is Chance, and he's their co-guardian *and* a cook? What the devil are the chances?"

"Well, I might have given chance a nudge," Vivica confessed.

"Chance? Or chance?"

"Both. Seriously, the girls have suffered an upheaval;

their parents are missing; they're meeting their guardians for the first time. We can't add another stranger to the mix."

"I suppose not, and they'll need more nutritious meals than I can give them. But did you see him? He looks dangerous."

"Physically, or dangerous to your heart?" Vivica chuckled. "He's gentle as a lamb. Protective. He can do anything that needs doing away from the house, in the event one of the girls has an emergency."

Queisha lowered herself into a hall chair. "I'll make a terrible guardian."

"Sweetie, their parents *chose* you."

"Yes, because they didn't know about my agoraphobia. Neither did I back then. I hadn't admitted to myself that I needed help."

"Sweetie, *you* wouldn't put them in boarding school. You know naturally that they need understanding, love, laughter, time, and attention."

"I see already that they need to learn to play."

"Right, so can you think of a better guardian for them? The Fitzpatricks knew what they were doing. Who better to raise them than you? You have a special bond, you and the girls. They lived inside you for nine months."

"I do love them, but I'll need to remind myself that their parents could be found tomorrow. For the girls' sake, I hope they will be." Queisha looked out the window. "Where are they? I should think my co-guardian would have rung the doorbell by now."

"I told Jaydun to bring them down by the water to give you time to get used to the idea of having them here."

"The Cove! That's dangerous. Call Jaydun now and tell

him to bring them to the carousel off the far side of the house. It's open." Plus, she thought, there wasn't enough time in the world for her to get used to the idea of having her babies here, or of letting them leave again.

Vivica made the call. "Since when do you have a carousel?"

"My aunt rescued it. It's a Rhode Island landmark from Rocky Point. A piece of history." Queisha checked her hair in a mirror. "The girls must spend a lot of time outdoors. They're nearly as tan as I am, and I'm half Kenyan."

Vivica cleared her throat. "They'll probably pale to a pasty white, if you make them spend as much time indoors as you do."

"Damn it, that proves I need the hunky damned coguardian." If only he weren't a man . . . with S-E-X written all over him. Or, maybe that notion, she admitted to herself, reflected her reaction to him. Damn.

"I have to *live* with him? Really?"

SIX

Unseen, Queisha watched the girls from just inside the entrance to the carousel, her hands shaking behind her back. She hadn't seen them since the day they were born, and she was sure she'd disappoint them.

Their wavy black hair ended in large curls that tumbled to their shoulders, a lot like hers, the Fitzpatricks being Irish, as was her own birth father, who Queisha never knew. She hoped the girls' parents would be found and need a vacation abroad to recover—for a couple of months preferably, before they came for the girls.

Greedy. She hadn't met them yet and she was greedy to hang on to them.

She wouldn't let herself dwell on their inevitable parting; she'd savor their time together. Never mind living for two, as the man who saved her life had charged her with; she would now live for four.

Her rescuer's death had hurt her. Only giving the twins

to their real parents at birth had ever hurt as much as realizing that the tunnel her hero dug for himself, but made her take first, had collapsed behind her and killed him.

But she wouldn't dwell on the negative. His heroism had allowed her to give the girls life, and she would dwell on the gift not the cost.

The lively carousel music reminded her of how lucky she was as Vivica led her from the sunroom.

Vivica gazed wide-eyed at the antique merry-go-round where mermaids, dragons, lions, and giraffes circled. "This is spectacular," she said.

"Too bad the girls don't think so." Queisha shook her head. "Look at them watching it with no expressions on their faces."

"They probably feel rather lost."

"Of course." Queisha gave Jaydun, working in the center of the carousel, a sign to shut it down.

As she approached the girls, they didn't look up, but Chance did, her heart fluttering as their gazes barely met and slipped away.

She focused on the girls. Since neither of the dears would look up, Queisha had to kneel, then sit on her legs to wink up at them. Meanwhile, she tried to hide emotions as dangerous as popcorn in an open skillet, flying unchecked and bound to burn.

Her babies, but not. "Let me see if I can guess which of you is Skye and which is Lace. You have beautiful names."

One of them raised a small stubborn chin and pointed at her sister. "She's Skye."

"That must make you Lace." A six-year-old using rebellion to hide fear, uncertainty, anger maybe. Almost to prove it, Lace crossed her arms in a forbidding gesture. Lace, the stubborn one.

Queisha took the hint. "You may call *me* Queisha."

Both girls shook their heads, curls slapping their cheeks.

"Your refusal seems serious."

Skye sighed. "Mother said no. Adults are 'sir' or 'ma'am' or 'miss,' unless they're a nun and we have to call them Sister Fister Blister."

Lace gasped. "Skye Fitzpatrick! You're going to hell!"

Skye's eyes widened. "You said 'hell'! *You're* going there."

Queisha coughed. "Neither of you is. So what should you call me? Queisha Felicia Creature?"

Lace dropped her gaze but straightened, as if she forgot for a minute that she was supposed to be solemn and feared the consequences. Perhaps Fister Blister had warned them before they left the school of their parents' uncertain futures.

Skye ignored her sister's mood and the playful light remained in her eyes. "May we call you Missy Queisha, if you please?"

Their co-guardian cleared his throat. "I've been dubbed Sir Chance."

Queisha raised a brow. "Methinks your armor needs polishing."

Chance tilted his head. "It is rusty, eight years' worth."

"Been out of circulation, have you?" Queisha quipped.

"Like you wouldn't believe."

"We'll get you back into the swing," Queisha promised.

"I couldn't hope for more." Sir Chance winked. "You don't happen to remember the name of the polka playing on the carousel when you came out."

"I do. It's called 'In Heaven There Is No Beer.'"

"You got that right." The knight's eyes fairly twinkled. "No wonder it sounded familiar."

Skye stroked Queisha's nubby silk jacket, the child's small amber eyes widening at the softness. This child had to work at being solemn, and as if to prove it, Skye took an involuntary step forward, slid her tiny hand up Queisha's shoulder, over it, and down her back—a near embrace. An amazing moment.

And as if that wasn't enough, Skye took bliss a step further by closing the distance between them and laying her head tentatively on Queisha's shoulder.

Queisha closed an arm around Skye, as if she were made of spun sugar and might break or run. Either way, she wanted Skye to *feel* wanted.

Sensing no resistance, Queisha gave her an unmistakable hug. Queisha's neck warmed with the release of Skye's held breath, a release of fear and an acceptance of caring.

Queisha could no more stop the tears welling up in her than she could have kept the high-rise from collapsing that day. In a way, having the girls here altered her as much as that horrible event, and even this would leave its scars.

Lace tried to pull her twin away, but Skye held tight to Queisha, with her cooperation. What Lace didn't expect, rigid as she stood, was for Queisha to drag her into the embrace. Still, there was no give in the reserved child. She might be stuck there, but she wouldn't return the embrace.

So be it. Never let it be said that Queisha Saint-Denis didn't treat her girls the same. Cramped legs or not, she would hold them until Skye, who'd initiated the hug, stopped trembling and stepped away.

What Queisha didn't expect was for Lace's head to fall, thump, against her shoulder as a soft puff escaped her lips.

Skye giggled, sounding as free and happy as the creatures who circled the heavens. "Lace is asleep," she said.

"I know," Queisha whispered. "She puffle snores."

"What's that?" Skye asked in Queisha's ear.

"She puffs the air out in little bursts, like a . . . puffle."

They laughed softly, brow to brow.

Lace was so stubborn, she wouldn't give in, unless it was to sleep. That way she couldn't be blamed for her weakness.

Queisha kissed each brow in turn, laid her cheek against their silky hair, and inhaled their scents, a pure, sweet combo of marshmallows and baby powder.

Frankly she lost herself in them and was surprised when Sir Chance knelt before her.

There, with the girls between them, they shared their first up-close-and-hungry eye to eye, heat-making and awareness-seeking— No. No, the warmth climbing up her neck must be from the girls' body heat.

But the man, oh Lordy. So very easy to look at.

Vivica stepped up beside the four of them. "Queisha, this is Chance Godricson, a generous, adventurous, no-nonsense hero, though he probably wouldn't agree."

Chance started to speak, but Vivica waved away his denial. "Chance, this is Queisha Saint-Denis. She has a fiery nature, scads of creative energy, and she lives a joy-ful, purposeful, and courageous existence."

"Vivica's deluded," Queisha said.

"I think not. I've heard a lot about you," said the per-fect specimen of knighthood. His long thick mane, dark as her own but straighter, seemed to carry some inner source of light that painted it in streaks of purple and navy. How odd. How sexy.

How bleeping horny was she?

"Let me take the girls so you can stand," he said. "With your permission?"

Queisha nodded, feeling speech impaired.

In taking the girls from her arms, he grazed her breasts, of course, leaving a trail of heat, like veins of liquid fire that branched out on their own, growing wider, deeper, all enveloping, like a full flaming tree taking over her body. Titillating. Frightening. Yet he made her feel safe, if only for a mindless second.

He certainly made the girls feel safe, because each opened her eyes during the exchange, and each let her head fall to one of his shoulders. "It's the time change," Chance whispered, his voice soothing in its own right, stroking, as well, but she wouldn't go there.

Celibacy. Can't live with it. Can't kill yourself.

Vivica helped her stand, and Queisha felt better, if a little stiff, until she stood face-to-face with *him*, his gaze holding her captive.

Angular features, sculpted brows, each the perfect half of a gull's wing, came together, nearly touching, in a frown that only served to exacerbate his masculinity. As much in need of an expression as a shave, the man had a dimple cut in his chin, deep set as his eyes, which held a fire in their fathomless depths. Jesus eyes, sapphire blue, all knowing, filled with *credible* promise.

Charismatic. So much so that Queisha stepped away from her physical reaction. She had only ever been attracted to one man, and he had given his life to save hers. She didn't know his name or have a picture of him in her mind except his face in darkness covered in dust and dry blood.

His eyes, though, reminded her of this man's.

Beware this gorgeous invader, she told herself, beware this alarmingly attractive male, shirt unbuttoned, tie now hanging from his pocket.

She denied the aggressive challenge that brought her singing heart to wild and shivering life, while sexual awareness battered the rocky shore of her resistance like waves in a hurricane.

She hated being tossed beyond her comfort zone, out of her element, subject to the whims of fate. She hated her own vulnerabilities, of which there were many.

No surprise, panic held her in its grip and squeezed the breath from her lungs. Not a phobic panic, but one more tangible, generated by the man, himself, his magnetism titillating her in hot, threatening waves, physically stroking her.

"We *cannot* possibly live in the same house!" Queisha declared in a rush of alarm.

SEVEN

"We'll discuss Chance's living arrangements later," Vivica, from Works Like Magick, told Queisha. And Chance appreciated the stay of execution, because he wanted to live here with her, however sensually dangerous.

"Queisha?" Vivica continued, "Where can Chance put the girls down to sleep? They must be getting heavy."

"Oh. Of course." Queisha suddenly acknowledged him standing there beside the carousel, a little girl in each arm. "I'm so sorry," she said.

Chance wanted to say she had nothing to be sorry for. He understood the magnitude of this event for her. She had given that jet-setting childless couple a gift she'd never expected a return on, and the gift—two wonderful children—had *literally* come back to her.

Nobody deserved it more, but that was beside the point, and not taking into account the heartache that could come of it.

He remembered the way she'd cried on the day of their birth after the Fitzpatricks left with the babies. The way she held her empty belly, her desperate sense of loss affecting him while he tried to comfort her by singing her to sleep, praying for her to be consoled by the knowledge of her generosity.

"Here," Queisha said, stepping into a small room off the carousel where sunshine poured in from both sides through facing windows. Odd that. On one side, sunlight reflected back toward the house off the water, he noticed, where a love seat sat beneath a window. On the mirror side, dust motes danced in prismatic sunbeams cutting through the opposite window and angling toward the matching love seat.

Chance stood in the center of the cozy room. "Your aunt must have had an outstanding architect to pull this off."

"How do you know about my aunt?"

"I filled him in," Vivica said, but Queisha's stance, hand to a hip, brows raised, said she wasn't sure she believed it.

Nevertheless, the room reminded him of the rainbow dome of pre-Everlasting.

"Set them each on a love seat," Queisha said, "so we can sit in the next room and hear if they wake."

As Queisha took one child at a time from his arms, he appreciated the touch of her hands grazing his chest as he'd grazed hers in taking the girls from her arms. Sweet torture.

But now, it was all he could do *not* to touch her in return, stroke her cheek, prove to himself that she was real, him standing beside her, after years of yearning. That he loved her. Foolish him.

Blasted, er, blessed archangels were right!

Queisha, too. He could *not* live here.

It would be impossible helping her and trying to remain angelic.

Taking the second child, she got close enough for him to inhale the scent of an English flower garden. Her unique scent.

He'd suspected the minute he got here and saw her, towering over him, literally, in person after all these years, that he'd been falling in love with her since before he sent her up the escape tunnel.

Seconds later, in the blink between the end of life and the beginning of eternity, he'd been there at the top to take her hand and pull her from the rubble, right before he found himself in Everlasting.

That day, he became her guardian. Before long, a lovesick angel in denial. Now, he found himself working with the gorgeous mortal who held his heart in her small burnished hands.

This arrangement would spell nothing but disaster. Angus had probably made a dreadful mistake in sending him here, praise be, but he'd make the most of it while it lasted. And if he had any say in it, he'd make it last, too.

Chance worked out the kinks from the weight of two six-year-olds as he followed his hostess, his gaze fixed on the sway of her hips.

In heaven there is no beer.

In Everlasting there is no desire.

On earth, desire pulses forth without the body's permission, because, here, one can look into the eyes or admire the figure of a loved one and want. And want. Here, he would be less sexually conspicuous wearing his robe of many colors.

Here, he feared, he would expire from lust and get swept back up to Everlasting. Yep, those urges came back the minute you got back to earth and faced the woman you loved, however unreachable she may be.

"Queisha?" Vivica queried, as if she were trying to talk her friend down off a ledge, which Chance understood, given the current strain on Queisha's emotions.

As her guardian, he knew what she must be going through, because he knew her as well as he knew himself. Well, better. Though the way he'd reacted to her biting her lip on meeting the girls had made him want to bite that lip, himself, which earned him the accompanying itch of a loose feather. Blessedly annoying things, he had no idea they'd fall off so easily.

He'd lost several on his way to earth. He'd lost rose feathers for lost patience and copper ones for lost faith. Now he wondered what virtue he'd lost or failed at to have another come loose and get caught in his shirt.

Probably chastity, given his physical attraction to Queisha, but whatever virtues he failed, losing the corresponding feathers bore the same consequence. For each feather he lost, he got closer to being human—and dead again—and farther from his angelic persona. Not that he didn't have scads of feathers in various virtues all coded with their own colors, but the consequences of losing them did, indeed, worry him.

Drat, whatever his concern, the loose feather was driving him crazy—tickling and scratching and generally relating archangels warnings with the annoyance—trapped in his shirt, until he could find a place to get it the blessed saints out of there.

Righteous folly, given his attraction to Queisha, if he *were* wearing his robe of many colors, he'd be dropping feathers all over the house. The triumvirate must be laughing their halos off.

"So, Mr. Godricson," Queisha said after they left the sunroom. "Vivica let slip in the carousel that you were a hero. In what way are you?"

"I am not. I assure you. Your home is beautiful," he said, and she tilted her head in such a way as to indicate to him her willingness to go with his change of subject. Fine, she'd only been making conversation. Now, so was he.

She brought them to her safari den, and he let her give the tour, acting surprised by her tribute to the land of her Kenyan ancestors.

She'd painstakingly hand-painted the "seemingly undulating" zebra-striped floor that, at first glance, appeared as if it might cause seasickness. The floor made you hope you didn't lose your balance if you stood on it, though it turned out to be as flat as any floor in the house. Queisha was quite the amazing artist, as her home attested.

He found the safari den to be the perfect room in which to keep himself from eating Queisha up with his gaze and revealing his long-standing and forbidden emotions. He was able to study, in every unique detail, the intricately carved ebony elephant, the amazing ceremonial tribal masks, and the leopard skin wall hanging.

He also needed to pretend that her entire home was a surprise to him, when in fact, he knew the effort she put into decorating it. He'd watched her doing it.

Vivica sat on the cordovan leather sofa and patted the

space beside her for her friend. "Queisha," she said. "Tell me why you think Chance should not live in. Does it have to do with the agoraphobia? I hope you don't mind that I told him. I felt that for you to work comfortably together, he needed to know."

"It's a bit disconcerting knowing I was discussed, but under the circumstances, I understand."

The way Queisha looked away from him and chewed her bottom lip gave the impression she was not okay with Vivica's sharing, when in fact there had been no need for the acclimator to share. He knew everything about this amazing, life-affirming, and life-celebrating woman with whom he had fallen in love.

Chance worked to keep from staring at Queisha while he wished he could tell her the truth. But Vivica did say that Queisha didn't believe in angels.

Twenty minutes in her company and he loved her zest for life even more, so he could easily forgive her for not believing in angels, something that many people considered as much a myth as a fairy or a pixie.

God, the She of Life, must be proud of Queisha, a work of art so beautiful she could inspire half the male angels to shed their wings, if they were set to guard her as he had been.

Torn between his duties as her guardian and her pull as a woman—the woman who possessed his heart—Chance worried about his acting skills. How could he pretend not to love her?

He should resign as her guardian, he supposed, go back to Everlasting, and mind his own business.

Except that Queisha had been his business since the moment he found her frightened and filthy, bloodstained but beautiful, crouched near a pile of debris, hands around her scratched legs, head on her knees, singing a sweet, soft version of "Over the Rainbow."

Head over heels, he thought. *In the deepest trouble any man can know. Crazy, madly, passionately . . . lost.*

"Actually, Vivica," Chance said. "I think Queisha is right. I shouldn't live here with her. She can handle the girls during the night. I'll commute."

EIGHT

"Chance," Vivica said, *"are you sure commuting will* be enough? You have a contract for the long term, don't forget."

How vague and oblique of Vivica. They were talking in riddles, and Queisha didn't like the sound of it. Chance had a contract with whom? The Fitzpatrick relatives? To do what? Keep an eye on her?

"How double-oh-seven of you, Vivica. I don't appreciate being left out of the conversation," she snapped. "Fine, you had to tell him about my phobia, my faults and idiosyncratic quirks, but I *am* in the room and I am not a child. You don't need to spell the big words."

Vivica crossed her lips with a finger for a second. "My apologies."

Chance scratched his back weirdly, and kept tucking in his shirt as he paced, but didn't he make a fine sight, anyway? She hated speaking in anger, but if forthright ire resulted in getting to watch the way Chance Godricson's body moved when agitated, then lucky her.

One thing she noted when Vivica said the girls must be getting heavy for Chance beside the carousel was that he had seemed to be glowing inwardly, the more so by the moment, for holding them, not suffering their burden.

Vivica and Chance might have some kind of secret between them, but they were not quite on the same wavelength. Curious.

As if sensing her turmoil, Chance stopped to look down at her. "Agoraphobia is an issue to be treated, not one to be embarrassed by. What I see in you is a charming, quirky woman, one I'd like to get to know better. Queisha, let me be frank. You intrigue me. Man to woman. *That's* why I hesitate to stay here."

Unable to sit still a minute longer, she shot to her feet intending to pace as well, which would reveal her angst over his admitted attraction to her. Rather than be so obvious, she went to the sunroom to check the girls, sleeping like angels. She smoothed the damp hair from their brows thinking she should have removed their blazers and ties, and unbuttoned their top buttons before they fell asleep, but now she didn't want to disturb them.

As for her, she was evading the issue: Chance Godricson. Chance hesitating to live here . . . for the same reason she didn't want him to.

Lightbulb moment.

She leaned against the doorjamb unbuttoning her own top buttons. They were attracted to each other. Mutual magnetic attraction?

This co-guardianship would most certainly *not* work.

Would it? Wait a minute, now. A handsome man interested in *her*? An adult to share this unique but potentially difficult time in her life. Someone with whom to share ideas. At first sight, she'd liked his manners and the way he handled, cared for, and spoke gently to the girls.

And, oh, his voice. It soothed her in ways she couldn't name.

She crossed her arms and ambled back into the safari den. "So, Sir Chance, do you think you *can't* be professional enough to cook for us and help me with the girls? Are you worried you'll cross the line? Or are you worried I'll cross it?"

"Oh, it's me," he admitted. "I can't lie. I'm worried about me crossing the line."

"Fine then," Queisha said. "Here's the deal. I'm setting down some rules. I'm allowed to cross the line, and you're not."

Chance chuckled. "What kind of deal is that?"

Queisha examined her rainbow nails. "It's a deal I'm comfortable with. Are you afraid of me? Worried about your virtue?"

He opened his mouth like a fish out of water and swallowed whatever he might have wanted to say. "Of course not."

"Do you think you can be a proper co-guardian? Because if not, you're right, you have to go." Queisha glanced at Vivica's bright, amused eyes and realized her friend was enjoying their role reversal, hers and Chance's.

He shook his head and bowed. "Don't think your phobia or quirks, as you call them, make you any less a woman in control, Ms. Saint-Denis. You just proved your strength as far as I'm concerned."

"I'll take that as a compliment."

"Please do. And on that note, I vow that I can be as good a guardian as you can."

"Oh, I don't know. I'm not convinced that you *can* do the job . . . to my satisfaction."

"I can."

"Let's say we share the care of the girls for a trial period of . . . two weeks?"

Chance nodded, his fists knuckle-white. "That would be acceptable. Care to make a wager?"

"What kind of wager?"

"If I'm a good cook and guardian, you have to take a step outside, on my arm, each of us with a toddler by the hand."

Queisha tilted her head and recognized either a strong adversary or a strong advocate. "Only one step?"

"Five steps then?"

"A full turn about the yellow-brick patio," she said. "And if you fail?"

He tilted his head with respect. "Name my forfeit."

A night in your arms, she thought, shocking herself. The warmth climbing up her neck made her turn away and scan the room, not sure where her unexpected desire had come from, especially at first meeting. "You'll hang from the ceilings and clean the chandeliers, especially the ones on the vaulted ceilings. I can never seem to get up that high."

"I can get up that high," he quipped with a misplaced wink, and Vivica swallowed wrong, so Queisha had to get her a glass of water.

Queisha and Chance shook hands, a simmering heat shooting up Queisha's arm straight to her heart, like a living jolt of well-being with a side of sincerity. This man could be trusted, though he did have secrets. Big bleeping secrets.

For the first time in her life trust was hers for the taking . . . and it frightened her.

Vivica nodded with satisfaction. "Now that's settled, we have to consider transportation. You'll need a car, Queisha, in case of childhood accidents, reactions to travel shots, that kind of thing. Chance will drive. I'll leave you my limo."

"No need. There are several cars in my carriage house out back."

"What kind of cars?" Chance asked, curiosity piqued. "Since you don't drive, I mean."

"They were my aunt's cars. She was quite the eccentric, hence the carousel. The cars are old, but collectors have tracked them down and made fine offers. I have an album with pictures of them somewhere around here. Anyway, there's an early Mustang, a rare one, evidently. The first Dodge Charger; weird-looking car. An early twentieth-century Mercury with a vase for flowers inside and etched-glass windows. A fifties convertible; I forget the make. My favorite is the DeLorean. And just for balance, one of Ford's first Model Ts. Evidently, it came with a picture of Ford taking Edison for a spin in the very car."

"We don't need your limo, Vivica," Chance said. "I can drive a different vintage beauty every day, except for the Model T, though maybe the girls would like a turn around the estate in that." Chance whooped, a Native American kind of war cry, high-pitched, celebratory. Chills-up-the-spine earthy.

A shiver ran through Queisha. A primordial physicality and sensuality; that's what Chance Godricson had brought to the Saint-Denis house, God help her.

She veiled her interest. "You act like you haven't driven a car in years. Or is it just vintage cars that turn you into a little boy on Christmas morning?"

His grin had Christmas morning written all over it.

NINE

"*Chance,*" *Vivica said, amused,* "*you can't drive a vin-*tage car with the girls inside."

"Why the hell not? Ah, excuse me." He cleared his throat. "Why the blessed saints not?"

"Vintage cars are not tricked out for twenty-first-century car seats, so we *will* have to trade." Vivica dangled a set of keys before him. "You get the limo, I get the DeLorean."

Queisha chuckled, feeling at ease for the first time that day. As if that wasn't enough, Chance gave her a peek at his boyish side. He pouted as he accepted the keys. "This is like a repeat of the Christmas my mother wrapped socks in a Lionel train box."

Queisha chuckled and headed for the kitchen. "I'll make tea so we can all get to know one another."

"Shouldn't I do that? I'm the cook."

"Tea is my specialty and I can make one thing: lady

cakes. It's meals I have a problem with, so, my treat. Relax. I think the girls are down for the count."

Vivica stood. "Do either of you mind if I get going? I have a couple of appointments I'd like to be on time for."

"Sure," Queisha said. "Chance can take the limo home."

"Home?" Chance and Vivica asked together.

"Well, I'm not ready for him to live in, not at first, anyway. For the two-week trial, I'd prefer that he commute. I know it seems like I'm sending mixed messages, back-pedaling, as it were, but think of it as self-preservation. I'm a loner and not used to having a man in the house." *Especially not one who reminds me that I'm a woman . . . with womanly needs.* "Let me take this in steps, okay?" Queisha parted her hands in supplication.

"I understand Queisha's reasoning, Vivica," Chance said. "But I'm not driving the limo unless it's an emergency. I'll take a boat or a water taxi back and forth."

Vivica opened her mouth to argue, but Chance raised a hand and she changed tack. "Queisha, may I have the keys to the DeLorean?" she asked, instead. "Please?"

"Because you are obviously so excited about driving it, yes, of course you can have them." Queisha went to her Aunt Helen's wall board, where rows of hooks held keys, and grabbed the DeLorean set for Vivica.

It tickled Queisha that Chance went outside to watch Vivica drive that car away while she made tea and arranged cakes on a tray.

"I'm not normally a tea drinker," Chance said a short while later, lowering his cup to the coffee table, making her cordovan leather sofa look better than it ever had. Comfy. Inviting. "But there's a taste here," he said, "that's refreshing and soothing at the same time."

His easy presence in her home improved the atmosphere, as if he belonged here, or had been here before. Impossible.

Still, the ceremonial masks, the Kenyan carvings on the mantel, none of it fazed him. He admired it but wasn't startled by it. "Mixing teas is something of a hobby for me. This one is Pomegranate Passion, and not only is it delicious but it's full of antioxidants, if you drink it warm."

Chance raised his cup. "I hope you'll like my cooking as much as I like your tea."

"Wait until you taste my cakes."

"I came here with nothing more in mind than to taste your cakes."

Judging by the stillness of the cup halfway to his mouth, the double meaning caught him off guard as much as it did her. Queisha topped off their cups so they wouldn't have to look at each other for a minute.

Sweet, creamy chai—the Kenyan word for tea—was no place to hide. She couldn't seem to dodge the kinetic energy zinging between them—like she wore a big dartboard where unwanted energy, ripe with sexual tension wrapped in pheromones, zapped her in shivery points.

She sipped and dared to peek at him over the rim of her cup. Zing! Awareness times infinity. "So . . . how do you know the Fitzpatricks?" she asked to lower the heat between them to a slow simmer.

"Who?" Confusion furrowed his brow.

She set down her cup. "The girls' parents? Why did they name you co-guardian if you don't know them?"

Chance Godricson cupped his neck, revealing definite discomfort in the face of her question.

And then knowledge dawned, in her mind, at least. "Ohhhh. Did you donate the sperm?"

He spilled tea on his lap. His don't-look-there lap, the term "hung like bull" coming to mind. She bit her lip, in lieu of licking it.

And she'd thought her libido was dead. So not.

She tried to act cool as the wet tea spread until she realized how long she'd been watching, and she snapped her gaze back to his face, too late, given his awareness of her interest.

In other circumstances, she'd want to explore the sparkle in his azure eyes, his dark lashes lowering to half mast, and turn that twinkle into major satisfaction. Oh, the possibilities.

Bedroom eyes. Bedroom, really? Because I dreamed *of them?*

Their silence lasted too long to be comfortable. She handed him a napkin.

"Do you have a blow-dryer?" he asked. "Wouldn't want the girls to think I had an accident."

Queisha slapped a hand to her mouth on a nervous titter. She never tittered. She was appalled she'd done so. "I'll show you to an upstairs bathroom. Follow me."

"To the ends of the earth," she thought he muttered beneath his breath.

"What?"

"Gladly, gratefully, best place on earth to repair such damage, a bathroom, I mean."

"The bathrooms down here don't have hair-dryers, though I could throw your pants in the clothes dryer."

He tripped on the stairs.

She caught him to keep him from falling.

He steadied her with an arm around her waist. Tight. Up close, his breath against her cheek.

"God, you have long lashes," she said.

"Thanks?" He stepped back.

Of course he'd tripped. Putting his pants in the clothes dryer would require him to remove them, including whatever he wore beneath them. Would they match his outfit? He seemed to have an eye for color. Was his hidden layer aqua? Gray? Bikinis? Boxers?

Imagination is half the fun. First bleeping day.

She hit the pause button on the underwear video in her mind. Maybe she *was* certifiable. "Sorry, bad idea," she said.

They continued up the stairs.

"So," she said, "you're the girls' guardian because?"

"It was a general consensus."

She indicated the bathroom. "With the Fitzpatricks' relatives? Their lawyer?"

"That's a matter of confidentiality," he said, rather abruptly before he shut the bathroom door in her face.

Maybe the Fitzpatrick relatives didn't appreciate having her, a stranger, as the girls' guardian. She should probably worry about this turn of events, but the mind video of him dropping his pants continued on its own. When she tried stopping it, she got stuck imagining herself blotting the tea off his lap the way she'd blotted it off her tablecloth earlier.

She heard the blow-dryer and wondered if he'd keep his pants and turquoise jock sock on, or take them off, while he blew himself dry.

Eek! Out, damned spot—out, damned vision. She hurried downstairs, fanning her face, to check on the girls and gather her wits.

That's what was wrong with a male co-guardian. The life of a semi-contented celibate went right out the window when a knight in rusty armor showed up.

Sir Chance, indeed.

TEN

As he returned, she tried very hard not to check his lap to see if the tea stain showed. "Why didn't you just change your clothes?" she asked. "Didn't you come planning to stay?"

"I didn't think that springing myself on you as a houseguest was a good idea. I intended to go back for my things, on the rare chance it worked out for me to stay, which it didn't."

"You sound as if you know me."

"I may sound that way, but it simply doesn't seem polite to show up at a stranger's house with a suitcase."

"We're agreed on that. Tell me more about yourself."

"I'll tell you the good, and you can figure out the bad as we go."

"Works for me; doesn't take long at all for the bad to come out."

"My ancestors are Irish, though I was born in Rhode

Island. I'm a simple man, adaptable, spontaneous, easy-going, resilient, broad-minded," he said, "and something of a failure."

"You weren't supposed to mention the bad, but how are you a failure, in your opinion?"

"In my last incarnation, I was an unremarkable lawyer."

"That's odd," she said, "I'm sure I've heard that before, but where?"

He shook his head. "It's one of those phrases you hear everywhere."

"Really? I only ever heard it once, I'm sure, but I don't get out much, so it could be popular."

"Don't let it bother you. Unremarkable lawyers are, by nature, nonjudgmental."

A little girl's cry put the period to their talk, but Queisha would prefer to describe herself later, anyway, after she had time to phrase it properly, so as to keep him from thinking her an escapee from a psych ward.

By the time they got to the sunroom, both girls were crying, disoriented, and sweaty from napping in the warm room.

Chance picked up Skye and it took her a minute to recognize him and slow her sobs.

Good thing Queisha remembered which girl she put on which love seat, though she'd have to find a way to tell them apart better, later.

Lace, the less trusting twin, struggled a bit when Queisha picked her up, until she gave in to that soft glow of after-sleep and let her back be stroked while Queisha whispered soft assurance. "I'll take care of you," she promised. "Not to worry. You'll always have a home here."

"No, we won't," Lace whispered back. "Mother gave us to the school. The school gave us to you. You'll give us away, too."

Queisha's heart about broke. Having been adopted, then thrown out by her adoptive father, she knew how it felt not being wanted, and she could weep that her girls knew it, too. "I'd only give you to your mother."

Lace sighed and rested her head on Queisha's shoulder. "Then we're safe here. She doesn't want us." Lace took in her surroundings, including her sister not far away, as if their whispered conversation had never happened.

Lace's ability to tune out her sorrow scared Queisha. It reminded her of her own ability to tune out the world. If she couldn't get over her agoraphobia for herself, she'd damned well better overcome it for the girls. "Chance, follow me to the water porch," Queisha said, wondering what Lace meant by her mother not wanting her. "It's one floor up, and there are two rockers. Great view of Salem Cove."

Chance gave a half nod. "Excellent."

The adults each chose a rocker, and for a while the girls were inclined to cuddle and enjoy the attention.

Queisha pointed out the sailboats on Salem Cove, some circling Paxton Island smack between Marblehead and Salem, though closer to Marblehead.

"Should we take off their blazers?" Chance asked her.

"Not right away. It's chilly and they're sweaty. I don't want them to catch cold."

Lace got off Queisha's lap first, to go and stand by the screened windows and look out at the water.

A minute later, Skye left Chance to do the same.

"Girls, how about a glass of milk or orange juice to hold you until dinner, with a lady cake?"

Skye shrugged, and Lace didn't even turn her head.

"I wish they'd say something," Chance whispered.

"Lace did," Queisha pointed out. "Tell you about it later."

He covered her hand for a second. "See, they're already getting comfortable with you."

Queisha almost wished Lace had said she wanted her mother, because that would mean they'd had a normal childhood so far. But they evidently hadn't.

"I'll get them a snack," he said. "Point me to the kitchen."

She gave him directions. "I'll take the girls for a walk up to the tower."

She took them, each by a hand, and described each room they went through.

A bit curious and a little less shy, they seemed interested in the rooms she had decorated to represent different parts of the world. When they got to the tower, they gravitated toward the tea party dolls, stopping beside the chairs the dolls sat in, though they didn't so much as touch them.

"I made the dolls with you in mind before you were born, but I never had a chance to give them to you. Go ahead, take them; they're yours."

The dolls were different from each other, and the girls did an odd thing. They each picked up the doll closest to them but traded without a word passing between them and cradled their dolls as if they cherished them, the way Queisha wished she could hold them.

"Thank you," they said together.

"You're welcome."

Chance joined them. "It's gorgeous up here. Hey, girls, nice dolls."

"They're ours," Lace said.

Skye pointed. "From that . . . from Missy Queisha."

"Oh Lordy, such a formal name, but I guess it'll do until we find something better. I knew you when you were born, which is why I'm taking care of you until your . . . until you're ready to go home."

"No one knows where Mother and Father are," Skye said and shrugged. "Do we have to wear uniforms while we're here and study every minute?"

"I make the rules here, and it's school break in this country, so no uniforms, and I insist that you play every day."

Little eyes got wide, and Skye nearly cracked a smile. "This is way better than Holy Angels."

Chance coughed and cleared his throat as he rubbed his hands together. "Lunch is ready. How about a grilled cheese sandwich, a glass of milk, and one of Queisha's lady cakes?"

"Peanut butter," Skye said.

Lace nodded. "And fluff. With potato chips."

Ultimately, they didn't eat much because their eyes kept closing, but they managed to stay awake for lady cakes with peaches and whipped cream.

"How long since you've had a bath?" Queisha asked.

"Tuesday," Lace said.

"No, Monday, remember?" Skye said. "Sister Oscar wanted us to hurry so she could *pray*."

Lace rolled her eyes and regarded them with a sarcastic look. "That means 'watch television.'"

Skye nodded. "It's true."

Queisha squeaked. "With all that traveling, you haven't had a bath in days? To the tub, young ladies, then I have a comfy bed for each of you."

Chance hesitated at the bottom of the stairs. "Should I wait down here?"

"Heck no. I've never given a child a bath in my life, much less two at the same time."

"Well, neither have I." He ran a hand through his hair in an endearing manner, like two little girls could get the best of him.

"Either way, two against two are better odds than two against one."

"Good point."

"Don't look so scared," Queisha said. "After baths, we're home free with bedtime."

"We're not tired," the girls whined, but Queisha herded them into the master bath and filled the huge oval tub with Jacuzzi jets for them. When they saw the bubbles erupting from every side, their clothes came off in a blink.

Queisha wrapped them in towels for modesty's sake until she got the water to the perfect temperature.

While the girls waited, Skye collected their uniforms, went to the window, opened it, and tossed them down two floors with the zing and determination of a strike-out pitcher.

"Yay!" the girls jumped up and down applauding while their modesty towels fell to the floor.

Chance turned with a chuckle and mumbled something about retrieving their shoes.

"That's probably best," Queisha said, "at least until we buy some fairy princess shoes."

"It's that way, is it?" he said. "Play, play, play. I'll be Sir Chance to two princesses?"

"Abso-frog-kissing-lutely. And I can be Lady Queisha,

their lady-in-waiting. We'll find princess dresses, too, shall we, girls?"

The twins' eyes lit up. They looked at each other, then Queisha, with reverential awe.

They needed to learn to play, Queisha thought, and by damned, she was going to teach them. "I wonder if there's such a thing as a princess rubber ducky for your baths. We'll get two."

ELEVEN

Chance got back from fetching the girls' shoes in time to watch them finish their baths. This was all new to him, since he'd never had children, and guardian angels weren't allowed access to bathrooms and bedrooms, unless they sensed dire circumstances.

The girls had lovely tans that would make a nice gauge right now, if not in winter. If they faded in summer, he'd know they weren't getting outside enough. He'd try to make Queisha aware of their need for sunshine, whether she needed it or not.

"Sir Chance," Skye said, her expression serious. "Lady Queisha said we need a bath every day, so could you buy us princess rubber duckies at a store tomorrow?"

Lace nodded. "We can't shop on the computer 'cause we can't wait. This is a mergency."

"Uh, sure," Chance said. "But they might not have princess duckies."

"Just make sure they're girl ducks," Skye said.

Lace nodded vigorously. "Pretty girl ducks."

He, a guardian angel fourth class, had been given the task of rubber ducky shopping. Fancy that.

Queisha's shoulders shook suspiciously as she knelt over the tub and washed each girl's hair, both of them looking a little like a white-haired pixie. Then Queisha filled two plastic pails with clean lukewarm water from the tap and poured them simultaneously over the girls' heads.

Screaming, and shaking, the girls shot to their feet, eyes closed, reaching for towels.

Queisha dropped the pails in the water and quickly wiped their eyes. "I'm sorry. I'm sorry. I guess I need to learn to do this better. Are you okay?"

"Drowned," Lace said. "You drowned us."

Skye giggled at her sister. "I was surprised. We always saw the hosey thing coming that Sister used."

Faces dry, hair rinsed, they sat back in the tub to splash each other, having learned this new form of sibling torture.

Queisha knelt beside the tub, again, to finish washing them, and when she was most focused on her task, the girls did that twin thing, communicating without words, and filled those pails with sudsy water to throw straight at her.

Queisha screamed, and Chance bit his lip, charmed as hell, well, Everlastingly charmed.

She could win a wet T-shirt contest, he thought, high-fiving each twin, bringing out their dimples, as he grabbed the thickest towel from the nearby stack to wrap around Queisha. "Do you need someone to wipe *your* eyes?" He blew suds off her lowered lashes.

She sighed. "Mmm, yes, please."

He hadn't thought she'd agree. A good sign, Queisha letting her signature whimsy out to play. He raised a corner of the towel and wiped her eyes, gently, thoroughly, the girls watching the two of them with unblinking focus.

Queisha opened her eyes, and the girls broke out in grins. "I got the message," she told them. "No more water surprises."

Chance stepped away, slipped on the wet floor, and landed on his rump.

Queisha applauded. The girls cheered. He'd entertained the women in his life. What a high, he thought, getting up. How could he go back to Everlasting after this?

"Chance," Queisha said. "Two pink bath towels. Grab a kid, wrap her up, and follow me into my bedroom."

Words he'd dreamed of hearing from her for years. *Follow me into my bedroom.*

"Yes, ma'am."

Queisha looked back at him and gave him a double take.

He returned a blank look that didn't feel as innocent as it should.

"Where's their luggage?"

"The airlines lost it," Chance said. "They checked their bags in late in Switzerland. It's probably in Uruguay about now."

"Okay, girls, pick out a shorty nightgown." She opened a drawer filled with secrets by Victoria, and before the girls got to it, Chance nearly had a heart attack until reality intruded.

Towel-wrapped munchkins rooted through bright-colored silks and satins, fabrics he wanted between his skin and Queisha's. The kind of nighties that made a woman seem feminine and kissable. Unless her man saw kids wearing them first.

The twins looked and sounded like magpies playing dress up. After their travels and hot baths, they'd sleep like babies.

Heck, they *were* babies. Queisha's babies—forever, *if* he could help her find the courage. He almost wished he didn't know her so well. When all was said and done, this was not going to be easy.

They'd made their choices, and they looked like angels in training, Skye wearing peach satin and ribbons, Lace in ruffled yellow silk, holding up their hems—shorties or not—to walk behind Queisha, like baby ducks following their mama.

Queisha had a bedroom on each side, adjoining hers. "This room," she said, "is decorated in English lavender—color and flowers." Its theme, Great Britain, given the castle paintings and collection of miniature thatched-roof cottage figurines.

"Mine," Lace said. "Everything matches."

"It's like I knew you were coming," Queisha said.

Chance picked Lace up and threw her gently into the lavender bed.

She bounced, and after a minute of shock, she raised her arms. "Again?"

"Once a night," he said, "then Queisha tucks you in."

"What's a tuck?"

"Scootch under the covers," Queisha said, her voice wobbly sad. Her little ones had never been tucked in. "There you go. Then I pull the covers up to your chin and tuck them against your body all around, down your side, around your cute tiny toes, and up your other side. Comfy?"

Lace nodded.

"Then I kiss you good night." She smoothed back Lace's hair and kissed her brow. "Night, sweetie. I'm glad you're here. Happy dreams."

Queisha led Skye toward the bedroom on the other side of her own. "This is my Irish bedroom. A mint background wallpaper with rainbows and shamrocks."

Skye applauded. "I like it. No matchie-matchies."

"I like it, too," Lace said behind them.

"What are you doing up? You undid all my tucking."

"I needed to know where to find Skye." Lace looked up at him. "I need to be tucked again . . . and stuff."

Skye giggled. "Faker." And raised her arms to Chance. "Bounce me, please."

He repeated the process and so did Queisha, but when it came time for a good night kiss, Skye puckered up. Queisha obliged, and just before she turned off the light, he saw the glow in her bright, happy eyes.

Because Lace needed her hard edge slightly sanded, she got the full treatment, again, and when she didn't pucker up, Queisha kissed her own finger and touched it to Lace's lips.

They heard her little puffle snore before they left the room.

"Jet lag," Chance whispered.

She put a hand across her lips—lips he wanted to kiss, especially in the middle of her bedroom—and left the doors ajar so she could hear the girls during the night. They tiptoed to her sitting room, his back feather-itching like the dickens, Queisha still damp from her soaking but glowing from her tucking.

"Good job, Mom," he said.

"Oh, don't call me that. It'll make it that much harder to let them go."

"Sorry, but you were magickal. The sleep costumes were an inspiration."

"Costumes? I wear those to bed every night—not all at once, of course."

He'd been afraid of that and he had the palpitations to prove it.

Now his back itched the more, so he went into the bathroom, rooted around beneath his shirt and pulled out three silver feathers. Silver for chastity, lust being the polar opposite of said virtue, hence the lost feathers.

He looked up beyond the firmament. "Are you kidding me? I'm gonna lose one every time I want her?"

He hadn't known he could drop feathers with his wings tucked away. They had scratched his skin as they worked their way out of the muscle sacs where his wings were tightly packed.

Of all the things to learn, when he should forget he'd been in love with her for years, was the kind of sexy nightgowns she liked to wear and the hidden depths of her sensuality.

"Why are you not married?" he asked, coming back to the sitting room. "Are the men of earth so dense?"

"The men of earth? What are you, a Martian?"

"It's an expression. Really, why are you alone?"

"This may come as a surprise to you, but I'm a vigilant, energetic, free-spirited scaredy-cat."

"You're a treasure."

"You've been duped. I never leave home, so I never meet anyone, and I wouldn't want to jail the man I loved in this house with me, though I have been trying to learn to come and go."

"You're selling yourself short. If you were mine, I'd never want to leave you."

Her eyes widened to luminescent liquid gold. "What did you say?"

Oops. Don't be saying what you're thinking, Angel Man. "I mean, if you found the right man, your phobia wouldn't make a difference to him. He'd understand and make a life here with you. Sure, he might have to go to work every day, but he'd sure look forward to coming home to you."

Angus would tell him to stop blatherin' and he'd be well within his rights to do so. "You're someone a man would want to be with, to take care of. He'd want to calm your fears. Show you the world."

"Hold it right there," she said. "I've tried to make peace with not seeing the world."

"Which is why you have a safari den, a Parisian parlor, shades of Ireland in one bedroom, Great Britain in another, an Irish pub, a telescope on Salem."

"That's me making the best of the life handed me," she snapped. "Frankly, I have good reason to live and love life. I live it for two, if you must know, and I'm proud of that."

For herself and for him, he knew. It was the last thing he told her when he boosted her up the tunnel: "Live for the two of us," and she'd been true to his memory in doing it.

She tilted her head, a query in her expression. "I didn't show you my Irish pub."

That woke him up. "Vivica told me about it."

"I had no idea that she was such a gossip. Or that you are."

Righteous folly, leaving this woman would kill him, again, body *and* spirit this time.

TWELVE

From her sitting room, the moon looked huge and close enough to touch as she watched Chance watch her, the two of them in facing easy chairs. A moment of sheer contentment. But she couldn't let it be. "Five bucks for your thoughts."

He chuckled. "Inflation?"

"In this economy? Do you doubt it?"

"My thoughts aren't worth a penny."

"Why don't I believe you?"

"Let me rephrase my answer. They're not for sale."

She raised a brow and attempted to charm him with a pout, but she didn't think it worked.

"I'll go clean the kitchen from the double snacks I made the girls, my choice of grilled cheese, and their choice of peanut butter and fluff. You're still damp from your dowsing. Change into dry things, get into bed with a good book, and if you'd like, before I leave, I'll bring you a cup of hot chamomile tea."

"Thank you; I *would* like." Queisha sat stunned as he left, because she thought he might have tried to kiss her, though their bet stated that only she could make the first move. Hmm. Did she have it in her? And suppose she'd misjudged his interest. One of those rare breeds, a gentleman, Chance would likely be polite if she tried to kiss him and he didn't want to kiss her back. How humiliating would that be?

Uncertain, bereft, cool and clammy, and in lust for the first time in her life, she grabbed a long nightgown and matching robe and went into her bathroom for a shower, hoping to wash away her disappointment.

When she came out, saffron satin robe tied around her waist, she made her way downstairs to the kitchen, taking the initiative, like the bet called for. Nothing like chasing a man.

"Hey," Chance said, turning away from reading the back of the chamomile tea box. "I thought you were going to snuggle up and get warm. The way I hear it, kids don't exactly sleep late in the morning."

"Neither do I."

"So, what? Breakfast at five?"

"You'd have to be here at four." It appalled her, the thought of working him so hard. "How about breakfast at six?" she suggested. "I can make hot chocolate to hold us, if necessary." She took the tea box from his hand. "Don't tell me you don't know how to make tea?"

"There's no bag in this box. It's like dry leaves. Give me a break. I didn't know whether to throw it into the teapot or pulverize it and look for a box of empty bags."

"You do sound like you're from another planet and not at all like you went to cooking school."

"No cooking school. Natural talent, and not much of that. Vivica can talk an Alaskan into a snow maker." Chance chuckled self-consciously.

And just hearing it, Queisha knew, with an inner shiver, what she'd missed not having a man in the house. Something about male amusement could inspire a woman to yearn for . . . all kinds of manly attention—from this man, in particular.

"Would you like a cup?" she asked, when the teakettle whistled.

"I'm beat. Mind if I have something stronger to keep me awake on the way home?" He made himself a cup of instant coffee, a rarely used staple in her cupboard, and she cringed.

He raised his steaming cup her way. "One for the road."

She raised hers. "For a peaceful night."

Thunder roared as if in answer, then lightning lit the room, and she saw that his yearning mirrored her own.

With a tilt of his head, Chance gave her a half shrug. "Guess the universe is saying you won't get your peaceful night, and I'll be boating across the water in a storm."

"Are you trying to play on my sympathy? Two weeks," she stressed. "We agreed. Take the limo."

He left his laptop on the kitchen counter, headed for the door, stopped, and turned back to her. "Honor to be working with you, ma'am."

"Queisha," she corrected.

"Lady Queisha, ma'am."

In the blink of an eye, he'd disappeared. She waited to hear the limo start, even ran up to the widow's walk tower to look out and see him safely away. But the car stood untouched.

Window to window, she went, but Chance Godricson was nowhere to be seen. She dialed his cell phone.

"Son of Godric," he answered. "Flying between lightning bolts. Be careful where you aim them, you crusty Scot."

"Funny, ha, ha," Queisha snapped. "The limo's still here. You're traveling by boat in a storm?"

"I have an umbrella."

"You have a death wish."

She loved the sound of his mirth, which seemed totally misplaced and over the top.

A few minutes later, the memory of his laughter, and of her babies' sleeping faces, made her relax as she closed her eyes to sleep.

Thunder and running feet woke her in the dead of night. Skye running through her room.

Of course, as twins they'd seek each other out if they were afraid, certainly not the stranger who carried them for the first nine months of their lives.

Acceptance topped her personal list of virtues, so Queisha turned on her side, toward the sound of little voices in the next room, and simply appreciated the fact that they were here.

As she began again to doze, the weight of the world landed on her chest. She tried to sit up to catch her breath and caught the little body that slid off her before Skye fell from the bed. "That was you?"

"I'm scared."

"What about Lace?"

"I can't wake her up. She's never scared."

"Lucky her. Here, get under the covers so you don't

catch a chill." For a June storm, the temperature had dropped quite a bit.

Quick as a wink, Skye snuggled up to her, head on her shoulder, little feet tucked beneath her knees. Queisha thought her heart would burst from her chest. Joy. Unbridled. One of her babies in her arms, trusting her.

Hail pummeled windowpanes and roof, and brought her second baby girl slowly toward her. Lace stood at the foot of the bed, cradling and rocking her new doll. "Dolly is scared."

Skye sighed theatrically. "Dolly is a *stupid* name for a doll!"

"I *know*!"

Queisha tried not to show her amusement. "Dolly can climb in with us, but I don't think she'll stop being scared unless you're with her."

"I can keep her from being afraid. Can I?"

Queisha lifted the blankets on her other side and Lace crawled in, yawning. The girls reached across her, their arms a welcome weight as they held hands.

No more storm, not in her heart, at least.

No more loneliness, not for Queisha Saint-Denis. She wouldn't let herself sleep or miss a minute of this time with them. No, they weren't kicking from within but wiggling from without. They had words now. Unique dispositions, Lace a bit more emotionally scarred than Skye. So said one day's observation. She'd see what the future revealed.

Why would their parents need to go mountain climbing for excitement? Why put these beautiful babes in an institution? Why did Lace think her mother didn't want them?

Queisha wasn't sorry she'd carried them for the Fitzpatricks, because they wouldn't be here if she hadn't. She could, however, tell the Fitzpatricks what she thought of their parenting when they came for the girls.

On the other hand, if she did, would they think twice about keeping her as the girls' guardian? After this, she'd want contact; would they agree if she spoke her mind? Something to consider.

Around five in the morning, Queisha slid from beneath the twins' hands, still clasped over her, and out the bottom of the covers. She chuckled after she shut the bathroom door, glad no one had seen her undignified exit from her own bed.

She usually woke about this time, so she didn't go back to bed. She watched the girls sleep, unconsciously gravitating toward each other until they snuggled in the way they'd been caught on her ultrasound pictures.

With the kind of contentment she remembered from carrying them, she went to the window, pulled the curtain aside, and saw Chance coming up the dock. She'd told him to come at six, but he knew what time she got up. Still, she wasn't ready to face him yet. She already wanted him to become a member of this temporary little family of hers, and that was just crazy.

She could have no man in her life as long as she struggled with her phobia. She would not. Especially not one she liked as much as Chance Godricson.

Like a fish swimming upstream, Queisha made her way back beneath the covers, footboard to headboard, and the girls separated in sleep to make room for her, never letting go of each other's hands.

She held them close while they slept, expecting the scent of breakfast to wake them.

THIRTEEN

Chance had spent the night in one of the apartments above Works Like Magick that Vivica used to house her clients until she found them work. So far he'd met assorted wee folk, a time-traveling Viking, a merman, and a werewolf. Altogether, despite the walls separating them, their combined snores sounded like a freight train in an echo chamber.

Good thing Chance chose to read about cooking for children in lieu of sleep. In Everlasting, he hadn't needed sleep, but when he'd hit himself in the face with a drooping, fifty pound tome, he realized that earth would be different in the way of sleep, as well.

He gave in to the temptation of Morpheus predawn, and an hour later, his alarm clock rang.

Oh, he knew Queisha said six, but she was being kind. She would have liked to eat earlier. Anyway, now that he was back in her kitchen, he was making them pancakes any little girl would love, including the little girl in one free-spirited guardian.

"Queisha?" he called from the bottom of the stairs. "Lace? Skye?"

No answer.

He went upstairs to find the twins' rooms empty and all three asleep in Queisha's bed.

His heart expanded in a way only Queisha had the ability to make it, but this time, it almost hurt. After having seen her bear those babies and give them up, this was the kind of sight that brought an ache to the back of a man's throat, to the heart he swore was made of marble, and it made him yearn. He knew he'd trade his life, again, for this woman, and now for her babes.

She opened her eyes as if she sensed his presence.

He raised a brow.

"Smells good, Son of Godric."

"Looks better," he said, not talking about the food but her.

She understood, because she blushed. "The storm scared them."

He knew he'd been smart to order it up. Angus had come through for him, again. Though answering the phone the way he had was a bit of a slipup.

She raised herself on an elbow. "That red shirt looks great on you," she whispered. "Same style as yesterday, right, but different color? The tie, too, this one matching this shirt."

He shrugged. "If I like it, I buy it in every color. It was always thus."

"Such a man. We'll shop online for you, too. I love your sense of color, but you need variety and more comfortable clothes. Mix it up a bit. Learn to relax."

The implication of a long-term arrangement in her suggestion alarmed him—when he knew it to be temporary—but he liked her attention. "Yes, ma'am." *Dearest Queisha. Shoot me now.* "Breakfast is ready."

"'Kay. See you in a few."

Before he reached the stairs, he heard the girls giggling. She must have tickled them awake. His heart lightened at the sound.

Queisha came down looking vibrant in a flowing flowered dress of every color. It made him miss his dream coat. But Lace and Skye made Queisha sparkle, not her clothes.

Refusing to have anything to do with uniforms, they each wore one of Queisha's T-shirts like a dress. Skye's, of neon pink, said "When" and depicted three little pale pink flying pigs. Lace's neon yellow bore a gingerbread man that said "Bite me."

Queisha helped set the table. "They picked out the shirts themselves."

"Okay," he said, "I'll get my sunglasses."

The girls high-fived each other. Animation. Already a change from yesterday.

"As soon as you eat your breakfast," Queisha said, "it'll be time for online shopping."

The girls hooted and applauded.

Chance winced at the sound. "Aren't you the lucky munchkins." He placed doll-face pancakes in front of them.

Skye licked her lips but sighed. "I'm lergic to strawberries."

Queisha tugged on his shirt. "So am I."

He replaced their strawberry noses with pineapple chunks. "Yes to whipped-cream hair and smiles?"

He got a resounding yes, hands down as the kettle whistled. "Perky Plum tea, my lady?"

"Don't mind if I do."

"Coffee milk." He set it before the girls.

"Does it have real coffee in it?" Skye asked, taking a tentative sip, then a deep drink.

"No," he said. "It has coffee syrup in it. Very much a Rhode Island favorite. I bought a case as soon as I landed."

"It's good." Skye licked her milk mustache.

That's when Lace tried it, and approved.

"I've never heard of it," Queisha said, tasting Skye's and liking it.

Chance drank some of his own. "I grew up drinking it. Wait until you taste coffee ice cream."

Lace looked up. "Can we put that on our pancakes?"

"No, but it makes a great caramel or chocolate sundae for dessert." He might not be as good a cook as he wished, but he'd aced breakfast.

"Now for shopping," Queisha said. "My rainbow room will make a fine playroom. It's on this floor and looks out over the water."

A rainbow room? Chance's radar went up. He'd never seen her there. "Care to take me for a tour?"

"Just let me grab my laptop so I can order what the girls need while they play."

"Have Mother and Father been found yet?" Lace asked as they headed toward the rainbow room.

That stopped him. He hadn't grasped the fact that the girls *knew* their parents were missing.

"Not that we know of, sweetie," Queisha said, "but it's possible they have, and we haven't heard yet."

Lace thought about that for a minute. "Okay." Then she was back to being a six-year-old discovering new toys.

Chance took in the room while Lace and Skye went straight for the dollhouse. "Queisha, you're ordering toys? There are more here than in Santa's workshop."

"Santa's a fake," Lace muttered.

"Is not," Skye said without looking up, indication of an ongoing argument.

Queisha nodded his way. "I'll buy them each a toy of their own, and give them one of these to remember me by. That way, I won't spoil them."

Chance smoothed his chin. "I think the toy boat has sailed on that one. Care to wager on whether you can stop at one toy?"

Queisha pointedly ignored him, probably because he was right.

"This room looks . . . familiar," he said. She'd painted a single swirling pastel rainbow around the soft white room. Colorful Care Bears lined a shelf on one wall. On another, a row of lifelike baby dolls, each wearing a different colored outfit, lined another shelf.

Chance especially liked the life-sized soft-sculpture fisherman sitting on a corner slipper chair wearing a battered bowler hat, worn leather vest, with a corncob pipe hanging from his mouth. His jeans were rolled up so he could soak his bare feet in a blue paper lake, and his fishing rod bobbed in a huge bowl filled with water, sea plants, coral, and one huge and excitable goldfish.

Queisha noticed the direction of his gaze. "That's Heirman Chumpster. I call him Chumpy. The fish is named Whale."

Actually the room wasn't cluttered, but tasteful, the dollhouse its centerpiece.

When Chance turned to look behind him, however, a wall mural about knocked him back to last Sunday. "Who painted that?"

"I did. Why?"

"How on earth"—and he meant that literally—"did the idea come to you?"

"I imagined it the morning the girls were born. To tell you the truth, I think I was a little out of my head at the time. I put this whole room together for them, shortly after. I think it's what kept me sane."

The painting depicted *him* in Everlasting, *if* his fears during Skye and Lace's delivery had come true, if he had not held them at the moment of their stillbirths, sprinkled them with angel dust, and put his mouth to theirs to breathe life into them . . . If he had not breathed life into Queisha, as well . . .

If he had not, this would be a picture of an actual event, rather than a dreaded possibility.

Queisha surely couldn't have seen the dread in his mind. True, he'd sat beside her during the girls' birth, sung to her, prayed for her, while a horrific fear of this scene filled his mind.

In the mural, he stood in his robe of many colors and carried two of his charges, who'd died at birth, the feathered stripes on his wings in the right color/virtue order, the gold feathers for love, the top row, glowing, bouncing off his features to the point of masking them from recognition. He was placing two kicking babes—Lace and Skye—with silk-soft dark hair, in the cherub nursery.

She'd painted the many-sided crystal walls, the iridescent cradles and the tiny wings you could see sprouting on the tummy-sleeping occupants, knees up, bottoms high. Some of the firmament's tiniest stars hung above the cradles like mobiles, the babes on their backs trying to catch them.

What human could see this sight and not be moved? Chance had been to the cherub nursery more often than he cared to admit, and it moved him still.

Queisha came to stand beside him, and without thought, he placed an arm around her shoulders, belatedly aware of it and surprised she let him.

She sighed. "But they *didn't* die."

He gave her a double take. "No, they didn't."

"You'll think I'm certifiable, but I believe I have that particular angel to thank for these two."

"You don't believe in angels."

"I say that to protect myself from accusations of idiocy."

"Give in to the idiocy for a minute. Humor me. What makes you think you have that angel to thank?"

"I floated above myself and saw him sitting next to me, saw this picture of worry in his mind."

So she knew she'd come close to dying with the twins. *That's* where she got her sixth sense. That place between life and death resonated with spirit power, and you never came back—if you came back—without acquiring at least a dollop of mystical wisdom.

In Queisha's case, it might have been a great deal more than a dollop of mysticism. She'd been out for a while, so it might have been more like a mountain—she should excuse the pun.

Now that he knew where her psychic ability came

from, a great part of it, at least, he'd watch her more closely.

Her sixth sense had often floored him, but until this moment, he hadn't realized quite how deeply close she came to joining him in Everlasting, or from whence her uncanny understanding of life and spirit had sprung.

This talented woman, this life-giving, effervescent woman, deserved to see the real Paris, and Ireland, and Africa, rather than painting rooms in her home to mimic them. Why should such a one as she suffer from agoraphobia?

He would make curing Queisha's phobia part of his purpose. He was, after all, a soul physician. And by not returning to Everlasting the minute he reached earth, he might as well admit that he'd fallen in with Angus's plan and become a multidimensional maverick, as well.

The humans had it right. Asking forgiveness was easier than asking for permission. Angus sent him here for some preordained reason. He might as well make the best of it.

Not that Angus could have known; the Scot acted on instinct. Excellent instincts, true, but Chance would never tell him so, or he'd go haywire, and maybe turn Niagara Falls in another direction.

If the wild Scot gave in to his every whim, the world would cry for mercy.

Skye came running over and tagged the wall. "That's *our* angel," she said cryptically, Lace nodding her agreement.

"What was that?" Queisha said. "Whatever it was, I'd like to see more of that kind of enthusiasm."

"So would I." They let the subject of the mural go, to

his relief. The girls played quietly, and were not the least greedy when Queisha began to shop for them, not what he would have expected from children raised in such a wealthy family. They asked only for a coloring book each and one set of crayons to share.

"Okay, now clothes," Queisha said. "Princess dresses and shoes to start, right here on this page, then this outfit, I think, one for each of you?"

"Please," Skye said. "Can we not dress the same?"

Lace got up to look at the computer. "I like that one, instead. It's got lace, like my name. Can I have shoes the same color? And socks, and pierced earrings?"

"All the same color?" Queisha asked.

"Yes, please. Oh, Skye, look at this shirt with kissing doxies on it. Miss Queisha, what does it say?"

Queisha tweaked each little nose. "Double the love."

"That's like us," Skye said. "We like doxie dogs. Our boarding school friend has one, and her mother brings it on visiting days."

"I assume that doxie means dachshund?" Queisha confirmed.

Chance leaned toward the screen from his chair. "That's one of my favorite dogs, too," he said. "Queisha, will you order the girls each one of those shirts, in their color choices, of course, from me?"

The girls scrambled into his arms and kissed him on opposite cheeks at the same moment. "A Sir Chance sandwich," Skye said.

"Why, thank you," he said, touching his cheek in awe. Had he ever been kissed by a child?

"I like that outfit," Skye said, looking back at the screen.

"This?" Queisha asked. "The tan sweater with the leopard collar, cuffs, and skirt?"

Skye made claws with her little hands. "Growl."

Queisha growled back. "Shoes to match?"

"Yes, leopard high heels, please."

"I think not. Besides, they don't come in your size."

Skye sighed. "Mary Janes, then, but can I have nail polish like yours, a different color for every nail?" She took Queisha's hand and touched each bright nail. "Show Sir Chance your toes." Skye turned to him. "She's got different colored toes, too."

"Does she now?" Righteous folly, he wished he could wear his wings on the outside so they wouldn't itch so much.

Queisha chuckled. "Ms. Skye, you want finger *and* toenail polish?"

"Yes, please. And don't forget our princess dresses should be different colors."

"Skye, you want princess shoes to match?" Lace asked.

"Not," Skye countered. "Silver or gold for me, to match everything."

Lace begrudgingly agreed with a shrug. "Skye gets gold, I get silver, and don't forget that her feet are bigger than mine."

"They are not!"

FOURTEEN

Chance made them a nutritious lunch, compliments of Vivica's computer cooking course. Crunchy, cornflake-rolled, baked chicken fingers with corn, cranberry sauce, and mandarin orange slices—after ascertaining that no one was "lergic."

The only area in which he cheated the nutrition fairy was dessert. When he realized he'd ordered unflavored yogurt by mistake, he crushed peppermint candy to mix in the yogurt.

The girls devoured it. Queisha raised a brow after her first taste, but she scraped the corner of the container before she gave it up.

The girls chose coffee milk over chocolate. Yes! Converts.

Queisha left him to clean up from lunch while she ushered the girls upstairs for finger and toenail painting, storytelling, and hopefully, naps. During which time, he was supposed to go shopping for rubber duckies and age-appropriate storybooks.

Thinking himself alone, Chance untucked his shirt, pulled a loose feather from a muscle sac, and tossed it in the wastebasket. Then he turned and found Angus leaning against the Sub-Zero fridge watching him.

Chance jumped and knocked a bowl of eggs off the counter.

Angus grinned. "Earth unsettles you a bit, does it?"

"The thought of picking up those broken eggs unsettles me, my sneaky angelic friend."

"Wise man, more or less."

Chance threw an unbroken egg at him, and the Scot caught it, without breaking it. "Figures," Chance muttered.

"What do you expect of a twenty-pound cherub with tiny hands?"

"You look bizarre."

"I know. Maybe I'd look better if I shaved." Angus tossed the egg back and it broke, square in the center of Chance's forehead.

"This," Chance said, grabbing a towel, "perfectly illustrates our friendship."

Angus whistled innocently. "Ach, and I'm here to share my wisdom, so stop distracting me."

Chance snorted.

"You know, do you not, that you're here as much for yourself as for Queisha, so do not be getting narrow-minded around the woman."

"Well, sure, I'm here for the girls, too."

"No, you're here for you."

Chance smashed an egg into Angus's beard. "You make no sense."

"Sure'n I do. You might not know it, or you just don't want to admit it, but you need to find meaning in your death. Closure."

"No," Chance said. "I'm certain I'm here to find meaning in Queisha's life."

"Because you gave her *your* life and you want her to use it wisely."

"And I want her to enjoy life, damn it. I care about her, in case you don't know it."

"Ach and we had this talk in reverse, my man, just before I knocked you down here."

Chance rolled an egg in his hand. "I'm thinking of one more place to shove this."

Angus flew back a bit. "Michael sent me."

"Crap."

"Crap and damn it," Angus repeated. "He'll love hearing that."

"Nonsense, he's got more important people to *listen* to. But what did he say?"

"He's furious with me for knocking you down here."

"Finally. *You* get your just rewards." Chance dropped the broken eggshells into the disposal and tried to get the goop from the floor back into the bowl.

"Looks like you're getting yours, as well. Michael *is* much annoyed with you for falling in love with one of your charges."

Chance looked up. "Do you know anything about rubber duckies?"

"Ignore me all you want. It won't change a thing."

"No, seriously. I have to go shopping for rubber duckies."

"The selection is endless. I had wee ones. Been there, drank heavily. Can I watch?"

Chance ignored the unholy glee on the crusty Scot's face.

"The consequences man. What do I have to deal with, Everlasting-wise, while I prepare Queisha to face her demons?"

"Hold on to your wings, but while you're here, I'm your guardian. I've also been demoted to messenger angel between you and the triumvirate. Since you're my *only* charge, I may have to annoy you occasionally."

"You've had plenty of practice. What about Queisha? Am I still her guardian?"

"Of course not. Seraphina has been named Queisha's temporary guardian."

Chance frowned. "They shouldn't punish Queisha for your stupidity."

Angus harrumphed. "Ach, and I was trying to do you a favor knocking you down here."

"Which is why we're in trouble," Chance said. "Seraphina will persuade Queisha to doubt herself in the guise of making her think things through. Sera is not what Queisha needs right now. Explain that to Michael, will you?"

"Sure. He listens to chastised messengers, aka bearded cherubs, all the time."

"Seraphina will not be good for Queisha."

"Who would be good for her?"

"I would, of course."

"I'll take you back, right now, so you can guard

Queisha and she can manage this situation with the twins on her own."

"No!"

"Fine, but you're in big trouble, in every way known to man and then some."

"Spit it out! How much is your interference going to cost me?" Chance straightened, ready to take his punishment like a fourth-class angel, unless he'd been demoted as well.

"You may continue to appear to Queisha in human form, get close to her, stay with her until she can settle the issue of the twins' future, at which time, you will return to us and turn her over to a new and permanent guardian. After that, you will never see or hear of her again."

Chance tried not to double over in pain, emotional, physical, spiritual. He'd lost her. In trying to help her— No, wait, he could still help her. She mattered more than he did. Her future had been his main concern since the day he died. Screw *his* future.

Angus patted him on the back. "Above all, you can't influence her. She has to make her own decisions. And you can't lie. Break either of those rules, and you'll be sucked up to Everlasting in a blink. If you're, ah, worldly, you'll lose the appropriate number, color, and corresponding virtue of feathers."

"My feather loss has started. I've noticed a pattern and it has to do with lust."

"Silver, hey?"

"Yep."

"No surprise there. The more you lose, the more human you become, as we've already heard, but there's an upside. Retain *one* feather, and you're still an angel.

Lose them all, and you're mortal, subject to an imminent mortal death, with no guarantee of reincarnation or of returning to the Casualty Corps.

"Seriously, if I keep one, I'm still an angel?"

"You've got it, but losing them will be like eating potato chips. Do you have the willpower to leave one last feather in the bowl?"

"I have thick wings, my friend."

"Not thick enough, I fear."

"Don't worry about me." Chance finished wiping the floor. "Worry about your own punishment. I notice you're still a cherub."

"But I don't crave worldly delights, though I wish I'd had that cigar when I craved it. How about you? What do you crave?"

"I'm losing my chastity feathers. What do you think?"

Angus grinned. "Some good news: you retain the angelic power to create the illusion of worlds, up to and including rainbows. Your assignment, should you accept it—"

"Cut the crap, Angus."

"You can stay to see Queisha through learning her children's parents are dead, and to see her safely to a decision about who will raise the twins, and, I repeat, without interfering in her free will."

"But what about a time frame? Do I have a maximum amount of time here?"

"The mighty three haven't decided yet."

"That's outright torture."

"And don't they know it? I'd say you could be recalled at any moment, so tread warily."

"Bloody hell."

"Ach, and you don't want to end up there, so stop calling hell into this."

"Blessed saints! Right. Gotcha. So, listen. If you're my guardian, and mine alone, you won't go peeking into bedrooms."

Angus grinned as one of Chance's silver feathers wafted to the floor. The Scot picked it up and twirled it. "Besides the fact that I know the rules, I will not be peeking into bedrooms. Ach, I'm already afraid of what I'll see. Best think twice, Angel Man. Do the deed and it could cost a peck of feathers. Do it once and you won't be able to stop, no matter how many feathers are left in the bowl."

"I'm dreaming. It can't happen," Chance said. "I'm an angel, she's human, but I might be willing to pay the price, if the opportunity arises."

Angus nearly swallowed his tongue. "Will you no shush your blatherin' mouth. They'll hear you!"

FIFTEEN

There had been no storm the night just passed,
Queisha realized on waking, except for children screaming and a chase through the house after Chance put a lobster in front of each girl at the dinner table. Peanut butter
sandwiches, it had been for them after that. Still, Queisha
woke that second morning hoping to find them beside
her—the girls, not the lobsters.

She didn't delude herself into thinking they'd become
instantly attached to her, but she liked that they trusted
her to protect them.

Fortunately or unfortunately, she'd slept alone. It
was good that the girls were adjusting to their new
surroundings.

Granted, the first night, they'd found themselves in a
strange house, a strange country, though the Fitzpatricks'
main mansion was in Greenwich, Connecticut, so why
their babies went to boarding school in Switzerland, she

couldn't say. It was a bone of contention, the girls being sent so far away, one she hadn't yet decided whether to mention to their parents, should the occasion arise.

She got up to check the girls and found them in the Irish bedroom like two peas in a little green pod, hands clasped, heads together, sleeping soundly. She blew them silent kisses and went straight to her bedroom window afterward, leaned on the frame, and pulled back the curtain to watch for the man who had the ability to change her. Not so much on the outside as within.

Anticipation, rather than loneliness, filled her. The girls inspired the same, of course, with more love than she had the right to expect. Tentative acceptance flowed from them in strengthening waves, and she ate it up.

With Chance, she ate up the sexual enticement of his presence. Possibilities: the pull of need and awareness, propriety vying with the lure of temptation and the power of the forbidden.

But prohibited why? Because she didn't deserve a man?

She did, damn it. As much as any other woman.

Yet there was an aura of the deeply illicit about this man, a self-driving sensuality that thrived on their attraction and grew stronger by the day.

She wilted. Had she been cut off from the world as some kind of consequence to her actions? God knew, her screwups were punishment worthy. Penalty for a teenage mistake—fed by the search for love missing at home— resulting in a babe who never took breath.

Silly, sex-starved her, thinking herself worthy of love. Not for any man, but for Chance, who probably had no such interest in her.

Yet there had been that moment on the stairs. A mutual inclination toward something that pulsed heavy and hot between them.

Her mind wandering to what that might be, she saw him coming up the dock.

Sir Chance, aka Sir Galahad, walking— Well, in her imagination, he was *riding* a trusty steed to her rescue, her heart pumping as if she'd raced straight into his arms, and found herself exhilarated at being there. And how could she experience, even in her imagination, feelings and sensations she'd never known?

She sighed and mocked herself for her one-day-old infatuation.

Wait. How did he get here? He couldn't be taking a water taxi. She saw no one motoring away. He must have rented a boat. A tiny one hidden by the dock? His weird travel plans simply added to her growing list of questions, like his doing double duty as both cook and guardian.

Vivica selling snow to Alaskans? Or Chance hiding his purpose?

If something happened to the Fitzpatricks, he could be the man to advise the family as to whether *she* might be a worthy guardian.

Would they take the girls away from her? On his word?

A moot point. Their parents would be fine. Mother and Father, as the girls called them, who should be home hugging their girls, and who Lace thought didn't want them.

Maybe she shouldn't have canceled on her therapist while the girls were here. Maybe she should have let the therapist speak to the girls, though treating them was not her decision to make.

Queisha only hoped the girls were not more Fitzpatrick collectibles, sitting pretty on a shelf to be brought out and admired when required.

She went to kiss each dark, wavy-haired head, pulled up the covers, and tucked them in. They'd held hands since the womb. She let them sleep and prepared to go downstairs, maybe learn Chance's true motives for being here. Maybe she'd find out more in a red satin wrap, a risqué bit of nightgown lace visible at the neck.

She changed and went down, the thrill of taking seduction into her own hands as powerful as the man she'd like to seduce.

Was she going to do this? Really?

He saw her, whistled, and handed her a cup of honey almond tea.

"I might whistle, too," she said. "A royal blue V-neck tee. I like. Brings out your eyes. Sexy." Did she say sexy out loud? Ah, she'd embarrassed them both. She gave her attention to sipping her tea.

Chance cleared his throat. "I heard you walking around upstairs. No patter of little feet, though."

"They're out cold, but not in my bed."

"Need someone to take their place?"

She tried to read his intent, but he'd turned back to the eggs. "They're perfect angels," she said. "I hope I can teach them to have a blast. I'd love to hear them tearing around the place, well, besides when finding lobsters on their dinner plates."

"Perfect angels is an oxymoron," he said.

"Is that a joke?"

"There are some who would think so. Never mind. The girls screaming in joy would be a beautiful sound.

Though their reaction to the lobsters was pretty funny. Anyway, if anybody can teach them joy, it's you."

She couldn't help but appreciate the compliment, and she probably was going loopy, but the world seemed brighter. "What makes you think so?"

"There's something magical about you. I think the girls sense it. They keep wanting you to play with them."

He offered her a refill with a lift of the teapot.

She held out her cup.

Second morning and they were in sync. Would this homey quiet time alone become a morning routine? Or would it make future mornings lonely?

She sat on a rattan barstool beside the counter and watched him stir the oatmeal and poach the eggs. On the table, he set custard cups of maple sugar, clover honey, and Craisins, as garnishes for the oatmeal.

"What?" she asked. "No peppermint stick yogurt?"

"One step ahead of you." He took it from the fridge when they heard the girls on the floor above. They came running. Chance winked at her when they appeared. Two days of no rules had made a difference.

Lace wore a belt wound three times around the waist of her mint green shirt sporting a regal frog. It said "Save a frog, buy your own crown." Her floppy green socks matched, as did the belt.

Skye's baby blue shirtdress had a lone crown with bright jewels that said, "Kiss me, I'm a princess." She wore striped socks of lavender and pink, and a yellow bow in her hair.

Queisha adjusted Lace's belt. "Your new clothes should come today."

Chance looked up. "So soon?"

"Overnight shipping. I also bought a few things no one's expecting."

Chance set the plates before them and everyone dug in. "That's a good look on you, Queisha."

She set down her English muffin. "What look?"

"The look of a wide-eyed little girl on Christmas morning with gifts to give. Your excitement is infecting us all."

"You're mocking me."

"I'm envying you. I probably looked like that when we talked about your vintage cars, which *you* pointed out. You're a teacup calling the kettle prissy. But it's your nature to be spontaneous. That's why it's so great. Why you're so great."

Speechless, breathless, Queisha allowed herself to be caught by his gaze, and held prisoner, while something that had nothing to do with compliments—and everything to do with a pulsing physical attraction—zephyred through her.

Muffled giggles broke the spell. The girls were watching, taking it all in. "Smoochie, smoochie, smoochie," Lace sang while Skye kissed her hand and up her arm to her elbow.

Lace fell into Skye's arms. "Sweetums!"

"Honeypot!" Lace replied.

Chance stood and fisted his hands on his hips.

Queisha cleared her throat. "I see nobody missed the elephant in the room."

Chance grabbed first Lace, then Skye, and carried them, dangling, one under each arm. "Morning showers?" he asked Queisha.

"Absolutely," she replied, throwing down her napkin.

"Then grab that bag of rubber duckies on the counter."

Climbing the stairs behind them, Queisha thought her heart would pound from her chest. Not sure what Chance intended, she followed him to her huge, doorless shower, where he set the girls down and turned on the warm spray, from all three directions.

They screamed so hard, they laughed, then they screamed some more, as if they liked the new sound.

"Hah," Chance said, "they have *your* sense of humor." He opened the bag and threw rubber duckies at them, one by one, queens, angels, princesses, and a saloon girl duck that he didn't think they'd mind.

They arranged the ducks around the huge shower, on the floor, upper shelves and lower ones, in soap dishes, too. Skye screeched, took one duck to the toilet and dropped it in. "A *boy* angel?" she said with such disgust, Chance barked a laugh. When she went to flush, Queisha and Chance screamed together, and Skye ran giggling back to the shower, the tease.

By then each girl had a "hosey" thing in their hands and they were trying to figure out how to get water out of them.

Chance took her hand. "Run before they discover they can turn the spray on us."

Last thing Queisha saw was Skye surprising Lace by pouring half a bottle of shampoo over her head.

They'd learned that from her.

SIXTEEN

～

*The girls stood in the toy room fidgeting with excite-*ment and anticipation while they waited for Queisha to open the packages that had been delivered.

Their fresh lavender T-shirts matched. One said: "I only sleep with the best." And the other said: "The best."

He'd roared when he saw them coming down the stairs side by side. Queisha beside them had worn a rust knit dress that made her pale mocha skin glow while it hugged her figure, her heels the same color, her femininity calling to him.

He'd chosen the T-shirt because it was easier to remove a loose feather with it untucked. It was also easier to drop them, of course. He'd found one in front of the stove and one beneath the breakfast table. He should take Angus's warning to heart.

Queisha armed him with a camera and a pair of scissors to attack the packages.

While he opened boxes, Skye hopped on one foot, and Lace scratched the mint green polish off her nails, never taking her eyes from the potential prizes.

Chance took pictures while the girls removed the clothes and toys from the boxes. They held the clothes in front of them and fake smiled for the camera.

Princess gowns and shoes came with crowns—surprise! The girls were beside themselves. Surprise number two: removable wings, so they could be fairies at will. Queisha was born to mother little girls.

"Ah," she said, unpacking a peck of princess panties. "Go put these on right now and forget you ever had to go without for even a few minutes."

The mini twins went behind the sofa and you could see their heads bobbing up and down as they pulled and tugged.

Queisha chuckled despite herself. "I meant that you should go and put them on in the bathroom."

"This is faster," Skye said.

Lace nodded. "We can't wait to see what's in the other boxes."

"I would have waited for you."

"Don't worry," Chance said. "I'm not taking pictures right now."

The girls disappeared and both yelped. They popped up rubbing their heads.

While Queisha ran up the stairs laughing, the girls climbed into his lap to show him their crowns. At their birth, he'd loved them with an angel's love. This . . . this was a father's love.

He came here to prepare Queisha to care for them, now he wanted to stay and take care of them all. Impossible.

Leaving them to go back to Everlasting was going to kill him. Well, not really. He was already dead.

Queisha took a few minutes longer than he expected and returned wearing a different dress. A red mini.

Skye tilted her head. "You peed your pants a little when you laughed, didn't you?"

"Yes, I did. Do not say a word, Chance Godricson."

He winked.

"Lace does that." Skye grinned.

Lace gasped. "I do not!"

Chance tickled them to stop an argument, but Skye gasped and slid fast off his lap. "'Scuse me, but I seem to pee a little when I'm tickled."

Lace crossed her arms. "Hah!"

Skye held out a hand to Queisha for a fresh pair of panties. "The bathroom?" she confirmed.

"Thank you, Sir Chance, for tickling us," Lace said, sorting through the fairy princess underwear. "We've never been tickled before."

Queisha turned his way, mirroring his surprise, and he knew himself to be falling, falling, falling—for Queisha, Lace, Skye, family, love, laughter, life, none of which fit the role of an angel. So why did caring for them feel so good and right?

He couldn't fool himself into thinking he didn't love them. At this rate, he'd be wing-bald and grave-bound in a month.

Skye returned and pulled him toward the sofa where Queisha sat, boxes on the floor in front of her, and pushed him down beside her. Then Skye crawled into his lap. "Open some more, please," she asked Queisha.

Skye looked up at him, almost as an afterthought.

"It's okay, I'm dry now." Then she produced a large silver feather, which she smoothed up and down.

He didn't say a thing. Maybe Queisha wouldn't notice, but Skye reached over to tickle her neck with it.

"What this?" Queisha asked, smoothing the feather herself.

"A feather," Skye said.

"I know that. Where did you find it?"

"On the floor, right"—she pointed—"there."

"Maybe a bird flew in one of the windows?" Chance suggested.

"We'd have heard it break a screen for sure. Is it yours? Some kind of good luck charm you're embarrassed about? You look guilty as hell."

Blessedly guilty, actually. He sighed. "Yes, the feather is mine."

Lace leaned around Queisha to see him. "Why do you have a feather, Sir Chance?"

Can't lie, can't lie, can't lie. He shrugged. "I'm an angel?"

SEVENTEEN

❦

"You're funny," Skye said. "Sir Chance, you can't be an angel." She smoothed the feather. "You don't got wings."

Lace pushed the hair from her eyes. "Do you remember the angel who took care of you when you were borned?"

Chance paled. "Do you?"

Skye nodded. "He was so handsome, he glowed, and he picked us up together and gave us his breath and his love. He wore rainbow wings and sprinkled us with angel dust."

"What do you mean by rainbow wings?"

"Well, the top row of feathers were a shiny gold."

Gold for love.

Lace nodded. "I remember the second row was the color of the pans hanging in the kitchen."

"Copper?" Queisha asked.

Chance swallowed. *Copper for faith.*

"The next color was light purple," Lace said. "Like that angel's wings right there on the wall."

Right, he thought. *Lavender for hope.* Like in the mural.

"The dark pink row is my favorite," Skye said.

For patience.

Lace pointed them out. "Then green, blue, and the silver ones are like Skye's feather."

Green—kindness. Aqua—charity. Silver—chastity.

They remembered him, so why didn't they recognize him? Dare he ask it? "What did his face look like, your angel?" *Please don't say like mine.*

"We told you, he glowed, and it was hard to tell, but he was beautiful."

"He?" Queisha asked. "Do girls have male angels? I thought girls had girl angels, and so forth."

"Old wives' tale," Chance said before he could stop himself. He shrugged. "I'm into that New Age stuff." And *big* into stupidity.

"If I have an angel, she's an underachiever," Queisha announced. "I remember a pretend angel, but she left when I was adopted."

"What's 'dopted'?" Skye asked.

Queisha took Lace on her lap. "Adopted is when a couple want a baby very badly, and maybe a baby's mother gets . . . sick, so she can't take care of *her* baby, so the couple who wants a baby adopts the sick mother's baby to raise and becomes its parents."

"So your parents wanted you very badly," Skye said.

"My mother did."

"Our father gets cross, too." Skye patted her hand. "It's okay."

"Our mother doesn't want us anymore, I think," Lace said.

Skye nodded thoughtfully, agreeing certainly, and Chance found that shocking. Now he wished he'd said more to the couple arriving in Everlasting.

"Lace, do you remember once, a long time ago, when mother said a lady we don't know cooked us in her tummy. Why didn't Mother cook us in her own tummy?"

Lace gave her twin a you-are-so-stupid smirk. "Duh, so she could keep climbing mountains, silly."

Chance worried that was true. He avoided Queisha's eye.

"So you were dopted, Lady Queisha, and we were— What is that called when you're cooked in another lady's tummy and not your mother's?"

Chance couldn't take watching Queisha's face change from shock to sadness. He put Skye on Queisha's lap, too, knelt in front of them, and took one each of their little hands. "It's not so much being cooked as being given a place to grow strong, snuggled, and loved, in a warm, floaty place."

"Think of it as being slow baked," Queisha said. She looked at him. "It's an easier concept for them to grasp."

"I guess."

"Why would any mother not want to bake their own babies?" Skye asked.

Queisha hugged her. "Some mothers are too sick."

"Not our mother. She's never sick. She gets mad at us when we are."

He wasn't liking these revelations.

"How long were we slow baked?"

"Nine months," Queisha said. "Nine wonderful months."

"It must have been boring in there," Lace said. "What did we do all day?"

"Oh, you danced. All day and all night, you danced, most of the time together."

"We do like to dance. What did we eat?"

"Unborn babies eat what the lady slow baking them eats," Chance said, "so they can grow strong enough to come out into the world. Obviously, your mother was honest with you, so I will be, too."

A squeak escaped Queisha as she grabbed his arm. "Chance, no."

He touched her cheek with the back of a hand, and she sighed in resignation.

"Miss Queisha slow baked the two of you," he told the girls. "That's why she's your guardian and why she loves you."

Skye touched Queisha's tummy. "We lived in *here*?"

"Right there," Queisha said, as a tear escaped a long, dark lash.

Skye leaned in and patted her shoulder to comfort her.

"Ack!" Lace clutched her throat. "We ate . . . *lobster*!"

"Yes, and you loved it. I ate it all the time when I was expecting you. I have an album you might like to see. Pictures of me with you in my tummy. Pictures of you in my tummy holding hands, like you do now when you sleep. I even have pictures of your parents holding you before they took you home."

"They're nice enough parents," Skye said.

"But why didn't you keep us?" Lace asked.

"Chance?" Queisha said. "You wanna help me answer that one, since you started this?"

"Sure. Well. Your mother's tummy didn't work, so . . ." He hesitated, seeking divine guidance. "Baby seeds! You were grown from your parent's baby seeds, and not Miss Queisha's, so Miss Queisha had no choice but to give you to them. After your parents took you home, Miss Queisha missed you so much, she cried for days and weeks."

What a look Queisha gave him. "And you would know that because?"

"You're you."

EIGHTEEN

After Queisha helped the girls change into their new clothes, she left them with their coloring books and crayons in the toy room and went looking for Chance. He'd left looking like he was nearly as ticked with her as she was with him. "What's wrong with you?" she asked as she approached him in the kitchen.

"Why do you think your guardian angel's an underachiever?" he asked, chip on his shoulder, as he slammed the refrigerator door.

"Why did you tell them I was their surrogate? You had no right."

"Don't give me that. You're glad they know."

He might well be right, but . . . "The jury's still out on that."

Chance slammed an empty pan on the stove. "I repeat: why do you think your guardian angel is an underachiever?"

"What are you, head of the angel union?"

"Sorry," he said. "Maybe I'm overreacting."

"Ya think?" Queisha snapped. "You want my therapist's number, maybe?"

"Snarky, smart mouth. Seriously, what do you have against your guardian angel?"

Queisha chuckled. "Angels are supposed to take care of us, right? Well, I'm a mess, an agoraphobic for starters. My angel's a screwup, and I dare you to deny it. Heck, maybe angels *don't* exist."

"Weren't you already agoraphobic when you got your last guardian?"

Queisha slapped the granite countertop. "You know, my angels forgot to check in with me at the changing of the guardian."

"That kind of snark is so not you." He opened the spice cupboard with an angry hand.

"Who are you working for?" she asked. "Should I be afraid of you?"

"I work for *you*, sweet cheeks. And why should you be afraid of me?"

"You know too much about me, defending my angel, indeed. Seriously, what are you going to tell the girls' parents about me?"

"Believe me, I'm not about to tell them anything." Chance chopped onions with a vengeance for the now sizzling skillet. "I was an unremarkable lawyer, because I went to law school like my father wanted. I should have become an architect like I wanted."

"What does that have to do with this conversation?"

"I'm defending your underachieving guardian angel

because he might not be able to make his own choices. Ever think of that?"

"Sure," she said. "I think about it all the time. Not."

"Lace takes after *this* side of you," Chance said. "Skye takes after your whimsical side."

Queisha gasped. "Stop with the curveballs, already. You got me in the gut with that one. I was only their surrogate and don't you forget it."

He pulled her against him. "Sorry. I'm not used to all these emotions zinging around inside me. Joy, anger, love, guilt, regret, hope, lust."

"Lust, really?"

He smoothed back her hair. "Forget you heard that . . . and forgive me?"

"You're forgiven." She relaxed, looking up at him. Mutual lust. "So if you're not reporting to the girls' parents, who are you reporting to?"

"You. I work for you." He kissed her brow.

"A cook is a far cry from a lawyer, just because you didn't get to go to school where you wanted. I didn't get to my dream school, either, by the way. I wanted to go to the Rhode Island School of Design."

"Where did you go?"

"Social services, ward of the state, foster homes, worked in a hamburger joint."

"How ashamed am I for feeling sorry for myself?" He did not, of course, expect an answer to that. "Why?"

"Story for when the kids are asleep, 'kay?"

"I will get my answer." He cupped her cheek. "I am honest to God not reporting to anyone. I'm just playing hooky and pissing off some archangels."

Queisha chuckled into the palm of his hand. "You're

making jokes when your presence as the girls' co-guardian makes no sense."

"I'm sorry about that, but I promise you that I will *never* lie to you." He tipped up her chin, which suddenly seemed connected to her wobbly knees. "You can take that promise to the bank."

Oddly enough, she believed him. "That's something."

"That's everything, sweet thing." He stepped back, as if remembering where he was, turned back to his cooking, slid the onions from the cutting board into the skillet, and added the beef.

"Did the Fitzpatrick relatives hire you? What are you going to tell them about me as guardian?"

"I had no idea you were so paranoid. Here, open this box."

"Taco shells? I thought we were having lobster rolls."

"You and I are. The girls are having tacos."

Oh yeah. "I'm getting a flashback to Lace's face when she realized I'd eaten lobster when I carried them."

Chance's chin dimple deepened. Amusement felt better shared. Sadness, too. But she wouldn't let him charm her from her purpose. "Do you live in Switzerland? I thought you were from Rhode Island."

"I don't think they make tacos in Switzerland. I learned about tacos at my grandmother's knee in Arkwright village."

"No, I mean, are you related to the girls? I see no human reason for you to be co-guardian other than that you could be a spy for relatives who might resent *not* being their guardians. It could come down to a fight, couldn't it?"

"I supposed there could be a fight." He tapped her

nose. "You see no *human* reason. *That's* the kicker. Think about it."

"Are you playing mind games?"

"Believe me, Queisha, there are other games I'd much rather play with you."

Queisha got lost in the possibilities for a minute and then she pretended she'd been watching him cook all along.

He added spices and sautéed the meat, and she knew she'd never eat Mexican food again without thinking of him, which probably meant he was leaving. No way on earth could he stay. Sometimes, she hated her instincts.

She was in this alone after all.

"Would you fight for the girls to have the best guardian possible?" he asked, taking her by surprise.

She didn't need to think twice. "To the death."

"I'd fight beside you," he said.

"Thank you, but know this, I'd fight for the best, even if it wasn't me," she said.

Chance nodded. "I meant the same, and that's why I'd fight for *you* to be their guardian. You're the best, hands down."

Queisha huffed. "Chance Godricson, you make no sense."

He reached behind him to turn off the stove. "Sorry about that. In answer to your first question, yes, you should fear me, but not for the reason you're thinking. You should fear me because . . . because I want to do this . . ." He took one of her arms in each of his hands, and she let him back her out of the kitchen and around the corner into the foyer, until he cornered her, literally, as if to hide them from the girls.

Kiss aforethought?

She had to admit that she found it very satisfying when he lowered his lashes over his hot, hungry eyes and came for her mouth, his lips grazing hers, his bottom lip against her top one, cool silk against trembling hunger. Parting them. Teasing. Testing. "Be afraid," he whispered. "Be very afraid."

Despite the corny cliché, Queisha couldn't seem to move.

When he actually took her lips in a full kiss, she moaned. Parched and hungry met trembling need. Manna from heaven, sustenance and blessing. The answer to a prayer.

The hair at his nape, soft against her hand, alerted her. She was acting on instinct. She'd fallen into his arms, into his kiss, body and soul. No thought, except *yes!*

No resistance. No pride. Who cared? Not him. Not her.

His hand at the base of her spine shattered sense to shards of ice that went prickling through her until it melted, warmed, and pooled in amazing places.

She shivered, they both did—wondrous in the midst of so much heat. Mouths opened, tongues accepted invitations, danced, a ritual mating. Symbolic. In, out. In, out.

Her entire being picked up on the rhythm, from her breasts to her hips, and deep, deep within.

A tug on her sleeve. "Sir Chance? Lady Queisha? The smoke from that stuff you're cooking is making it hard to breathe in here."

Queisha pulled from the embrace. "Skye, where's Lace?"

Buzzers. Smoke detectors started going off all around them.

Chance ran into the kitchen, moved the smoking skillet from its bright red burner, and shut it off. He also shut off the burner he'd turned on by mistake, thinking he was turning the first off.

Another minute and that skillet could have burst into flames.

"Girls," he snapped. "When you smell smoke, or you hear smoke detectors go off, you don't stop for anything, you leave the house. Go. Now. Outside! Wait by the angel fountain, and don't move from that spot."

The girls ran.

Queisha's heart began to pound and she began to shake. "I can't leave the house. I can't."

"The patio," Chance said. "Go there. I'll follow the girls and take them around to meet you."

Thank God she'd mastered the patio, she thought as she ran.

When Chance finally brought the girls around the house, they ran into her arms, and she kissed them all over their faces, making them scream and giggle.

Some guardian she was, she thought, holding on to them. She didn't know what to do in case of fire. How far should she run from one? Could she do it? Actually leave the house? The yellow brick patio?

It seemed to her that she could do anything for the girls, but her current chills and the tightness in her chest were telling a different tale. On the other hand, the girls were safe, and she was allowed to panic. Wasn't she?

If the Fitzpatricks had seen this, they'd know she'd make a lousy guardian.

"Why did we have to leave?" Skye asked. "There's no fire."

"None that we could see," Chance said, "kneeling to their level. Queisha, is your alarm system connected to the fire department?"

"I'm afraid not."

"Okay, here's the rule. Nobody goes back inside until I check the house. I'll turn off the smoke detectors and open windows as I do. Do not go back inside until I tell you it's safe."

She watched him disappear into the smoke-filled lower level. A window onto the patio opened. Chance waved before he disappeared.

Skye pulled on her hand. "Lady Queisha, let's go play tag in the grass until he's done."

She'd never felt more like crying. "I can't go in the grass."

"Are you lergic to grass?"

"Well, sweeties, I'm kinda lergic to anyplace except inside my house and here on my patio."

"What if we need to go to the doctor?"

"Chance could take you." *For however long he stayed.* "The doctor comes here for me. He could come for you, too."

"That's weird. I went to a hospital for stitches on my chin. See? Does your doctor come for stitches?"

A defining moment. A taco fire had become proof that, whatever happened, she could never become Skye and Lace's permanent guardian, unless Chance stayed forever, except he must have some kind of life to go back to. He hadn't appeared out of thin air.

Vivica drove into the yard and the DeLorean's gull-winged doors couldn't go up fast enough before she was headed their way. She didn't look good, not at all. She paled further when she saw the girls.

Queisha got a sinking feeling. "Skye, Lace, go play near the fountain. Stay where I can see you."

They raced. Queisha couldn't stop her heart from doing the same. "Their parents?"

Vivica grasped her hand in a bone-crushing grip. "They've been found. They . . . didn't make it."

NINETEEN

When Chance opened a tower window, he looked down toward the patio and saw Vivica and the stricken look on Queisha's face. Nobody needed to tell him that the Fitzpatricks' bodies had been found.

Cue the complications.

Because no one could see him, he played the angel card, and waved a window-raising arm to get them all open, and to air out the entire back of the house so he could go quickly back down to the patio.

"To what do we owe the pleasure, Vivica?" He pretended he didn't know why she was there.

"I wish this was a social call," she said.

"The girls' parents?" he asked.

"Their bodies were found."

Chance put his arm around Queisha. "Now I understand the look on your face. Or is that panic?"

A tear slipped down Queisha's face and it about broke

him. "I lost my mother when I was eleven," she said. "I know what it did to me. I'm worried about what it'll do to Skye and Lace."

"You can handle it, Queisha," Vivica said. "You have a lot of love to give. You'll make them a great mother."

"You tell her, Vivica," Chance said.

"No, no, I won't. I didn't even know what to do in a fire."

"So you'll take parenting lessons. I'll send Jaydun over with a set of computer courses. Everything you ever wanted to know about being a parent, and a lot you didn't think you needed to know. No parent is born with the knowledge."

Chance squeezed her shoulder. "Listen to the woman."

"It's kind of you to say so, Vivica, but I couldn't step away from my own house if it caught fire."

"You don't give yourself enough credit," Chance said. "If I weren't here, you would have gotten those girls to safety, panic attack or not."

Vivica covered her hand. "He's right."

"I'm glad you're both so certain," Queisha said, walking to the edge of her outdoor safe place. "I'm not so stupid as to stay and get flash fried, but panic freezes me, and I'm not the sensible Queisha when it does."

"Why are you okay here on the patio and not on the grass?" Chance wanted to know.

"As a kid, the yellow-brick road in *The Wizard of Oz* seemed like Dorothy's safe place. Later, I had a near-death experience, and there had been some event going on where I got trapped, gold tape marking what must have been some kind of procession route. I followed it, looking down and away from the carnage to keep myself sane. It led me to the man who saved my life. Years later, when I finally got a therapist, she let me pick where I wanted to start leaving the house. I picked the yellow-brick patio. Look, the bricks are laid in a circle like Dorothy's road."

"A yellow-brick circle," Chance said.

"I walk it every day. I even sit on the top step because they're yellow brick, too. See . . ." She crossed her arms in a self-protective gesture. "I'm certifiable."

Vivica stopped biting her lip. "We should have your yard paved in yellow brick."

Chance watched Queisha process the suggestion, tilt her head, consider it, and frown. "I'd headline the wacko news."

He had an idea.

"We're still hungry," Lace said, coming back toward them, Skye nodding behind her.

Vivica agreed. "I haven't eaten since I got the call."

"Lady Queisha," Skye asked. "Are you lergic to restaurants?"

"Yes, sweetie."

"Chinese takeout," Vivica said. "It's starting to rain, though, so we can't picnic out here."

"I know where we can eat outside and not get wet," Chance said, his mind still working on a way to get Queisha into the yard to play with the girls. "Queisha will love it."

Skye clapped. "Mother and Father bought us Chinese food on our birthdays."

"It's our favorite. I like chicken teriyaki and gold fingers."

"I like boneless spareribs and crab raccoons."

Queisha blinked. "Crab? But you don't like lob—"

Chance pulled her hard against him and touched her ear with his lips. "Shh," he whispered, bathing her neck in the warmth of his breath.

"So," Vivica said, pointedly, "I'll call in the order and go get it."

"Look, more feathers," Lace said, collecting two from the brick at his feet, and handing one to her sister.

Vivica tilted her head and raised a brow his way, a cocky grin on her face.

She knew he was an angel, figured he was losing his wings, and she must have a saucy idea why.

He turned to the house because he didn't want them to see him blush. "Follow me, but put your hand over your nose and mouth while we run through the house. The smoke is thicker nearest the kitchen, but thick or light, it's not good to inhale."

He heard them behind him, the twins giggling. "You're supposed to cover your mouths," he called back.

They were having such a good day, the near fire notwithstanding, he didn't have it in him to tell them about their parents. He didn't know what to say. He'd have to discuss it with Queisha later.

"This isn't outside," Queisha said when she got to the carousel where he waited. "And it's still a bit smoky in here."

"Not for long." Chance rubbed his hands together. "Miss Skye and Miss Lace, would you come and help me perform a feat of magick?"

The girls raced over to him.

"Put your hands on this panel, below mine, and do what I do. I'll need your extra strength. Now push."

Together they pushed the wall panels out and in, like a fan of glass doors, folded back and forth, one against the other, into a one-panel-wide wall, thick as six panels. On the opposite side of the carousel, they did the same; until it looked like an amusement park carousel open to the public.

"I'll never use it closed again." Queisha twirled. "Unless it's winter, of course."

Chance started the carousel and set it to go slow, the music low, and lifted each girl up to ride. Skye sat on a cat with a fish in its mouth. Beside her sister, Lace chose a beauteous—her word—mermaid.

Queisha stood between them, an arm around each.

From behind her, Chance caught her around her waist, though she never let go of the girls, and put his lips to her ear. Okay, he was taking advantage of the need for discretion in his speech, but he believed that Queisha liked getting kissing close as much as he did. "Let's give them one perfect day before we tell them," he whispered.

"Yes, please," she said, and it seemed as though she were saying yes to so much more.

TWENTY

Floating as close to Everlasting as one could get on earth, Chance savored a flare of euphoria so he would remember it for eternity.

On the moving carousel, standing against Queisha's back, he inhaled her lilac scent, as if flying without wings to "After the Ball"—a bit of poetic justice that, for this ball would surely end.

But as the carousel turned, Queisha between her giggling girls, hugging them as they rode their whimsical steeds, she looked his way, leaned in, breathed warmth into his ear, and kissed his lobe. "My hero," she whispered.

"More later," he said, pulling away, despite a magnetic need to stay. One: because the girls were watching them. Two: his physical reaction would soon be obvious. And three: feathers on the carousel floor at his feet.

Glad Vivica wasn't back yet, he tried to kick the feathers aside without looking before he left to ready their picnic.

After a while, Skye yelled, "Look! More feathers!"

"Those three must be magickal," Lace said, looking down, too. "They're gold and glowing."

Gold, not silver. And glowing? Chance set down the antique card table.

Gold for love.

Yes, he loved Queisha, and of course he'd fallen for the girls, but shock turned him cold. He'd stepped on the feathers, blindly tried to foot-slide them from sight, but he might have tried to pocket them if he'd seen their color.

Three was a big loss for a cuddle, and they glowed even after he dropped them. That had to mean something— probably not good, like . . . he might be shedding his angelic energy with them. He'd see what Angus knew, his big worry being whether he might have to leave Queisha and the girls that much sooner just for loving them.

Chance put angst aside when Vivica returned with their Chinese picnic. "A table? Not for a picnic. I got plastic plates and forks."

"Good idea," Queisha called. "No dishes to wash."

"Glad to see the girls are still smiling," she whispered.

"We'll tell them tomorrow . . . or the day after. They need some fun in their lives."

"You're right. This is no Swiss boarding school."

"Praise be."

While they ate and listened to the girls' stories, all about their time here, Chance threw a rainbow out over the Cove.

"Look," Queisha said, and the twins cheered and ran toward the water.

Queisha screamed for them to come back, and Chance ran after them, but Skye and Lace knew well enough to stop and watch the rainbow beside the dock. He stood them side by side in front of him. "You scared Queisha by running toward the water like this. Until you can swim *and* she can come out and watch you, you can't be scaring her like that."

Lace put a hand to her rounded mouth. She understood on the instant and ran back shouting to Queisha that she was sorry.

"Is Lady Queisha lergic to the whole wide world?" Skye asked.

Just about, Chance thought, lifting and carrying Skye back to the carousel. "I have an idea about how to help her get better," he said. "But shh. That's our secret."

"Can we help?"

"Yes, tomorrow morning when Lady Queisha is taking her shower, meet me on the water porch, you and your sister." Now he couldn't wait to get started.

Back in the carousel, after the girls apologized sincerely to Queisha, Chance twirled them, giggling fast. "That's for being so thoughtful," he said.

Vivica said good-bye. "I've had a much better afternoon than morning, and I'm so much less worried about the girls now. Good job, Queisha."

Her shoulders literally relaxed at the compliment, but she would surely restore the weight herself by doubting her guardianship abilities once more.

"It's nearly dinnertime," she said, "but we just finished lunch. We've really thrown the girls' schedules off."

"What say we dance with the stars for a while, get them salsa tired, give them a light snack, a hot bath—

throw in a duck race—and a couple of stories?" He would have liked to punctuate his words with a brow wiggle, but they didn't have a hot date planned for after the girls went to sleep. They had to discuss how and when to tell them they were orphans.

"No, don't frown," he said, realizing Queisha had come to the same conclusion. "One great day."

"Right. I'll find them some glitz and glamour to wear, some boas, and maybe gold and silver feathers, to make it fun."

"Great." Yes, he'd been sarcastic, but only he knew it.

"Girls, we're going to dance," Queisha called. "Let's go raid my drawers and closets to see what we can find for you to wear."

"Let's wear our new princess gowns," Skye suggested.

"Oh no, sweetie, those are not to roll around on the floor. They're for a special occasion."

"Like our birthdays. They're coming up, you know."

"I thought I remembered that," Queisha said.

"I know," Lace said. "Let's wear them when Mother and Father come to pick us up. Won't they think we've gotten pretty?"

Knife to his heart, Chance thought, grabbing Queisha around the waist with a squeeze for courage.

The girls saw and looked worried, so he and Queisha had to pull themselves out of their funk. Chance opened her closet and saw, above the shelf, a wooden sign. It said: LIVE FOR BOTH OF US. His last words to her. Humility hit him in the gut.

Lace broke the solemn moment when she pulled at the hem of a silver strapless gown with glitz and glitter all over it. "I want to wear this."

"Sweetie." Queisha swept her long hair back, then up on her head, just for the fun of playing "dolls," he thought. "You'll break your neck dancing in that. It's too long."

"Noooo, you can't leave it there. Every day a fairy gown hangs in a closet, an angel loses its wings."

Chance turned and hit his head on the open door. "I think you're a little storyteller."

Skye crooked a finger for him to bend down and when he did, she kissed her finger and touched his head with it. "All better," she said.

"Why, so it is." He acted shocked. "Thank you. Does that make you a nurse?"

"No, that was fairy magick," Skye confided.

He took the gown off the rack, uncurled its shawl, and lowered it to Lace's shoulders. "Never, *ever*, let an angel lose its wings."

Lace hugged his legs. "Deal."

Skye borrowed the boas off two hat racks.

Queisha put makeup on the girls "for play," and wore the silver gown, herself.

When she came out wearing it, Chase wiped the drool off his chin and kicked a feather beneath the bed.

TWENTY-ONE

Chance took Queisha's hand and walked her in a circle to show her off. "Wish I could partner you with a cane and top hat," Chance said, "to compliment your ravishing beauty."

"I can arrange that." Queisha swished off toward the tower, her adoring public following.

Standing guard in the upper hall, a Cary Grant–type hat rack raised a cane to tilt his top hat. "This, my friends, is Sir Laughsalot."

The girls curtseyed. Chance bowed, and asked the British hat rack if he would allow his accessories to be borrowed. Laughsalot made no protest.

"This is my entertainment center and dance studio." Queisha led them to her simplest and biggest room, pale sage on three walls, white on the wall facing, a white half-circle sofa against the sage corner, and behind it, a six-foot onyx oriental vase of peacock feathers.

She worked a couple of remotes, two-handed, like a mad text messager, and the white wall became a television, the dancers big as life.

Beside the indirect lighting, soft ceiling spots angled toward the spacious dance floor and made it the focus of the room.

"Watch and dance," she told the girls, jiggling Skye by the hips and Lace by the shoulders. "Jump in whenever you're ready."

He and Queisha waltzed, eerily in sync, like he dreamed of them doing every time he watched her dance alone. During his time here, and no less so at this moment, life surpassed his expectations. He did not remember a pulse-pounding exhilaration at being alive, even in the best of times.

This felt more like love set to music than dancing. Slow, calculated, bodies swaying toward and away, back again, a mating dance, ritual, tradition, life at its most elemental.

Music. He would never underestimate its power again.

He caught the dip on the screen and executed one of his own, lowering Queisha, protecting her in his arms, over her, hovering; ready to make love to her, pushing his body closer and closer against hers. Reacting to the embrace, to his sex against hers, his lips aching for hers, there was nothing between her and the floor but his arm.

Like a swan, she made the dance look easy, even bending to his will, then she raised her hips and touched her center to his.

After years of celibacy, he short-circuited. Zap! That fast, his manhood morphed from a spring sapling to a mighty oak. Wood and plenty of it! Well, everything still worked, and so blessed well, too. He'd felt it happening, but this. Kudos to him.

His newly awakened libido threatened to undo him, until he looked at Queisha and got harder. Dancing pelvis to pelvis, she bit her lip, raised her hips, realized what she'd found, judging by the catch in her breath, and she succumbed to a full-bodied shudder.

The program erupted in applause, bringing them both a dose of stark reality, but not as far back as the place they'd started.

Somehow, they'd crossed a metaphoric bridge that dissolved behind them, and by the look in Queisha's eyes, she didn't care to go back anymore than he did.

The girls in their stocking feet, in a world of their own, were dancing the jitterbug, imitating the couple on TV, pretty much throwing each other around the room, and loving their slides across the floor. He liked their concentration. It left him free to enjoy his dance partner.

Standing hard body to soft with Queisha, both catching their breath, Chance slow waltzed her to jitterbug music, because he liked her in his arms, not to mention where his woody nestled against her. And he could tell that she liked keeping the woodster happy by the purposeful movement of her hips.

Her parted lips spoke of a seductress discovering her power. Resting her head on his shoulder and entwining her fingers with his said she was trying out that power. "Was that as good for you as it was for me?" she whispered.

Chance chuckled and executed a turn, keeping her plastered against him. "Kitten, I've never been happier, though I am in the middle of a *long* dry spell."

She shook out her hair and regarded him beneath her lashes. "I noticed."

"What was your first clue?"

She blew in his ear. "The submarine in your pants," she whispered.

"Watch us," Skye yelled. "Watch what we can do."

Chance looked into Queisha's eyes and they both sighed and watched the girls while clutching each other, though after a few minutes, sanity returned.

The girls did the jitterbug amazingly well, and they got fancy with dips, twirls, high kicks, and for Lace, a near split—ouch—though it didn't seem to bother her.

Skye ended their demonstration with one fantastic somersault.

Queisha showed off a hot and sexy cha-cha while Chance stood back to admire her, the life in her, the beauty radiating from within. Sweet heart light, no wonder he loved her.

The program ended with a tango, which they all tried, and the twins ended up on the floor and out of breath from giggling, because Queisha tried to dip him, and she dropped him.

The girls' final moves reminded him of a rain dance. All they needed were . . . feathers . . . all over the dance floor.

While the three of them caught their breath, Queisha went around collecting them. "What the heck is this? It's like some new kind of infestation. Or some large colorful bird, who shall remain nameless, got a gold and silver paint job and is hiding here in the house. Have you seen a big nest anywhere?"

That set the girls to giggling again, while Chance got

up to help Queisha pick up boas, wraps, top hats, and such. They had really made a mess, but it was worth everything to see the girls in such high spirits.

Besides, he and Queisha had a fabulous time, especially with that unexpected bit of foreplay. That unexpected bit of folly, madness, idiocy. But he couldn't stop the tide pulling them together. He didn't want to . . . whatever the consequences.

"Seriously," Queisha said coming up to him. "Where do these feathers come from?"

"I told you. They're mine."

Queisha tucked one deep in his waistband, like she'd use any excuse to get in there.

Chance dropped another feather.

TWENTY-TWO

❧

A late, light summer supper after an extraordinary day. Family around the table. Conversation. Jokes. *She* knew the meaning of family. Her cup runneth over.

The twins nearly fell asleep in their custard and didn't make it the entire way upstairs. She ended up carrying one, Chance, the other.

Skye sighed in her sleep and shifted her weight, so Queisha faltered.

Chance slipped an arm around her to keep her steady.

They put the girls in one bed. One would go looking for the other, anyway. Baths in the morning, Queisha thought, as she and Chance tiptoed from Lace's bedroom.

In the hall, Queisha shut the door and let herself wilt against it.

Chance's hands came to rest high on either side of her head. Their gazes locked like radar. Ping. Ping. Zing!

She caught the hunger in his eyes, sexual heat radiating from him in ravenous waves.

He didn't make a move, as if giving her a chance to get away.

"Please," she whispered . . . and he came for her.

He worshiped at the altar of her mouth the way she worshiped at his, lips and tongues exploring, mating, more primordial, more vigorous, than their first kiss, so hot and smoking, it nearly caused a fire.

Chance's hands stayed on the door, as if waiting for her to make the first move.

If she wanted, he'd pull away. She knew that.

She wanted, ached, but not for him to pull away, so she wound her arms around his neck.

He groaned, lifted her off her feet and away from the door, turning her while he kissed her. Then he looked around as if he didn't know where to take her.

"Across the hall," she said. "We'll hear them if they wake up."

"And they'll hear us."

"We've been quiet so far."

"Listen," he said, as he got close to the door and she reached for the knob. "This is more that just putting off the inevitable. This is *us*." He said "us" with capital letters. "There's still *them*." More capitals. "We still have to discuss what to say and how to deal with their grief. You know that, right?"

"I want us." She used caps, too, then she parted her lips, touching her bottom one to his top, parting his, readying him for her invasion, a trick he'd taught her. "How about one perfect night for us?"

One perfect night.

"Such a small request," he said. "It doesn't matter when we tell them. Nothing's going to change."

Queisha released her breath. "Let's lose ourselves in each other."

"I've dreamed of that. Of you suggesting it."

She tilted her head, confused. It wasn't possible. "We just met, silly." Yet she'd known him forever and accepted the knowledge as a gift from the universe. She opened the guest bedroom door, the room across from hers. A man's room, she now saw. Taupe walls, black lacquer furniture, a king bed, striped taupe-and-black bedspread, which she found beneath her, Chance hovering above her, ready to make love to her.

Slake their mutual lust? No, make love, weird as that seemed, considering the time frame of their acquaintance. Forever?

She'd never admit how wet and ready she was for him.

How hard up was she to react so easily and quickly to his advances?

How scared was he to be hesitating? Given his reinvigorated boner, she knew she had his attention, so she'd take the initiative. Problem: it had been years for her. How did a woman of the world take the initiative? The truth. "I'm not sure I know how to be a seductress."

He fumbled at her buttons. "You were doing great on the dance floor."

"Well, there you go. You were leading. But I remember how this used to work." She raised her hips and made Chance hiss while he got harder and seemingly longer. "Still does," he whispered against her lips.

She slipped her hands between them and began to knead that lovely, hard, and growing harder, place. One finger along his length.

He groaned.

Two fingers slow up his length. Her thumb at its base.

Chance took deep, purposeful breaths.

"You like?"

"Like?" he rasped. "So much, I'm going to die of—" He gritted his teeth, covered her hand with his, raised it, kissed her knuckles, and rolled away. He lay on his back, a hand over his brow, his breath coming fast. "Kitten, if I'm going to last long enough to get the woodster from my pants, I need a distraction."

She got on all fours above him, looked down, and gave him a look filled with promise. "We can talk first," she said. "No touching."

"But even that's tempting. Full breasts," he said, "hard nubs, heaven in two hands full. Forgive me, but I can't help myself."

"You're hard to distract."

"That's the problem. I'm hard."

She caught her breath when he filled his hands with her, her silver fairy dress crinkling between them.

"You're not wearing a bra!" He removed his hands like they'd touched a hot plate instead of her breasts, soft and naked beneath her gown.

"It's a strapless gown. A bra would ruin the lines. I should think you'd like the feel of my breasts."

"I like. Too blessed much." He looked a little peaked. "No bra could ruin me."

"Sir Chance, methinks you're sending mixed signals.

The equipment is ready, but I'm not—not to finish in a blink, anyway. I want to make this last."

"Problem: I have a lance with a mind of its own."

"You have a cloudy case of trouser brain?"

"Funny you should mention clouds."

TWENTY-THREE

❦

Clouds? Who cared about clouds? She had a man in her bed.

Handsome. Rugged. Kind. She wanted soft touches, sensuality. Sex play.

Perhaps Chance was toying with her, and she should be appreciating it. After all, sex was not all action, but talk, patience, teasing, and discovering. "Let's clear your clouds, then." Queisha straightened. "This is called a side zipper," she said, raising her arm and indicating the implement on her dress. "It's not considered sexy, so you can regroup while I make use of it."

"I think you're years too late to slow me down. Pardon me if I can't wait." He licked his lips and slowly lowered her strapless top to expose her breasts.

"Now, only my manhood is regrouping. Happy, *happy* Sir Chance," he declared. "Happier submarine."

"I'm sorry," she said, regarding her breasts overflowing his big hands. "I've been overly endowed. It's so embarrassing."

"Please remember for a future conversation—I'll tell you when—that you tend to overreact and apologize for your assets, as if they were deficiencies."

"I'll remember." Inside, she danced. An asset, not a deficiency. Her father had made her feel bad for being well-endowed, like she utilized her breasts specifically to attract attention. Negative attention. The kind that caused babies. And she all but gave him proof.

"Now back to your regularly scheduled assets," Chance said, reclaiming her attention. He reached for her breasts, again, but stopped short of touching them. She thought she might scream.

"How do you feel about a man who drools?" he asked. "Ah, I see you appreciate my attention. I personally love a woman with a twinkle in her big, amber eyes."

He'd taken his hands from her flesh, damn it, but remained utterly focused on her breasts. She adored his robust lust, she loved being responsible for it, so she upped the brazen factor and lowered herself toward his mouth. Just a nipple away from unbelievable ecstasy; she knew because she pulsed just knowing it.

"Ah . . ."

"Yes?"

He licked his lips. "Forgot what I was going to, oh yeah, maybe we should hang up the dress? Please say no."

"And let an angel lose its wings?"

Chance's amusement got entirely out of hand. "You do believe in angels?"

"No, do you?"

"Yes. Angels appear when we've lost our way."

"Like in the dark when we're buried alive? I can almost believe it."

"You of all people should."

"I'll tell you what I do believe," Queisha said. "I believe you've gotten your libido under control. Now we can take it slow."

His body stiffened . . . everywhere. "You changed the subject to keep me from short-circuiting?"

"I hoped you'd last for a minute or two longer."

Chance's eyes narrowed. "Off with the dress."

Queisha pulled the silver dream over her head. "Nothing like challenging a man's staying power to get him to focus."

Chance winced. "Guess I'm giving you a glimpse at my recent lack of experience."

Queisha winked. "As long as you give me a glimpse of your submarine."

When she cleared her dress, he came for her breasts with his mouth, and at the anticipation of imminent contact, she tilted back her head, closed her eyes, and let him work his magick. Her breasts were in Chance's hands, his miracle-working fingers hardening a nipple, slow, thorough, creating and increasing pleasure. Her breath came in bursts, sporadic like her pleasure, his mouth pulling her closer, closer to an intangible crest. She dare not open her eyes for fear she'd break the burgeoning spell.

She moaned.

He groaned, suckled her while sliding his hands down her hips, inside her panties, lower, a hand on each cheek, squeezing, sliding tantalizingly toward the front, his thumbs seeking, abrading, making her rise above herself as he kneaded her, sensitized her to his touch, and separated her folds, finding her slick, making her slicker, bringing her higher.

Someone whimpered.

Her?

She found him, that pulsing mound of manhood beneath his zipper, while he brought her to a place from which she never wanted to return.

She heard herself pant. Embarrassment rushed her at the sound of her need to ride the crest for as long as possible before falling off the precipice, so she went for his zipper, anticipation granting her desire to receive pleasure as much as to give and increase it for them both.

She crested, and rather than rise again, she looked to see what she was doing to him, but his eyes were closed, his face contorted. Pain. Pleasure. She came again at the thought of her own tactile aggression. She caught her breath as she unzipped him, and his hard wooden length jumped into her hands. Long, thick, pulsing. She rubbed the telltale droplet around the tip and nearly raised him off the bed.

"Queisha," he whispered, like a prayer.

He breached her, again, with his fingers, both of them sliding deeper into sexual abandon. She savored and rode the waves of pleasure, rising slow and filled with the promise of the highest peak.

Amazing how sharp and serene gratification could become, nearly unbearable, when one with your lover.

She cupped his balls, thumbed his base, closed a hand around his thickness and began to work him.

Their rhythm fell into sync, slow at first but growing stronger, faster, a rise to fulfillment, nearly unbearable.

"No!" he shouted, surprising her.

She saw only the tilt of the room as he switched their positions, kicking off his pants as he did.

Him on top, he stroked her hair, finger-combed it from her brow and clutched a handful. At the same time, he re-sought her center, and worked her until she pulsed to receive him. When she cried out, he entered her, fast, hard, both of them ready, hot and slick, and he matched her greed.

She wanted this. She wanted him. Chance. Son of Godric.

"I'm sorry," he said, kissing her eyes, her lips, her ear, nipping her lobe. "I'm moving too fast." He tried to slow his pace, his face a mask of concentration, as he held himself in check.

She'd climaxed several times, and now she wanted to watch him come, to release him to the ultimate pleasure.

She raised her hips, rotated them, swallowed his groan with a kiss, and milked his sex so he rushed toward his climax, her wallowing in the power of his final orgasmic thrust.

Whomp! The muffled sound filled the room, bouncing around them with a slow, lowering echo: *Whomp, whomp, whomp, whomp . . . whomp.* Flying debris rained down on them.

Queisha covered her eyes for protection.

When the sound stopped and the debris stopped raining, she peeked between her fingers.

Red-faced, Chance raised himself on his hands . . . and picked a gold feather from her hair.

Then she looked beyond his face and saw the *big* picture.

"Wings?" She scrambled from beneath him, until she came up against the headboard at her back. "You've got wings as wide as the bleeping bed. Rainbow wings. Hah!" She pointed. "Colored feathers."

Chance got off the bed with dignity and stood as if at attention, two feathers crossed before his tired privates. "Are you talking to me?"

TWENTY-FOUR

―⁓―

Queisha moved from the bed so fast, she stubbed her toe on the nightstand. Even jumping around the room naked holding her foot, she looked sexy. He didn't know whether to be turned on or to hurt for her.

He didn't want to think about the picture he made standing there with a re-stiffening dick and huge, gaudy wings.

She stamped her sore foot, too mad to hide her wince. "Really?" she snapped. "You're horny again? Now?"

He dropped the feathers and used his hands as a codpiece, or a cock piece. "It's been a long time for me." Long being the operative word. Damned thing was getting too big for his hands to cover.

Who knew that an angel's muscle sacs couldn't contain his wings on climax? When he got back, he'd have to record it as a footnote in the handbook. "Do you want to do it again? I'll leave my wings out."

"You think I'm having sex with a . . . a . . . perv?"

"I'm an angel. I told you I was."

"Sure you are. So am I. Didn't I tell you? I left my wings in my other ball gown."

"So you really don't believe in angels?"

"Yeah, well, looks like one's pointing his handy-dandy at me."

"There could be another explanation." He fluttered his wings. "These could be fake."

"Are they?"

He sighed. "No."

"Turn around." She enunciated her request in such a way as to make him obey. He faced the wall like a naughty child, which Michael would probably applaud.

Good thing Angus didn't invade bedrooms; Chance couldn't handle an amused cherub right now. "Queisha, listen."

"Are you molting?"

"Excuse me?"

"One, two three . . . seven."

He turned to see her face. "Have the girls been teaching you to count, again?"

"There are seven feathers in the bed. Gold and silver."

"So, that's the cost of having sex. Seven feathers. Gold for love. Silver for lust."

"There are more gold than silver," she said, her voice less hostile, making his lavender feathers glow. *Lavender for hope.*

"Get on the bed," she said.

He turned his upper torso her way. "So you can have your wicked way with me?"

"The bed is now neutral territory," she declared.

"That's unfortunate." No wonder he'd fallen in love with her. "Yes, ma'am."

"Don't get smart with me. You're not off the hook. Sit in the *middle* of the bed."

Queisha knelt behind him, not exactly what he'd hoped for, until she stroked his wings. He could feel every feather she touched. Top to bottom, side to side, color to color, feather by feather.

He didn't know he had feelings in his wings. Must be the virtues connected to them, the magick with which the She of Life imbued them.

"Chance, these look real."

"There's a reason for that."

"Sweet sassafras tea, I'd go to hell if I seduced an angel. You know, the row of silver feathers is kind of ratty."

"Yeah, well, that's why I'm going to hell with you. Silver are for chastity, and I've been spreading a bit too much lust around since I got here. How many silvers do you think I have left?"

"Too many to count."

"Oh good." He turned to face her. "We can have a lot more sex."

"You sure look like a perv. You smirk like one, too." She turned him back around and slid her hands into his wing sacs, one hand in each, and he winced at the pain, until she grasped his wings at the roots and yanked, her whole body behind her.

"Ouch, ow! Stop, no. That hurts!"

She was off the bed again, moving a bit like a grasshopper, but looking wondrous, and doable, in her nakedness. She pointed an accusing finger his way. "You are an . . . It's not possible. You're an angel?"

"I thought we'd established that. And it's worse than you think. I'm your very own underachieving guardian angel."

"No wonder you were so angry when I said that. But I didn't mean—wait, yes, I did. I've had a pretty sucky time of it."

Across the hall, one of the girls started crying.

"Hide," Queisha said. "Get in the closet."

He pointed his thumb back toward his wings; they should have a WIDE LOAD sign on them. True, he could slide them back into his muscle sacs, but that took energy, and Queisha had sucked *that* right out of him.

"Coming, babies," she called, slipping his blue T-shirt over her head, her long legs a sight to behold.

She scowled at his leer as he watched her struggle to pull her panties up beneath it.

"Stay!" she ordered.

"Aw gee, I thought I'd go buy more rubber duckies while I was waiting."

She growled as she slipped out the door. "Hey, sweeties," she said in the hall before she could close, er, slam the door. "I was chasing a mouse," she told the girls. "A rat, really. Don't go in there."

"We had rats at the boarding school, too," Skye announced with pride. "We're hungry."

"I'm not surprised. Let me go get a robe on and we'll find you a snack. We messed you up today when we burned lunch. I'm sorry."

Chance appreciated this extra time so he could get started on his plan to get Queisha out of the house and into the yard.

He went up to the tower and looked down at the yellow-brick patio, concentrating on setting down the same exact bricks. He used a finger to draw in the air, with the yard as his canvas, circles, maybe thirty to forty bricks wide, curling them around the angel fountain, then around the rose garden. He curled the path at the water and planted the bricks root-deep in the sand, part of it beneath the water. Sure, she'd have to sweep her yellow-brick way to the beach once in a while, but the girls would be able to play in the sand, Queisha nearby, getting over her fear of the water.

From there, he took her "magick" path around the gazebo, up to each and every door of the house, going so far as to spread a veneer of yellow bricks on every set of steps, bringing the path away from each door in an opposite direction.

It bounced into the carousel and curled around it to the other entrance, as well. From there, it rounded the front yard, climbed the front steps, and covered the circular drive, winding its way back to the side of the house where he started.

Chance circled every ancient tree and flower garden on the yellow-brick path's route, allowing for Queisha to become acquainted with the beauty of her own yard. The path went so far as to kiss the fence at the gate separating Queisha's property from the private school next door—which he'd learned from Vivica that Queisha supported—before his magick path wound its way back to the base of her yellow-brick patio.

That way, if the girls stayed, she could walk them to school mornings and pick them up afternoons.

If she ever walked the whole thing, Queisha might put in a mile or three, given the curls and swirls.

When he finished, he added yellow-brick benches along the route, and filled in some random curls with bricks for garden parties or picnics.

Now Queisha could hopefully begin to lose her fear of the world outside her door. The girls could learn to ride bicycles, depending on how long they stayed. He was unfortunately not aware of the master plan, but he did know how Mrs. Fitzpatrick's family felt about Queisha being the girls' guardian. The shoe of battle was likely to drop soon.

Chance rested, slipped his wings back in his muscle sacs, and took a shower while he waited for Queisha to come back upstairs with the girls.

Afterward, he realized how tired he was, so he slipped between the sheets of the bed where they'd made love and went to sleep.

He heard them coming up the stairs around two, Queisha coaxing the girls to stay awake long enough to get to bed.

He imagined her in his shirt, which caused his, er, submarine to resurface, and he sat up to wait for her.

She didn't come back.

Some good time later, at the click of the door, he looked at the clock. Three. An hour had passed since they came back upstairs. He'd lived in Everlasting for years, yet this had been the longest hour of his life.

She stood beside the bed, still wearing his blue shirt, the musk of their sex calling to him.

"Time for breakfast?" he asked, raising himself on an elbow. Periscope, going up.

She folded back the blanket. "Dessert first," she said, pulling off her shirt as she climbed in with him. "Which does not mean that I forgive you for lying to me."

"I didn't lie. I said the feathers were mine. I said I was an angel. Twice."

"Damn, you make me mad. This time, I'm on top."

TWENTY-FIVE

He loved how she slid her naked body along his, until they became like one piece of humanity, all their parts having once been melded in the grand scheme, formed by the She of Life in a single mold then forced apart to live their respective lives, though their souls had never stopped seeking their mates.

Blessed glory, he couldn't help comparing their fit to a magick commenced in Everlasting. A fit ordained. Never to be parted.

He wished the triumvirate believed in the two of them together as much as he did. Never mind the small hitch that she lived and he died.

Her mind on the physical plane, Queisha cupped his butt cheeks and purred. At the small of his back, she made a circle, or was she . . . "Are you writing on my back with your finger?"

"Yep, I wrote: M-I-N-E. So whoever gave you your wings will understand that things have changed."

"You think you can influence God? She's a pretty strong personality, you know."

Queisha sat straight up, her blanket clinging to one, only one, breast. The other made his mouth water. He moved so his erection poked her in the thigh.

"God's a woman? Hot damn."

"Queisha, saying damn about God is like missing her point the way you're missing mine. Yes, God's a woman, but she'd rather be blessed than damned."

"God's a woman," she repeated, her grin rather glorious. "Bless her. You know, I've always suspected that she could have done the period thing better, don't you think? That, and maybe put a man's balls in some kind of protective—"

Chance pictured Queisha giving God biology lessons. "I'll give her your suggestions."

"Thank you." Queisha lay facing him, watching the way he watched her, and he thought, *Okay, this is it. This is where we get busy and start making love again.*

"This is amazing, us as a couple."

Ah, he'd always hated the call to brutal honesty. "You know, don't you, that us as a couple was over before it began, right?"

She denied his assertion with a shake of her head. "I've always been more interested in the here and now. I'm a work in progress, myself."

"Great progress."

"Thanks," she said, rising up to kneel on the bed. "Roll over."

Brain blip, probably due to the natural beauty of the goddess before him. "Please explain."

She huffed and rolled him to his stomach.

"Ouch, careful. You're going to sprain my dick. It's hard as a pikestaff, in case you didn't notice."

"Pikestaff?" she repeated. "What did you do, reincarnate from medieval times?" Meanwhile her hands were all over his back, a pretty gloriously terrific experience.

"We do reincarnate, don't we?" she confirmed. "You said you'd been an unremarkable lawyer in another life."

"Sure," he said. "I was a divorce lawyer for Henry the Eighth. You saw how that went."

She sat back on her heels. "Was Anne Boleyn terribly beautiful?"

"Get a grip, Queisha. I was a lawyer, before I died."

She scrambled back so fast, she fell off the bed.

He turned on his side, head in his hand, to give his erection a break—well, to keep it from breaking—and to wait for her to pop up off the floor. He loved the sight of her all café-au-lait naked.

She must be embarrassed, because at first, she was a no-show. He had a moment of panic, then he saw her hands on the side of the bed, the top of her head, her eyes, wary and looking in both directions, her pert nose, that luscious, eminently kissable mouth, her sculpted chin, which she set on the bed.

"Are you dead . . . now?" she asked.

"Do I look dead?"

"How would I know? You said you died. I never saw a ghost, though I'm pretty sure that my mysterious Aunt Helen is still here. Then again, none of my other lovers ever sprouted wings at orgasm."

"The whomping wings were unfortunate. How *many* other lovers?"

"One."

Chance bit the inside of his lip, hard, to keep from insulting her with the knee-jerk bark of laughter he suppressed.

Oblivious to his relief at her lack of lovers, she seemed to search inwardly before speaking.

"In retrospect," she said, "your wings whomping out like that was a shock, a bit creepazoid, but fantasmaglorious, too, all at the same time."

Chance waited, certain she wasn't telling the whole truth, hoping she'd reveal more. "On *second* thought?" he coaxed.

"Well." She pursed her lips and worked her brows in a brain-scan-ish sort of way. "Maybe on *fiftieth* thought."

That's what he got for digging deeper. "I want the bald ugly truth. You've been in your room trying to talk yourself into coming back in here, haven't you, ever since you brought the girls upstairs an hour ago?"

The talking head grinned. "Wrong," she said, popping up like a jack-in-the-box. "I was trying to talk myself into *not* coming in here."

"Why?"

Her lips fake trembled. "You scare me."

"Likewise," he said.

"Let's talk about this dead business," she said, hands on hips. "When you were dead . . ."

Chance sighed in resignation, pulled himself up against the headboard, and softly tented the blankets over his erection. He didn't want her to see his dick weeping or begging or trying to hang itself.

She got into bed, settling across from him, against the black wrought-iron footboard. He thought that was fine, until she caught the sheet up beneath her arms to cover her breasts, molding them in a highly sensual come-and-get-it way.

So, there they were; her in his bed . . . but not. His dick doing the here-I-am-dance . . . for nothing. One side of her sheet beginning to droop, his hope rising as uselessly as his dick.

"So," she said. "Tell me how you died the last time, and when."

TWENTY-SIX

Chance never thought they'd have this talk in a bed.

Mentally preparing himself, he grabbed another pillow and shoved it behind him, sat straighter, and sighed. "We've already established that I was an unremarkable lawyer. Let me be more specific. I sucked as a criminal lawyer, but the day I died, I had an interview for a job as a corporate lawyer."

"So did you get the job?"

"The company doesn't exist anymore but I'm getting ahead of myself."

"Sorry, you died on a job interview? Literally?"

He was sorry, too. "Not quite. I got there nearly two hours early, having flown there from Providence. Filled with nervous energy, I decided I'd look more successful if I showed up carrying an indecently expensive briefcase. The company was located in a building with a mall below ground level, so I went shopping."

Queisha shivered involuntarily. Her eyes widened, and she pulled the blanket closer around her as she bit her lip. He could practically see the description alone insidiously working its way into her subconscious.

He wished he didn't have to tell her, but it was time, for so many reasons.

"With time to spare," he continued, "and to keep calm, I went looking for a leather goods store."

Queisha sat forward.

"I bought a briefcase, sat in the middle of the mall to nail clip the tags. No scissors, of course. As I threw away the paper stuffing to replace it with my letters of recommendation, the building shuddered, more than a little. The sky was falling; stairways and elevators filled with fire."

"No," she whispered, going pale.

"Yes, Fiskville Crossroads Center, Los Angeles, July 2000." He opened his arms.

She flew straight at him.

He pulled her, blankets and all, tight against him, and kissed her brow. "*You* know the rest."

"I do not. What happened to you?"

He gave her a double take. "I died."

"How?"

Denial, he thought. He'd humor her. "I dug my way out, forming a tunnel going straight up. I had a clear path, but I knew that if one more piece of debris fell, the tunnel would collapse."

"You knew that?"

"I did."

"So you took it and it collapsed too soon?"

"No, I encountered the most beautiful and frightened young woman I'd ever seen, and I told her to go first."

"I don't believe you."

"Queisha, why won't you admit that it was you?"

Her eyes filled. "It was bad enough that I killed a stranger. I don't want to have killed someone I love. That was not us. It couldn't have been. Chance, you're here. You're *not* dead. You haven't said a thing to prove it was me."

"You clung to me like a spider monkey, arms around my neck, legs around my waist, and cried until I yanked you off me and forced you up the tunnel."

"No! That could have been anybody."

"Fine, I'll tell you something that couldn't have happened to just anybody. Someone grabbed your hand at the top, after the tunnel had collapsed behind you, and when you got your footing, you looked up and thanked the person whose hand you grabbed, but there was nobody there."

He held her tight to stop her trembling.

"You know how people say they float above their bodies in the hospital when they're having a near-death experience? Well, there's this blink of time between life and death where you're present but outside yourself. I used that time to pull you through from the top, despite the tunnel having already collapsed behind you. Then I was in Everlasting in a crowd of hundreds."

Queisha wept openly.

"I didn't care," he whispered against her brow, "because *you* were alive. You became my first charge." He caught her chin and brought her gaze up to his. "Contrary to popular belief, Queisha, there are people and things worth dying for. You and the girls for instance. Now, let's get you past this unjustified guilt. You didn't kill me. I made a choice. I saw you from quite a distance away. I could have gone up that tunnel before you saw me. Let's call it destiny and move on."

That was as close as he'd ever gotten to lying to her. Michael told him that he'd reversed their destinies that day. She was supposed to die and he, to live, but she didn't need to know that. Besides, Skye and Lace wouldn't be here, if all had gone according to the greater plan.

He only regretted that Queisha had probably died more on the inside than he'd died on the outside that day.

God had tried to right the mistake when Queisha gave birth. No go. He'd saved her that time, too, with the twins. It was a wonder *he* wasn't a messenger cherub like Angus for all the interfering he'd done in Queisha's life.

"Why were you there that day?" he asked, handing her a tissue.

She wiped her eyes. "I had been refusing to leave the center, acting afraid of everything, so my social worker took me shopping to show me that I had nothing to fear. She didn't live to find out how wrong she was."

Ah, Chance thought. Her social worker had sealed Queisha's phobia instead of proving it didn't exist. "The good news is that I'm a better angel than I was a lawyer, but I lost track of you for several months during angel orientation."

"That's when I miscarried, though not because of the Fiskville disaster. One nurse told me that my baby had a shock of red hair. He would have been one-quarter Kenyan and three-quarters Irish. I wish they'd let me hold him. That's all I wanted. One minute with him in my arms."

Chance sat straighter. "During orientation, Michael sent me down to pick up a cherub. Holy angels hospital, October thirteenth?"

"Yes!"

"That's why they sent me, because I was your guardian and he was your boy. It was also my first trip to the cherub nursery. Queisha, you painted a picture of your son. He's in the mural. We called him Connor."

"I named him Connor in my heart."

"Then that's where we got it. You were young to have a child."

"Sixteen. My adoptive father threw me out for getting pregnant. That's why I was in the custody of social services."

"You haven't had it easy."

"Neither have you. At least I lived. Where in the mural is Connor?"

"He's the redhead on his back, gurgling, kicking, and reaching for the stars. The thing is, Connor often catches the stars, throws them, and bounces them off the nursery angels, members of the Granny Brigade. He'll stay tiny forever but his mind and heart are expanding. He'll do great work someday. He has an aptitude for love. Everybody says so."

This time he just gave her the box of tissues.

"Do you know what my adoptive father said when he heard I lost my baby? 'Just as well.' Said I could come home. I told him to go to hell. That was the last time I saw dear old dad."

"Social services didn't make you go with him?"

"No, when the man who adopted me threw me out, he shook me so hard, he broke my arm, and they took me from him."

"How did you end up here?"

"At the first year anniversary of the Fiskville tragedy,

a news crew revisited the event, and I was interviewed with the survivors. Aunt Helen recognized me. Evidently my adoptive parents kept her in the loop, sent pictures. She got in touch with my ex–adoptive father, and he told her where to find me."

"So she took you in?"

"She changed her will in my favor and had started the process of bringing me here when she had a stroke, which I didn't know at the time. I worked at social services as a live-in until she passed two years later."

"How did you get here, physically, I mean, from there to here, if you were afraid to leave your home?"

"I'm wealthy, thanks to Aunt Helen. You figured that out, right? I hired a doctor to tranquilize me and accompany me on an air ambulance, then he did the same when we took a regular ambulance from Logan airport. The man's still my doctor. His office is here in the house. I'm his only patient. I came, I stayed."

"One thing I don't understand. Why did you become a surrogate? You'd lost one baby but agreed to give away two more? That just doesn't sound like you."

"It makes a certain sense, and we didn't know the procedure would result in twins, but basically it's your fault."

"I told you, *not* my sperm."

Queisha elbowed him. "You said, 'Live for both of us.'"

"I did."

"When Vivica proposed the surrogacy, I saw an opportunity to give the world a life for a life. I did it for you."

"I'm sincerely humbled."

"I'd been pregnant; so everyone knew I could conceive. The Fitzpatricks had everything they wanted, except a baby. We had a private contract drawn up."

"So, you're just generous?"

"And you're just an angel—*co-guardian style*—who's here for . . . how long?"

"About that . . ."

TWENTY-SEVEN

Chance composed himself. "*You should know that I* greeted the twins' parents when they got to Everlasting, and I knew what a mess you'd be in as their guardian."

"You knew I was their guardian before I did?"

"Yes, and I knew you'd need my help."

He took her hand and brought it to his lips. A powerful love, so very much more than the physical, shot through him, weakened him, made him want the impossible, to be with her, forever. "Queisha Saint-Denis, I've been in love with you since the day I died. I watched you grow into a soul-beautiful woman with a heart as big as Everlasting."

"You watched me? So you knew everything I just told you?"

"No, I watched *over* you. The miscarriage happened while I was in orientation, and I never made the connection. I have other charges who take my attention on a regular basis. I keep track of my charges on a grander scheme."

She folded her arms, moved a bit away. "Keep talking."

"In the last couple of years, though, I tended to favor you, to the annoyance of the archangel triumvirate, and the good friend and fellow angel who sent me down here."

"Do tell."

"I love you, Queisha. You think I'd take just anybody to bed?"

"I've never been loved," she said, almost to herself. "I don't know how to love you in return."

"You don't know how *not* to love."

"I take it you haven't taken anybody to bed since you died, or you wouldn't have popped your wings?"

He cupped his neck. "I had no needs, urges, hungers of any kind in Everlasting, just love, and I directed most of it your way. So call me crazy, I'm human again, and I want to be with you in every way a man can be with a woman."

"For how long?"

"Ah, we digress. In the way Connor, the cherub you sent to us, became my charge because he's yours, Skye and Lace did, too, because you bore them. So I wasn't lying. I am their co-guardian, but in an angelic way."

Queisha touched her brow, frowning as if she were computing a tough math problem in her head. She pointed at him. "*You* were at their birth. You sat with me during labor."

"Me on one side, Vivica on the other."

"Where did the idea for my mural come from?"

"It's a picture of my fears."

"Skye said you were their angel when she pointed to the mural."

"She's so bright. I breathed life into them so I wouldn't have to take them to the cherub nursery. They saw me. They'll forget. Adults don't believe like children."

"I'm not getting rid of the mural."

"You don't have to. It's a wondrous reminder. Besides, Connor is in it."

She had so many questions about her son and the angelic world of Everlasting, he never noticed the light growing bright behind the blinds. Suddenly the girls were giggling and opening and closing drawers across the hall.

"Munchkins are awake," Chance said. "Aren't they supposed to have a bath this morning?"

Queisha checked the clock. "They overslept. Breakfast first, bath after."

"Works for me. I'll get breakfast started." They hadn't made love again but he felt strangely satisfied after their meeting of minds and souls.

She threw on her robe and went to the door but stopped with her hand on the knob.

"What?" he asked, pulling on his jeans.

"When do you have to go back?"

He glanced up, hoping for a whisper, or shout, of "never."

None came. "After you and the girls are settled, but I could get called back anytime."

"Let's make every minute count, for us and the girls."

"Haven't we been doing that?"

"I don't want to tell them about their parents yet. Their

futures are anything but settled. I've seen no paperwork. We don't know where they belong or to whom. What could we tell them now but they're orphans with an uncertain future?"

"That's true." They should belong to her now, but she wasn't used to getting good news, so she hadn't grasped that. On the other hand, she didn't think she was good enough to raise them, because of the agoraphobia.

Blessed conundrum, he had his work cut out for him.

Well, first things first, a walk for Queisha on the yellow-brick path, right after breakfast . . . if she stepped foot on it without breaking a brick over his head.

It was a nasty trick, taking her by surprise with the yellow-brick path. And if she refused to step on it, she'd be denying the girls, not him.

The ultimate test.

TWENTY-EIGHT

Before breakfast, and after a two-minute meeting with the girls on the water porch while Queisha showered, Chance heard them shouting for her to "come and see the yellow-brick road."

He slipped bacon and fried eggs between fresh sandwich rolls, put hot cocoa into a thermos, and individual apricot yogurts in a small thermal bag. He collected hot cups, plates, napkins, a quilt, and went to wait at the bottom of the stairs. The girls charged down a second later.

"Where's Lady Queisha?"

"She took the elevator."

"Oh, oh. Did she see the paths around the yard?"

"Yep," Lace said, Skye nodding behind her.

The elevator door opened revealing Queisha plastered to the back wall, arms spread wide, every inch of her touching, from the top of her head to the palms of her hands.

He stopped just outside the elevator. "Though you look the part, you'd never make the Martyrs Brigade."

"Whomp you."

Getting her out of there was going to be like prying that spider monkey from his arms and sending her up a tunnel. "Girls, here," Chance said, handing them the quilt. "Follow the path to the rose garden, and lay this out. I've got breakfast right here."

"No!" Queisha yelled, but the girls ran toward the patio and disappeared.

Queisha charged from the elevator and followed the direction they'd taken. "I can't *see* the rose garden from here!" she shouted, feet firmly planted on the patio.

He didn't tell her that he had his angelic radar on the girls and knew they were perfectly safe, or that he'd told them to stay out of sight, unless he called for them to come out.

When he got close to her, she shoved him so hard, he landed on his butt. "Hey, these bricks are hard."

"My girls are missing."

"They're setting up our picnic breakfast near the rose garden."

"I can't see them." She charged back toward the house.

He raised an angelic hand, and the patio door shut and locked in front of her. All the doors locked.

Queisha walked his way with such purpose, she backed him up against the balustrade. If she pushed him again, he wouldn't bruise his butt.

She smacked his shoulders with a scream of frustration that could curdle milk, putting the entire force of her body behind her.

With the balustrade behind his knees, he toppled ass over wingtips into the thorny bushes on the other side.

She called the girls twice as he extricated himself from the clawing greenery, scratched bloody, but proud as punch, because, whether she knew it or not, she was so busy shouting for the girls, she'd taken two steps on the walk.

Lace and Skye, no fools, stood just out of sight at the very corner of the house.

She might seem unaware, but her hands were trembling, her breath short, and she was fanning herself with a hand. "Come here, you two," Queisha called, taking another step their way.

With the next step, Queisha doubled over, a hand to her stomach.

Chance flew to her side, put an arm around her, and worried he'd gone too far.

She straightened, fisted that hand, and socked him in the jaw.

He worked his chin and grinned. "I never wanted to take you to bed more than at this moment," he whispered.

She turned to look behind her. "Look at how far I am from the patio. This is your fault."

"I hope so."

"I hope I puke on you."

Perspiration dotted her pale upper lip and brow.

Torn between guilt and success, he fell into step beside her, waves of fear radiating off her, and tried to help her by putting an arm around her.

"Don't touch me," she said, which he took as a backassward request because she clasped his hand, tight, crushing his knuckles in her trembling grip.

She turned on her heels and caught the twins peeking around the corner.

She raised a brow. "I'll get you for this," she told them. But for every step Queisha took in their direction, the twins backed up one.

As he and Queisha rounded the corner, they saw the two innocents sitting on the quilt waiting for them.

"Girls," Chance said, "can you get the picnic basket off the patio?"

Queisha tried to turn back. "Let's all go back to the patio."

But Chance pulled her up short. "Forward, my love, not backward."

"I hate you."

"I could tell last night."

"Shush."

"I don't pop my wings for just anybody."

"Be quiet," she hissed.

The girls each held a handle of the picnic basket as they passed him and Queisha. By the time he and she got to the quilt, breakfast was laid out, though Queisha was too queasy to eat it.

He hadn't quite realized how physically debilitating the phobia could be.

Skye curled against her, and Lace rubbed her back. "You did good," Lace whispered. "You came far."

Sky patted his knee. "Sir Chance, did you build this path so Lady Queisha won't be lergic to the yard and can play out here with us?"

"Yes, I did."

Lace nodded. "Our Queisha is brave, taking this magick path so far from the house."

"But the path leads back to the doors, see?" Skye asked. "Easy out, specially in a fire."

Queisha hugged them together. "What did I do to deserve you?"

"You must'a slow baked us *real* good."

TWENTY-NINE

As Chance packed the remains of breakfast, Queisha took the opportunity to look up at the front of her house for the first time. She'd needed to get out here for the girls. This was good. Her symptoms were receding. She was feeling almost normal, but she wondered if that would last.

She'd done it, and she was still alive. Nothing awful had happened.

Chance sent the girls up to the carousel. "I left something in there for you. You'll know what when you see it. There's one for each of you. This path is a great place to use them."

Queisha poked him. "What did you do?"

"Will you stop being so physical?"

"You liked it last night."

"Give me a break. My wings'll go bald."

"Seriously, what are you going to torture me with now?"

"They're kids," Chance said. "They need to learn to play. You're not sick anymore, are you?"

"I'm steadier. Feeling not quite happy but pretty proud of myself." She pointed toward the house. "It's a pretty nice house, isn't it?"

"Sure is."

"I never thought I'd sit in my own yard."

"You're welcome."

"The jury's still out as to whether a thank you is in order." She bumped his arm, just to be close to him, to touch him, and she didn't know how to initiate that out here, with the girls in sight. "My insides are still quaking."

"They'll quake less when we take this walk tomorrow."

"And when you're gone and I'm facing this path alone? Chance," she said, resting her head on his shoulder. "I don't want you to go back."

He slipped an arm around her waist. "I'll always be in your heart. You'll always be in mine." He cleared his throat. "Listen, now, this is interesting. This path has a twofold purpose and one of them is about us. It's a picture of our love, going on forever, but running in crazy circles."

"That's us, all right, all over the yard."

He tapped her nose, then he kissed it. "It's also a picture of you living in the world, knowing that wherever you go, you'll find your way back home safe again."

She acknowledged the wisdom in his words with a nod, touched his cheek, appreciated his thoughtfulness, but she couldn't speak beyond the lump in her throat.

He was going to leave her. How far could she travel to keep him?

Not a choice, but surely something to think about.

Chance held the palm of her hand to his lips while she tried to figure out how to kidnap him from God. Pretty risky.

That was when Skye rode a red and blue tricycle from the carousel building.

Lace, butt in seat, pedals turning on their own, walked a lavender three-wheeler down the path behind her twin. "Mine won't go," she called.

Skye rolled her eyes, and got up to put her sister's feet on the pedals and physically turn them with her hands until Lace got the idea.

Lace promptly passed Skye's abandoned bike.

"No fair!" Skye called, trying to catch up.

Falling behind, Skye looked around, grinned, lifted her feet off the pedals, legs straight out, and let gravity take her flying down the hill . . . straight toward Salem Cove.

Queisha screamed.

Moving fast, Chance stopped the flying twins in their tracks and sent them to Queisha while he carried the tricycles back up the hill.

Queisha paced their picnic area like she'd always been doing it. No fear, no palpitations. However easy she felt now, she wondered if she'd be able to take the first step to get here tomorrow. She turned to the girls, who had been looking more afraid the longer she remained quiet.

"The way I see it, Sir Chance has to build a connecting path to keep you in this part of the yard, up here near the house, where you can ride your bikes on the flat side of the rose garden and not on the hillside. And, girls, hear this: You ride only when there's an adult present."

Lace tugged on Chance's shirt. "Sir Chance, since *you*

built our yellow-brick road, does that mean you're friends with the Wizard of Oz?"

"No, but I might get the stuffing torn out of me."

"Damn straight," Queisha said.

"Of course I'll build a safe path to keep them up here, unless one of us takes them down to play in the water."

Queisha's head came up, and fast. "Neither of us will ever do that."

Chance rubbed the back of his neck. "Discussion for another day," he said. "Right now, let's walk up here and let the girls ride their bikes in front of us."

Queisha looked at him as if he had two heads. "Sure, as soon as the path is built to connect this part of the path to that one."

"You won't walk the path that loops beside the water and back up again to connect to the other side?"

"I don't like the water."

Chance shook his head, swept her into his arms, and carried her to the opposite side of the path, bypassing the path to the water.

Queisha held on to him and sputtered. "I'll get you for this."

His lids lowered the way they had in bed last night.

Tingles ran through her.

"You bet you'll get me," he whispered.

Squee. "Now get the girls' bikes."

They had barely begun their walk, her tummy jiggling like a Jell-O mold after being carried, when Vivica came out of the carousel addition.

"Sorry," Vivica said, "I came through the house, and you can imagine my surprise, Queisha, when I saw you out here. Congratulations, Chance."

Queisha caught her breath. "Hey, how about congratulating me?" She hadn't pulled the faint and twitch, or barfed like a beer-bellied barfly, which only happened in public, of course. They had no notion of the strides she'd made this morning.

Vivica raised a cheering arm. "Go, Queisha, she's my girl! Seriously, I'm wild with excitement that you got this far from the house."

"It's his fault. He sent the girls into the wilds of the yard, and I had to make sure they were okay."

Vivica looked from one to the other. "Queisha, I see a difference in you, as if you've come to life. And Chance, you seem less surly, as if you've found a purpose."

"I've found purpose in our two small, sweet loves," Chance said, looking over at the girls, then his expression about melted when his gaze turned to her, and he winked at her, and Queisha knew they were both thinking about last night when they'd made love.

"And I've found a new and gratifying passion," he admitted to Vivica.

"Whomping angel wings!" Queisha elbowed him. "Shush!"

He lost a feather.

THIRTY

Vivica cleared her throat. "In the event the sensual sizzle I sense is correct, you might be glad that I've come to borrow the girls, with your permission."

Queisha's heart did a phobic somersault as she clasped her trembling hands behind her back. "Borrow with what purpose in mind?" She could not project her phobia onto the girls. They had traveled the world and should continue to happily do so.

"My cousin McKenna and her husband, Bastian Dragonelli, Jaydun's brother, are giving a birthday party for McKenna's friend's daughter, Whitney. It's at the Dragon's Lair, McKenna's Salem inn. She's planning clowns, a puppet show, kite races.

"Since I'm going, anyway, I thought Skye and Lace would enjoy playing with some other children their age. I'll watch them like they're my own, Queisha." Vivica raised a hand. "I swear. Every kid will have a set of parents, who'll also be watching everyone else's kids. I wish you could come, too . . ."

Queisha clenched her fists. "Maybe next month." She didn't want to let the girls out of her sight. How foolish when she hadn't seen them since their birth. Not to mention the fact that they'd heard the invitation and were jumping up and down beside their bikes, hands clasped her way, as if in prayer, silently begging her to say yes.

What kind of parent, er, guardian would she be to deny them the world, just because *she* couldn't face it? "Vivica," Queisha said. "There isn't anybody I'd trust more."

The girls rushed her, slammed into her, and thanked her with hugs and kisses.

"Queisha, are you sure you can't go yourself, on my arm?" Chance asked.

She gave him a lethally withering glance, with which she hoped to shrink his balls. "Does the pope pee in the woods?"

The girls dissolved into giggles.

Chance cleared his throat. "Like Smokey Bear is Catholic."

"I rest my case."

They changed the girls into picnic party outfits.

Skye chose a fringed play set with a pointy-waist polka-dot top of turquoise and teal on aqua, her capris having one turquoise leg and one teal. She wore her new waterproof kid Crocs in pearl.

Lace chose a frilly yellow sundress with matching leather Mary Jane–type Crocs and a shoulder-strap purse.

"Blessed saints, do they ever have minds of their own," Chance said. "Good thing you over-shopped."

Queisha displayed her snootiest I-told-you-so smirk in his honor. The girls mimicked her perfectly.

They each chose a still-packaged toy from the over-abundant supply she'd bought, always two of each. In this case, a Barbie and a Barbie car, the girls assuring her they'd play with the other Barbie and car together.

A maternal pride overwhelmed her as she helped them wrap the gifts. "Can we invite our new friends to our birthday party?" Lace asked.

A little light-headed here, she thought. "Are we having a party?"

"We always do," Skye said. "Even in boarding school."

"Then, we'll darned well have one here," Chance said.

Wake me from this nightmare, Queisha thought. She hated crowds. Though the guests would be here in her in own home and yard. With Chance and Vivica's help, the twins, too, she supposed she could keep to the yellow-brick path.

Vivica tilted her head thoughtfully. "We'll need to get addresses while we're there. I'll bring a notebook and make a list. Better yet, I'll get the list Whitney's mother used. Queisha, can I give them a date to put aside?"

"Our birthday is July twenty-third," Lace said. "Maybe by then, we can invite Mother and Father, too."

Panic rode in on her roller-coaster stomach, as far as Queisha was concerned.

"Well," Vivica said. "Your parents might not—"

Skye waved away her words. "Once they've been found, I'm going to ask Mother and Father if we can live here and go to that school next door. Can we?" she asked Queisha.

Queisha knelt in front of the girls and pulled them close. "I'd love nothing better." She wasn't sure she should keep them because of her agoraphobia, but she'd stepped outside today, and for them, she'd go out again tomorrow, no matter how sick the thought made her right now.

"If we go home with Mother and Father before the invitations are sent out," Lace asked, "will you send them?"

Queisha nodded as she stood, but the girls clung, Skye rubbing her leg, which made her feel like a real mother. She clasped their shoulders and bit her lip so she wouldn't cry.

One panic attack coming up. No, she could do this. "Of course, sweetie."

"Are we set, then?" Vivica asked.

They climbed into the backseat of the limo and buckled themselves into their car seats.

"Hey," Jaydun said, looking miffed. "You made me fumble like crazy to get you out of those seats when we got here."

"We were scared," Skye said. "We're excited now."

Jaydun shook his head as he went around to drive.

As they pulled away, Queisha stood in the yellow-brick driveway beside Chance—which she wouldn't have done yesterday—to wave their girls off.

Chance pulled her close against his side. "Has it only been a week, not a lifetime, since they stepped out of that limo somber and silent?"

"I'm nervous," Queisha said. "I hate letting them go even for a child's party. Never mind *giving* a child's party. I don't much like being railroaded."

"I'm not sure Lace saw it that way. They're already feeling so at home here, they're treating you like a mother.

You may have to start doing some of the hard mom stuff one of these days, like disciplining them when they do things like fly down a hill on their bikes."

"Horrors."

"One thing I can promise," he said, "they'll have a better time at this party and their own than they would have had in boarding school. And, they'll still love you if you treat them as a parent should, performing the easy and the difficult roles. You did good to let them try their wings."

"I'm not too overprotective? Because I don't have a right."

"Love gives you the right. You never stopped, even when they were away from you. Same way your aunt loved you all those years and proved it by leaving you her home."

"That's likely who's calling to me right now. It's my aunt. Like it's time to learn more about her and get some answers about myself. While the girls are gone, care to explore the attic with me and try to solve the mystery of Helen Grace Chege?"

"That wasn't the proposition I'd hoped for," Chance said.

"I feel this need right now, deep inside me, to find my past. I'm sorry," she said, tracing his lips with a finger, and getting that finger kissed, and practically devoured, weakening her resolve, yet her inner mandate didn't waver, despite her sexual awakening.

"C'mere." He pulled her close, and mouth to mouth, right there in her driveway, his kiss didn't lose any of its zing. If anything, he'd upped the zing ratio in a devilish, uber-non-angelic way.

Their demonstration of affection turned deeper and

hungrier on both their parts, probably warming the bricks on the yellow-brick path.

"What could be more important at this moment than me taking you to bed?" Chance cajoled.

While he must look, from the road, as if he had his hands on her waist, his thumbs up front were teasing her beneath her breasts, heightening her need more than a little.

"Perhaps not more physically important, but more spiritually so, would be helping me search for my past. If I discover my past, I might be able to move toward the future, as in away from this house, as in the way the guardian of two little girls should be able to move."

Chance lowered his teasing thumbs. "I hate it when you make good sense."

"Chance, sometimes I think the past is what's holding me back. My therapist said my phobia was rooted in something deeper."

"I apologize," Chance said, stepping away from her and running a hand through his long dark hair. "Sometimes I think you've bedeviled me."

She grinned. "I'm not the one with a horn."

"Point taken and pun acknowledged. Now, what deepset issue eats at you or pops into your mind over and over again?"

"Why was I given away by my birth parents? Was I considered not worth keeping? Garbage? Junk? Did they suspect my phobic flaw?"

"Definitely a priority, getting that crap out of your head. Where do we start?"

"The attic above the tower. There's a locked room I've never been able to get into. Sometimes I stepped up to that door and got the sense I was being warned away. The night I dreamed the girls needed me, I felt compelled to get in that room, and I tried, believe me. I have a broken sledgehammer and the scar to prove it, but I went away believing it just wasn't time.

"And now?"

"Now I don't care if you have to take an ax to it. At this moment I feel more compelled than ever to see what's in there. Getting into that room has been haunting me since the girls got here, like it's the key to *their* futures. Does that make any sense?"

"Yes," he said. "It does."

"With you on my side, Son of Godric, I feel as if I can do anything."

"I've never had a sexier or more awe-inspiring offer."

Ten minutes later, flashlights in hand, Queisha leading the way, they climbed the attic stairs. "You okay back there?" she called.

"What, you think a mouse will take me hostage?"

"There are no mice in this house. I have a contract with a pest control company."

"Well, this isn't life or death, and good going on the pest control. Now get contracts for fire and burglar alarm systems and we'll all sleep better."

"I called Vivica for references this morning. Probably the reason she thought of the girls for the party, which was kind of her."

"It was kind. Hey, it's pitch-black up there. Want me to go first?"

"The staircase is narrow for such a big house, and they really skimped on the wiring. You'd think they'd put a switch at the bottom."

He came up close and cupped her butt with both hands. "Then we really should trade places."

Queisha liked him rubbing against her, before and during the switch. She also liked it when his mouth came for hers, halfway around.

He nipped and nibbled at her lips, and with his free hand, he stroked, titillated, and caressed some interesting places. She considered it only polite to reciprocate, and so she went right to the source of his interest and pleasure. The woodster.

He fumbled the flashlight when she cupped him and caught it pointing down . . . toward a trail of feathers.

"Yeah, well, I was watching your ass while you climbed the stairs."

"Does that mean I'm enough to bald an angel's wings?"

"Well, you've been turning my *head* for years. The wings were an earth surprise. You know, if we don't get this mandate of yours completed soon, we won't be able to take this foreplay to its inevitable conclusion before the girls get home."

"Do you mean you're hoping for multiple wing whomps?"

"You're never going to let me forget that, are you?"

She caught his earlobe between her teeth. "Why would I? No girl has ever been so satisfactorily . . . whomped."

"If we replaced a well-known four letter word with whomp, nobody would know we were cursing," he said, "like whomp you! Whomping A. What a whomping mess."

Queisha bit her lip. "We wouldn't need a middle finger.

"Your grin," she said, "and that pulsing cattle prod

against my middle, tells me that I haven't distracted you at all, but I'll accept it as a promise for later."

"You'd better," he called as she turned and ran up the stairs.

By the time he got to the top, she'd turned on the lights.

"This is amazing," he said. "If it wasn't for the attic ambiance, it'd look like a small cabin in the woods, rustic bed, hand-stitched quilt, and all."

Queisha looked up. "As for the ambience, I don't get the chairs and pictures frames hanging from the ceiling."

"That's a space saver, an old-fashioned way of storing excess without taking up floor space. Why would your aunt set up a small cabin in her mansion attic?"

"Panic attacks. There are days when even the house you feel safe in is too big. Twice, I've needed to come up here."

"When?" Chance asked. "How did I miss that?"

"The first time, when I suspected I was in labor, because my separation from the twins was at hand. Then on their first birthday, when I wanted to go to Connecticut to get a glimpse of them, but I couldn't get in the cab I'd called to take me to the train station."

She crawled into the center of that old bed, crossed her arms, pulled her knees up to her chest, and shivered. "It doesn't feel as comforting as it used to."

With anticipation, she watched him take a spare quilt off a rough-hewn chair, open it, and tuck it around her. Then he got in with her and added his arms to her security wrap.

Queisha sighed. "Now, my safe place feels safe again."

"If you think you're safe with me in the same bed, you're delusional."

She rolled over to face him, joy filling her at his words. "Let's bookmark this spot and come back to it after we've done what we came up here to do."

She kissed him, and he cooperated fully, his hands finding their way to bits of bare skin, everywhere.

"What *did* we come up here to do?" he asked. "I forget."

"My past."

"Your past is right here."

"Beneath my bra? You're thinking with the wrong brain."

"It's been dormant so long, it's working overtime."

She tried to get up, and he pulled her back down, pinning her to the bed. "I always feel Aunt Helen's presence strongest up here," she said. "I believe she's smiling down on us right now."

Chance quit the bed in one leap, his hands raised to show his innocence.

Queisha knew where they'd been, though. Her nerve endings were weeping.

"This room is an amalgamation of your past," he said, "right out in the open for you to see."

"It's not; my psychic instincts tell me that my past is there, behind that locked door, and though I've tried often enough over the years, I just can't seem to get to it."

"What's stopping you?"

"The truth? Don't freak now. I think that my aunt's ghost doesn't want me in there."

THIRTY-ONE

Queisha collected the feathers he'd left on Aunt Helen's quilt—more gold than silver—and stuck them in her pocket.

That surprised him. "Have you been keeping them?"

"I'll want something to remember you by."

Her words hit him like an arrow to the chest. For all he'd been married for a short time, once, Queisha had been the one to teach him the meaning of abiding love, of a love beyond death.

"I suppose you'll start decorating a feather room the minute I say good-bye."

"An angel room, maybe. Will you say good-bye? Or just disappear?"

"I don't know."

She turned to look out the window, slipped her hands in her pockets, and let her brow touch the glass. He took a step closer to her, a reminder to them both of what it had been like before he came from Everlasting. Her living her life, him watching over her. She'd survived before. She'd survive again.

But would he?

He heard a weak sniff, as if she might be trying to hide her emotions, so he tried to ignore it and picked up the sledgehammer with the broken handle, the result of her last try at getting into the tower attic. "Want me to bash the door in?"

"With that? You'll break your wrist."

"Nah. Let me give it a whack."

A framed picture fell, smack between them.

Queisha caught it. "See," she said. "I told you things happen when I try to get into that part of the attic."

"That's a pretty little girl in the picture. It looks hand painted. Who is she?"

"I never noticed it before. The back says, 'Mouse, age one.'"

"Let me see." He checked the bottom corners but couldn't find a signature. "I think it's you."

She looked at it. "I suppose it could be a picture that my adoptive parents sent my aunt, though I don't see the resemblance."

"I do. Give me a pout."

She pushed at him, trying not to laugh. "Give me a hand with this door."

"Sure. Why don't I just try the door handle?"

"I'm not stupid. I tried that the day I moved in." It was too hot to touch. She opened her palm to reveal her faded scar.

He traced it until he made her shiver. "Looks like Aunt Helen doesn't play fair," he said, raising her palm to his lips.

"Or she plays for keeps." Queisha retrieved her hand, a matter of self-preservation for them both, he thought, reaching for the handle to the locked attic chamber, but Queisha curled her hand around it before him, without getting burned and without opening the door. "It's locked."

"Holy halo, somebody's toying with you."

"I told you." Queisha raised an admirable brow. "You never listen."

"Sweetie. I've spent hours listening to you, before and after I came from Everlasting. I especially enjoy your off-key rendition of 'Let There Be Peace on Earth.'"

"I like that song."

"I do, too."

Chance started taking the latch and lock apart, stripping them from the door, but when he got close, the screwdriver's plastic handle got soft and melty in his hand so he couldn't work with it. When he gave up, the lights went out. "I think your aunt is mocking me."

Icy air came whooshing around them. "I'm cold," she said, and he got her the quilt.

"It's June," he added. "An attic is supposed to be hotter than a house in summer and colder in winter."

"I think this is Aunt Helen's way of telling me she's here."

"Yeah, well, if she gets any friendlier," he said, "we're gonna need gloves and a parka."

"It's usually only cold when I first come up, then when I curl up in the bed I warm up and feel cozy and unusually safe."

"That explains it," Chance said. "She wants *me* to know that she's strong and can protect you from me."

"You think so?"

"I do." He looked around. "Tell her, Aunt Helen."

The lights blinked.

"There. She's telling you I'm right." He went for the ax leaning against the wall near the picture that fell.

"Aunt Helen?" Queisha called. "It's time to let me in. I need to know the past to face the future. I have my girls to think about now. Let me in. Please."

Cool air swirled about them.

Chance raised his chin. "You know, if I can't take apart the handle and lock, and you broke the sledgehammer, I'm using this ax." That fast, he swung, and when he brought the ax forward, he was left holding a handle. The ax head had gone flying behind him and embedded itself in a cabinet across the room. They turned to see the cabinet teeter, and as it did, something slipped off the top and landed on the floor with the distinctive sound of tinkling metal.

They walked cautiously over to it. Chance picked up a key ring. Besides a key, he found a charm: a gold feather nearly as long as the key.

Queisha leaned against him. "I think you should move in."

Short circuit. The ax handle fell from his hand. "After all these years, you think you need protection?"

"No silly. This was a . . . momentous event. A ghost just handed me the key I've wanted for nearly ten years. I liked sharing the event with you, and I'm greedy. I want every minute we can have."

"I want the same. Yes. Where should I stay, so we don't make a bad impression on the girls? Up here? I can live up here. I like it."

I can't stay forever, Chance admitted. *I'll see you when I get back to Everlasting. Meanwhile, can I send Angus with questions if necessary?*

The triumvirate permitting, Queisha's aunt said, and she vaporized, laughing. Damn, she must have heard him and Angus talking in the kitchen that day, or maybe all of them on the day they arrived in the billiard room. Glory, he hoped she'd stayed out of the bedrooms while she was here.

Queisha looked up from the album. "It's getting warmer in here, warmer than it's been since I moved into the house." She looked around with suspicion.

Chance sat down, and found, at eye level, something like a dollhouse, except it was a single-floor hut, with a room like the one in the attic, down to the print on the quilt. Centered by a cooking area, it had other rooms or sections without walls, beds in some alcoves, even an area for chickens. "Queisha," he said. "I believe your attic room, like this miniature, is part of your heritage."

"Something feels different, suddenly, here, in this room. Different from when we walked in. She was here, wasn't she, and now she's gone?"

He didn't need to ask who. "She had to move on. She said she'd see me in Everlasting, because you didn't need her to watch over you anymore."

Queisha stamped a foot and pointed a finger. "You *saw* her. *Communicated* with her."

"I'm sorry, but yes."

"What did she look like?"

"You, a bit older. Beautiful. Perfect. And not the least afraid to leave the house."

THIRTY-TWO

It took several trips with a hard-sided piece of avocado green luggage—no wheels—to get all of Aunt Helen's journals, diaries, and albums to Queisha's bedroom. By then, she could do nothing but pace.

"What's wrong?" Chance asked, sure she was fixating on losing the spirit of the aunt who'd been watching over her for years.

"It's the girls. I'm worried about them."

"Do you want to see how they're doing at the party?"

Her eyes filled. "That's a mean thing to say."

"No, I have the ability to transport you to locations that exist within this world. For instance, I couldn't take you to Everlasting, but a local party, piece of birthday cake. We'll stand in your yard, with my arms tight around you and yours around me."

"Is this a come-on?"

identifying her. Helen Grace Chege. She was half white, like me."

Chance touched her cheek. "Such a gorgeous color, your skin."

"Neither white nor black," Queisha said. "That can be a burden sometimes, especially to a child. Children can be cruel."

"I think it's jealousy. Your skin color is enviable. Luscious. Do you know how much people pay to get burnished like that? They bottle it and call it things like sun-kissed, honey-dipped, and bronze beauty, and you have it all the time, whether you go outside or stay in the house."

Chance suddenly got his answer as to why the room seemed lit from within. They were not alone. However much Aunt Helen—the female ghost facing him—had toyed with them, they had somehow managed to gain her favor, because she was watching them, and smiling.

Magickal supernaturals often saw each other for what they were, Vivica had pointed out, and he now understood. *Aunt Helen, I presume?* he said telepathically while Queisha looked at family photo albums.

The woman nodded. *I've been waiting for you.*

You have the sight?

As does Queisha. Do right by her and her girls.

Chance winced inwardly. *If she's willing to keep them.*

She needs to read my journals while you're here. Now is the time, for the sake of the twins. Make her read them.

Will you be here if I have questions?

No, now that you're here, and she has learned her purpose in life, I am called to move on.

"There are other choices. Above the carriage house. In the opposite wing. Or in the room you slept in last night."

"Did we sleep?"

He looked at her while he waited for her to come to the right conclusion. *Across the hall from you would be good.* But he'd let her come to that conclusion. "The choice is yours, Queisha."

"The room you used last night?"

He practically went limp with relief, well, most of him did. "I thought you'd never ask." He kissed her, heavy on the passion, and had a hard time letting her go, but she needed him to help find her past.

"Thanks, Aunt Helen," he said, handing Queisha the key.

"Here goes," she added. The key slid into the lock like a knife into butter.

The tower section of the attic seemed bigger than the tower, but the roof did hang over it quite a bit, like a mushroom cap, to support the larger room above it.

Overflowing bookshelves covered the windowless walls with print books and handwritten journals. They found diaries written by a young girl, framed photos, and picture albums. The occasional souvenir, both Kenyan and American, stood among the book stacks, the raw wood of the shelves dark, foreign, a wood Chance didn't recognize. Because it was so naturally dark, he would have expected the room also to be dark, but it seemed lit as if from within.

As an angel, he understood that, but the possible light source escaped him.

"These pictures must have been taken in Aunt Helen's village in Africa," Queisha said. "Oh, here's one

"Check out the games they're playing. We'll have to host some of them."

The look Queisha gave him might as well bear arrows, Chance thought. "I may not have you or the girls with me on their birthday," she said sadly. "Do you realize that? I've never been so scared."

"Sure you have. And still no panic attack." Chance applauded even as he kept his arms around her. "Sounds like progress to me."

Pride transformed her features. "Damn straight, Angel Man."

"Speaking of progress, I never made your request and my answer official. So yes, I'll be your *live-in* co-guardian."

"Don't you mean my live-in cook?"

"Cook, co-guardian, lover, you name it. I'd like to be here for you and the girls around the clock."

Their lips had barely met when the people at the party they'd invisibly invaded started saying good-bye. It was breaking up, which made them step apart, and when they did, the vision of worlds dissipated.

Queisha looked disappointed. "We're back in my yard."

"In a way, you just got home from a trip. What did you think of seeing something other than the inside of your house?"

"I see the world on my TV all the time."

"But you don't stand in the middle of it. You're off to the side. Alone. A nonparticipant."

"That's harsh, but I was a nonparticipant at the party."

"We heard the shush of the leaves in the trees, smelled the hot dogs, even the earthy scent of the barn when the wind was right. The party was alive to us. TV is not. That's a fact, Queisha."

He knew she tried not to be hurt, but some truths needed telling.

"I have Mrs. McGillicudy and the hat racks," she said. "Chumpy and his family."

"Soft-sculpture people? No matter how whimsical and joy-filled you make your private world, my bronze beauty, it isn't real. For the first time in years, the girls have made it so. Take the gift forward, not backward."

"This from a man with wings on his back and feathers at his feet. Now that's reality."

So she was using snark to hide her hurt. He could take it.

"The girls are everything, Chance. They've brought me to life. They give me purpose. And in case you haven't noticed, my girls are pretty whimsical themselves."

"Are they *your* girls? Have you asked yourself what their parents' deaths means to you?"

"Maybe I'm afraid to count my chickens, or in this case, my twins, before they're mine." She shoved his shoulder with the heel of her fist. "There's nothing angelic about you right now."

"I'm trying to make a point, pretty lady. Stop letting life happen to you. Join in. Be proactive. Fight for the girls. Go out into the world, if you have to."

"Whomp you. I'm agoraphobic, butthead. You don't just decide to stop."

"I am a butthead. I apologize."

"Forget it. Go pick out a bedroom, and don't bother to tell me which one it is."

THIRTY-THREE

A wild wind came up off the water and her dress flapped around her legs as she walked to the house, leaving Chance behind.

"You don't just decide to stop being phobic," he called after her. "You take baby steps, like looking in on that party just now. Congratulations!"

"Whomp you." She didn't look back.

Upstairs, Queisha shut her bedroom door and sat on the floor with her aunt's albums and journals. She tried to read, but all she could think about was Chance and his rotten statement about her life not being real before the girls arrived.

He'd cut her deep. She'd forgotten the danger of letting someone into your heart. Then again, if you didn't, maybe you *weren't* really living.

There was probably some truth to his words.

If anyone else had said those things, she'd ignore them.

But what he thought mattered. Lordy, she'd fallen in love with her own guardian angel. And he could disappear at any time. How bitchin' craptastic was that?

If she didn't love him, his opinion wouldn't hurt so much. Nothing could come of a love between them. She was alive with her girls to think about, and he was an angel, dead, actually, here temporarily, with Everlasting to think about.

She went out to walk parts of the yellow-brick path and wait for Vivica and the girls. At the far end of the property, she saw something she'd never quite made out. From the house, she'd thought it was a garden, but it was a cemetery. The walk wasn't set down close enough for her to read the names clearly. She was just trying to make herself step in the grass to look more closely when the limo pulled up.

Wow, did the girls run once they hit the ground, right into her arms, knocking her into the grass, climbing her like a mountain. Skye called her Mama Bear, Lace avoided calling her anything. They showed her their prizes, sea monkeys and crystal kits, and their personal favorites, guns that shot mini marshmallows.

She got shot about forty times, all three of them rolling around in the grass, while snacking on the ammunition.

Lace emptied her gun and set it in her lap. "Whitney's daddy uses two canes to walk, but Whitney's mommy says that he'll be walking without them in no time. Whitney says it's because Mr. Bastian fixed him; he's Mr. Jaydun's brother. We met everybody. You would like Mrs. Kira. She has twin boys and twin girls, too, and some other kids, and an orphanage. Her husband is a great kisser."

"Excuse me? Vivica?" Queisha shouted.

Vivica hadn't been far away. "Jason Goddard won the reality show *Best Kisser in America,* in his NHL days," she explained. And darned if Queisha didn't recognize the name because she'd seen the program.

"Miss Vivica told Mrs. Kira that you would be interested in the orphanage. You're not gonna put us there, are you?"

"No, you silly girl," Vivica said. "Queisha helps schools and orphanages with money donations."

"Are you rich?" Skye asked Queisha. " 'Cause we are."

"Hello there," a beautiful redhead said as she rounded the corner, the Best Kisser in America, himself, on her arm. "I'm Kira Fitzgerald and this is my husband, Jason."

Queisha rose from the grass to dust herself off and shake their hands. "It's wonderful to meet you. I hope the girls weren't a bother at the party."

"They were angels," Kira said. "Like our twins and singles were." Kira laughed at her own joke.

"Where are they?" Queisha asked.

"Still with McKenna and the gang. We're spending the night at the Dragon's Lair. My best friends both happen to be in Salem at the same time: Melody Seabright and Vickie Cartwright. Bit of a vacation. Vivica thought that you and I might like to talk for a bit, though."

"Yes," Vivica said. "I'll take Jason in to meet Chance. Girls, come inside."

The twins balked, but they followed Vivica and Kira's husband.

Queisha, not knowing what they should talk about, led the way along the yellow-brick path.

"I'll get to the point," Kira said. "When Vivica and I

had a minute alone, she told me about you, that you were doubtful about being good enough to be the twins' guardian because of the agoraphobia."

"Oh, I see. Wow. Am I embarrassed."

Kira took her hand. "Don't be. I have a bit of experience in choices for children's lives. We run an orphanage, two now, actually. A home for girls and one for boys. I gave birth to a girl and a boy of our own, two single births, and we adopted both sets of twins."

"That's why Viv thought I should talk to you?"

"You doubt yourself," Kira said. "So did I. I didn't think I should have any more of my own than the one. Didn't think I was good enough to adopt my twin girls at their birth. I thought they'd probably be better with someone who had fewer children and more love to spread around."

"That's crazy."

"I know, because love never runs out. It's like the loaves and the fishes; there's always enough to go around. The point is, we always doubt ourselves, but if we love those kids, have patience, and we can laugh with them, and discipline them, at the appropriate times, they're better nowhere than with us. I've overseen lots of adoptions. Matched parents with children. And I watched your girls run to you. Watched you with them for quite a while. Add to that the fact that they talked nonstop about you all day, and they're yours, sweetie, heart and soul. No one would make them a better mother. Plus you're conquering your phobia. Look at you. Last week, I heard, you never left the house?"

Queisha nodded, inhaled the sea air to calm herself but couldn't help her overflowing tears.

They embraced and both needed a tissue. "Let's set up

some playdates. Both my sets of twins are smitten with your girls. And the day you can travel, which I predict will happen, come to Newport and stay with us. I'll give you a tour of the mansions and the orphanages."

"I'd be honored," Queisha said, wondering if it would ever happen. "Thank you for your hard-earned wisdom, your offer of friendship, and for your belief in me."

"It comes from you and your girls, Queisha. It's called love. Ready to go find our men?"

Jason and Chance had talked and bonded as equals and fathers of twins.

Queisha, Chance, and Vivica, with Skye and Lace beside them, said their reluctant good-byes as Jason and Kira got into their pristine, '63 white Rolls-Royce limo. "It's my grandmother's," Jason said, going around to the driver's side. "She begs us to drive it and keep it in good shape. Now that she married her adoring limo driver, I finally get the seat behind the wheel."

Chance chuckled as they watched their new friends drive down the road and back to the Dragon's Lair.

"Everyone's coming to our party next month," Lace said as they turned toward the house. "They can't wait."

Skye executed a somersault. "We're inviting Whitney and Wyatt, Zane and Travis, and Elizabeth and—"

Queisha laughed. "What did you eat, raw sugar?" Kira was right. She should fight for these beautiful babies. She could be as good a mother as anyone, agoraphobia or not, hopefully.

Vivica chuckled. "I was amazed to see you rolling around in the grass with the girls. The grass!"

"And I lived to tell about it," Queisha said. "Kira suggested a playdate, you know."

Vivica nodded. "Expect a lot more requests."

Chance coughed. "Jason said the girls handed out your telephone number like candy. But I'm sure no mother will mind having playdates here."

"I'm hungry," Lace said.

Chance hauled them up beneath his arms. "You've been eating cake and ice cream all day and now you want supper?"

Queisha squeezed each girl's chin. "They played hard. They need fuel."

He jiggled them. "You'll eat boiled jelly worms and pond scum soup and like it."

"No, no."

"Ack, phooey!"

"Let's sit on the water porch after supper," Queisha said, sensing that Vivica had something on her mind. The girls ate their dinner, a thin cheese pizza sprinkled with mango salsa, and went right to the playroom.

Vivica wouldn't even take a rocker. She stood facing them. "I got a call at the party. It's bad news."

"I've been half expecting it," Chance said, cryptically.

Queisha looked from one to the other, her frustration focused on Chance. "Expecting what?"

He pointed his chin toward Vivica.

"The Fitzpatrick relatives are fighting your guardianship. On the plus side, they're also fighting each other, so they'll be airing some dirty linen."

"While my dirty linen is already out there—my fear of the world beyond my door. Will I have to go to court?" Queisha felt that old panic rising, then she looked up at Chance. "Because I will if I have to."

Panic nipped at her heels for the rest of the evening, long after Vivica had gone home.

Later, she read the girls stories, then they kissed her and Chance good night.

"Mama Bear," Skye called as Queisha switched off the light.

"Yes, Skye Bear," she replied, backlit in the doorway.

"Do you want to know why I'm calling you that?"

"If you want to tell me."

"There were lots of kids and mothers there today. None of the kids called the lady who loved them Lady or Miss or Missus."

Big words. Bigger thoughts. "Is that right?" Queisha leaned against the doorjamb and crossed her ankles, but said nothing.

"We had a teddy bear tea party, and while we did, Whitney called her mother Mama Bear . . . *a- n- d*"— Skye stretched out the word—"I thought that fit you, so I thought I'd try it out. If that's okay with you. Is it?"

Queisha flipped on the light so they could see her pleasure in their decision. "It so is. You might have noticed my shelf of Care Bears. I've always thought of myself as their mother, so . . . of course I like it. Let me know if you settle on that."

Queisha heard a sigh and Skye's enthusiastic change of position as she settled in the bed. "I will."

It had done them good to be with other children today, to see how kids live outside of boarding school.

Now that they were asleep, she wanted to go and find Chance, especially knowing he was asleep, or awake, somewhere in the house, but she wasn't ready to face him after he'd slapped her upside the head with a few home truths today.

True, his words had perhaps a miniscule basis in fact, but that didn't mean she'd liked hearing them.

She changed into a nightgown bordering on angel torture—though she had no intention of leaving this room—which probably made her more than slightly nuts. Yet she hated for this sheer, pleated baby-doll nightie in gold chiffon with lace triangle cups and a matching thong to go to waste.

Around nine, she climbed into her own bed, picked up her aunt's journals, and started reading. At nearly midnight, she started looking through the picture albums, stopping to read the back of each photo.

Before she knew it, her bedside clock read three in the morning and her life—well, her past, and her future—had taken an unexpected turn.

There'd be no sleeping for her tonight, and there was only one person with whom she wanted to share her news and upon whose shoulder she wanted to lay her weary head.

Knowing him, he'd picked the room across the hall, because they'd hear the girls when they were together. She tried to open his door quietly, but upon ascertaining that the bed was indeed occupied, the door clicked too loud when she shut it.

"Took you long enough," he said without moving. "I'm here all naked, alone, full of apologies, and this is one boring ceiling."

She stood by the bed looking down at him, a piratical angel, dark eyes narrowed, filled with love, an apology on the tip of his tongue, and just as he was about to give it, she crossed his lips with a finger.

He kissed it.

"No need for regrets," she said. "You were brutally honest, and I guess I needed that, though I could do without the hard edge in the future, home truth or not."

He caught her around the waist. "Come down here, woman. Dressed like that, you're poking the tiger."

"A winged tiger. Will wonders never cease?" She let herself be pulled down on top of him, and before she told him her news, their lips met, more than a few slow, sultry times.

"I don't know who's poking who here."

He chuckled against her breasts.

"So," she said, snuggling down on her manly mattress, a striped spread between them, while all her mounds filled his valleys and his submarine teased her center pulsing in anticipation, yet she had things to say first.

"You probably know this, but Aunt Helen was my birth mother. As if that's not enough, my birth father—who cheated on his wife with my aunt Helen—adopted me with his wife. The father I've always known, who threw me out when I got pregnant as a teen, was my biological father. Who was he to judge? What could Auntie Mom, or whatever I should call Aunt Helen, have been thinking? That man was *no* prize."

Chance kissed her brow. "The portrait of an American family."

"Wise guy. Oh, Auntie Mom used to call me Mouse, by the way. Isn't that odd? Do you think I was a scaredy-cat from the beginning? Almost makes me want to rebel and get ferocious. Paint the town red. Travel to distant lands. I am so *not* a mouse!"

"Incredibly glad to hear it."

"So get this, the only person who ever loved me, worried and cared about me, was my adoptive mother, who got two-timed by her husband, and by rights, should have hated me."

Queisha rose up and let her knee slip a little too close to the angel jewels when she was really aiming for Angel Central. "You knew this, didn't you?"

"A little to the left, please," Chance asked. "What makes you think I knew?"

She tickled his fancy in the direction he indicated. "Because you're not saying anything."

"Watch the man bags, sweet cheeks. They might not be filled with hibiscus flower tea but they're precious all the same. And I have plans for them tonight."

"You're changing the subject."

"I'm protecting the family jewels. Now, as for your mother, I *didn't* know your aunt was your birth mother until I saw her, in spirit, yesterday. No one who saw her could doubt the mother/daughter resemblance."

"Why, thank you. Because you said that Auntie Mom was beautiful."

"You gonna keep calling your birth mother that?"

"My real mother raised me and died when I was eleven. Auntie Mom left me this house. The fact that she carried me is about as important as—"

"You carrying the twins?"

Queisha slapped a hand to her heart. "Ouch!"

"Home truths, baby. I'm full of 'em."

"Well, you're full of something."

THIRTY-FOUR

Queisha did not like hearing the truth any more than anyone else, she supposed. "If I want the girls I carried to love me, I have to . . . be there for them, like my adoptive mother was there for me. And that's what I'm doing, now, at this first opportunity I've gotten, right?"

"Right."

"It *isn't* necessarily one way or the other, it's nurturing. Love. Not birth mother versus adoptive mother. I didn't understand that until I talked to Kira."

"Well, I've been thinking—"

Queisha rested her head on his shoulder. "Always a risky proposition, you thinking."

"Right, but let me just say that the part about your father is a shock, especially since he was so rotten to you when you got pregnant."

"I know," Queisha said. "So why did his wife love me so much? Why did my birth father dislike me?"

"I know the answer to some of this gleaned from your adoptive mother in Everlasting. She couldn't have kids of her own, but she had a nurturing nature, and while she was mad at your father for cheating on her, she loved you unconditionally. Problem was, she transferred her love from your father to you, which he might have resented you for and taken out on you.

"You're very lovable, you know. Your adoptive mother is one of the guardian angels who loves babies and likes to get the ones she'll guard on the day they're born. She says it makes up for never having a newborn. Babies see their angels before they can see their parents, so there's a short, personal relationship between them that's quite loving. Your mother got you when you were a year old, by the way."

"Did you know all this when we went up to the attic?"

"No. I called on my friend, Angus, a messenger angel, and he talked to your adoptive mother. She sends her love."

"Oh, you're making me miss her. I really loved my mom, the mom who raised me. Now, after finding the one who gave me life, wow. Two mothers who loved me.

"Wait, if my birth mother loved me, why did she give me up when clearly she could afford to keep me?"

"Ah, I was afraid you'd ask that."

"Spit it out!"

"She didn't want you to suffer from her agoraphobia. She didn't think she'd be a good enough mother."

Queisha paled and shivered and showed some of the physical signs of a panic attack.

"Come, love, get warm beside me beneath the covers, and we'll talk."

She silently did as she was told.

"Talk to me," he said, rubbing her arms. "You shouldn't

be cold. It's half past June and we don't even have the air-conditioning on."

"I'm cold from the inside out. I think it's because someone is trying to take the twins away from me."

"Several someones," Chance said. "No, let me clarify that. Several couples are fighting over the girls. You do know that Skye and Lace come with a hefty inheritance, a fortune nearly as big as yours."

Queisha twirled the chest hair around his nipple. "I have one worry."

"Well, color me surprised, worrywart."

"For an angel, your grin is evil. Sexy, but evil."

"More of both later. Continue. You must have had a hard time when you gave the girls to the Fitzpatricks."

"I didn't have a choice; I had a contract. What agony Aunt Helen must have suffered, even if she thought she was acting in my best interests, especially since she gave me to my birth father."

"The jerk," Chance said.

"Guess she didn't know him very well. In retrospect, I think he resented the attention and love his wife showered on me. My adoptive mother was a good mother. My birth mother had a good reason for giving me up." Queisha turned to look at Chance. "Are you a wise angel?"

"Horny. I'm a horny angel."

"Stop fooling around and be serious."

"Okay. Turning serious and moving into wise. Here you go," he said, covering his face with a big, capable hand, sliding it down to reveal a serious expression. "Wise angel at your service."

"You don't think my birth mother did the right thing, do you?"

"Are you glad your mother gave you away?"

"No. I sometimes felt like I'd been thrown away. Unworthy. Like so much trash. I yearned to meet my birth mother. More than that, I dreamed of it and prayed for it."

"So maybe staying with your birth mother would have been the best decision all around?"

Queisha sat up. "Because she was agoraphobic, Aunt Helen, also known as Auntie Mom, didn't think she could take good enough care of me. She decided with love and suffered for losing me. As the one who was given away, I suffered, too." She cuddled against Chance. "I'm thinking the agoraphobia is a bad reason not to keep Skye and Lace, for their sakes. Maybe. Mostly. Almost surely."

"You're making progress. I'm proud of you."

"Oh, but if my real mother was half Kenyan, that means I'm only one-quarter Kenyan."

"I forgive you." Chance lowered first one shoulder strap, then the other. He removed the quilt from between them.

"Such talented hands," she said as her lover worshipped her with his fingertips. "And, aren't you perfect, naked? Randy, too."

"Years of celibacy does not allow for satisfaction in one night. But before this unremarkable lawyer makes mad, passionate love to you, he has two requests."

"They must be serious if they come before sex *and* Son of Godric, the unremarkable, speaks of himself in the third person."

"Seriously serious. One: I'd like to read your surrogacy agreement. And two: will you marry me?"

THIRTY-FIVE

Queisha always thought that a marriage proposal was the kind of moment a girl dreamed of. She didn't expect the dream to be a nightmare. "But you're dead."

"Technically, not at this moment."

"Can an angel legally marry?"

"Let me deal with archangel tantrums when I get back to Everlasting."

"Oh, happy day. I marry you and you leave. One day, I wake up, and my husband will have disappeared. No body. No funeral. Could you *try* to leave me a note? Two words: The End." She swiped at her eyes, angry at her crazy emotions.

He caught her hands, though she'd put up a good fight. "I know the situation isn't ideal. But this way, we could fight for the girls as a couple. It would be couples against couples. An even playing field. They're related to the girls' parents, but you've been named their guardian."

"Dead men can't get a marriage license," Queisha said, thinking she had him there.

"Vivica has connections who rescued my Social Security number from—let's call it 'the book of the dead'—because my body was never found, and I'd only been *presumed* dead, so she reinstated me in 'the book of life,' shall we also say?"

"Your point?" Queisha asked.

"I looked into getting a marriage license here in Massachusetts, in anticipation of such an emergency. Vivica knows a judge and arranged for me to apply for one for both of us, because of your agoraphobia, and we can be married in three days. Whaddya say?"

"How bleeping romantic of you!"

"I'll give you romantic." He settled her on top of him, pulled down one side of her nightie, exposed a breast, and took it in his mouth. And after he made a feast of her, he kissed his way to her navel, sliding her gown further down as he did, discovering something he'd never noticed before, a pearl belly button ring. "What's this?"

"Something special. Just for you."

"You had it pierced today?"

"When I was sixteen. Today, I put the ring on."

He got instantly harder, she noticed, just knowing she'd intended to turn him on. Because of that, while he worked his kissing way back up to her breasts, she found and pleasured him. "God, I love this," she said. "You're spoiling me for any other man."

"Damned straight I am. Don't make me watch you with another man."

"Whoa, careful there, Angel Man. You're not here for

the long haul. You want me celibate and lonely after you leave?"

"I want you to be mine, forever, selfish as it sounds."

Oddly, that made her love him more.

"I want you to be happy, so find a man who loves you. You deserve that. I can't be your guardian anymore after this anyway."

She cupped his face and kissed him, slid her hands through his hair, down his face, over and over, faster as his kiss deepened. She couldn't get enough of him, and felt the sentiment was definitely mutual.

He took a breast again, worshiped it, made her whimper in satisfaction, only because she didn't dare cry out and wake the girls.

He understood that and gave her a look of approval, pulled back, and gazed at her full and ready breasts glistening from his mouth.

"Like what you see?"

"You're mine and I want you."

"Inside of me. C'mon." She slipped out of her gown, crouched low, found his big, thick, ready length, and put him where she wanted him. One upward thrust on his part, and they both groaned in satisfaction. He took it from there.

"You're a psychic wonder, sweet cheeks. How did you know that's what I needed? I wouldn't get enough of you in three lifetimes."

"Then we're really going to have to make the time we've got count," she said, undulating her hips, "which doesn't mean that we have to rush. Sometimes slow is better than fast." Hungry, she had to go in for a kiss as she rode him, his head in her hands, kissing and riding, loving his hands as they roamed up and down her body, cupping her ass, finding her sweet spot.

Deciding to get married had somehow morphed him, set him on a new course. His movements became unhurried, profound, unselfish, memorable. He set his sexual compass on her, not him. He moved with the intention of giving pleasure rather than of taking it. This was less about sex and more about making love, less about the body and more about the heart.

Spiritual and emotional lovemaking made her come, and come again.

He reveled in her responses and urged her on.

She'd never had an orgasm that lasted so long.

Chance seemed to be riding a groundbreaker, himself. She could tell the way he was breathing and trying to make it last for her sake.

The longer she watched him, the hotter she got, the closer her next climax.

When he opened his eyes, and their gazes met, she couldn't hold off a minute longer and let go.

He followed her into oblivion. *Whomp shwomp shhh!* "Ow. Ow. Get off. Get off!"

She rolled off him. "What's wrong?"

"I think I broke my wings." He tried to roll to his side and groaned for every inch he progressed. "Are they in or out?"

She got up to look. "Yes."

"What?"

"Some in, some out. All crooked and backassward. Maybe you should have been on top."

"Ya think?"

"How are you going to get dressed tomorrow?"

"How am I going to pee tonight?"

"If we could get you on top, we could try again, and when you came, maybe they'd all come out."

"It's gonna hurt," he said, "but I'm game." She lay beside him, arms down, like a sacrificial virgin, while the inept high priest tried to scale her. "Just call me Mount Queisha."

Sure, mocking his clumsy attempts made it harder for him to get up there, and he said "ouch," and a few other choice non-angelic words more often than not, but she managed to tease the hell out of his cock in the process, and he had a boner that wouldn't quit, so he was motivated in a very big way. "Super Woodster."

"Will you please shut up and show me some mercy."

She stopped teasing the daylights out of his woody. "Really, you want me to neglect this hungry big boy?"

"No, just help me over the hump?"

"What hump?"

"Queisha?"

She grabbed him beneath his armpits and yanked.

He shouted, but he mounted her, breathing heavily for more than a few minutes. Made her nervous. "Don't go back in the middle of sex, 'kay?"

Such a look he gave her.

Sweat beaded on his forehead, and frankly, she was hurting for him by then, so she grabbed his dick and slipped him home. For every thrust, he groaned, and it wasn't always with ecstasy.

After a while though, she could tell that he was getting into the groove, and she got into it as well, careful not to move her hips the wrong way.

Finally, they were in sync, the world disappearing around them, and she came, and came again, her hips rushing up to meet his, and *whomp!* "Ack! Ouch! No!"

A lopsided angel. Wings on one side only. "Does this make you a half wing? Sorry, I can see why that would hurt."

He looked like he might pass out.

"You're scaring me now," she said. "No, don't fall on that side." She guided him to the left. "Fall on the side without wings."

"Whomping A!" he snapped and fell over like a defective Weeble.

She rubbed his de-winged shoulder. "Does it hurt, sweetie?"

"I'm bare assed in the fetal position. You think this is a choice?"

"Do you want me to call my doctor for you?"

"No. Hell no. Wait. Put on a robe."

"Why? I haven't sprained my wings. Or will a lack of lust make your wings recede? I can go get ugly. Sweats, curlers, you name it."

He started to chuckle but stopped because it hurt. "I can call Angus, my guardian angel. He might be able to fix this."

Yikes. She grabbed her robe. "Okay, give him a call."

"Not until you cover my ass with a blanket, please."

"There." She tucked his ass in all around. "Comfy?"

"Remind me to beat you later. Angus?" he shouted softly. "Angus, come down here! I'm in a bit of trouble."

Queisha lay behind Chance and wrapped her arms around him.

"What are you doing?"

"Vision of worlds," she said. "I want to see this angel friend of yours."

Angus appeared, saw the pain etched on Chance's face, removed the blanket, and laughed his ass off.

"Hey," Queisha said. "I like this little angel."

"I suppose that's a good thing. Angus, this is Queisha. We're getting married. Re-cover me, Queisha, will you?"

"Ach, that's quite the bit of irate-archangel news," Angus said as she did. "Do the big three know about your wedding?"

"They will when you tell them."

"Hello, missy," Angus said, hovering in front of Queisha.

"I didn't know that bearded cherubs existed," she said. "Will my little Connor grow a beard?"

"Ach, no, this is my punishment for sending Chance down here, but he was pining for you more than doing his job, so it was worth the price. They'll turn me back, eventually, right, Chance?"

"Angus, this hurts."

"Oh. Sorry." Angus hovered over his friend and placed his hands on the spot between Chance's wings. It took a while before the missing side began to peek out. Finally, the tip of his wing was visible, but that's where it ended.

Chance now had one big wing and one baby wing.

"Will that make him tilt when he walks?" she asked.

"Queisha Saint-Denis!" Chance snapped.

She guessed jokes didn't help. "I love you anyway." She knelt on the bed beside him and began to massage his back, hard in the center between the sac openings, and very slowly, and only a bit sore, his half wing slid all the way out.

"Well," Angus said. "You didn't need an angel. You needed great hands."

Chance slipped his wings back in the sac, out, then in, again, easy, slow, but with little effort, and turned in the bed, careful to keep the blanket over his lap. "Thanks, sweetie."

"Glory, and you're welcome," Angus said, snark with a Scot's accent."

Chance rubbed the side of his nose. "Thanks, Angus."

"Ach, not a problem. I needed a laugh." He snickered at the rumpled bed, poked the fitted sheet where it sat popped up at the corner, and pulled at the corner of the bedspread on the floor, all while grinning. "How exactly did you sprain your wings, I wouldn't mind knowing."

"Farewell, friend." Chance saluted.

The small winged Scot disappeared, leaving a trail of raucous laughter behind.

THIRTY-SIX

*Queisha and Chance's June wedding day dawned per-*fect and beautiful.

"The flower girls wore princess gowns," Queisha said when she stood back and looked at them.

Skye curtseyed. "And the bride wore silver."

"A silver fairy gown," Lace clarified. "Which," she said, "if worn as a wedding gown will repair the wings on eleventy-seven angels, all at the same time."

Skye raised an arm. "Yes!"

"Ohhh," Lace said, clasping her hands. "Wear a pair of our wings, Mama Bear. You'd look beauteous."

"I am marrying an angel." The girls' wide, hope-ful eyes were so beautiful. The idea sounded perfectly whimsical. "Why not? Go get 'em."

She had never seen two more excited flower girls. She kissed each dear head, then she bent down for some big-time hugs. *Yes,* she thought, *I'd die for them, but more important, I'd live for them.*

They smoothed their gowns, examining themselves, and each other, in the standing mirror.

"Sir Chance is going to love you," Lace said.

Skye gave her sister a "duh" look. "He already loves her, silly, or he wouldn't be marrying her."

Queisha knew he was marrying her to give her a shot at keeping the girls, though he *had* said he'd loved her for years, that was a fact. Love just didn't account for their wedding in the usual way.

Still, this must be living because her heart was both filled with joy and breaking at the same time. She was marrying him because she loved him knowing, someday soon, she would lose him.

Elated and saddened, she marched with her girls down the main stairs and out to the yellow-brick patio. They followed the path until they reached the flowered arch near the rose garden.

The groom, drop-dead gorgeous in a navy tux—he couldn't bring himself to wear black—excused himself for a few minutes when he saw her walking his way.

He needed to remove the loose feathers from his dress shirt, she realized, worse since she hadn't whomped him since he sprained his wings.

"I'll marry you for the girls," she'd said over early tea the next morning. A weak protest at best, and she knew it.

He'd nodded. "I'm doing it to get whomped." The truth. Precisely.

He was so due. Past due.

Queisha winked at him. She'd added a peck of silver feathers to her hope chest since.

Speaking of chests, Chance looked straight at hers, until the judge cleared his throat. "Who gives this woman?" he asked.

"We do," the girls said, one rainbow and one lavender princess, bedecked in jeweled crowns of the finest plastic.

Vivica and Jaydun stood up for them as maid of honor and best man.

Guests in lined chairs on the lawn included the friends they'd made on playdates since the birthday party at the Dragon's Lair. Kira and Jason Goddard; Melody and Logan Kilgarven; Bastian and McKenna Dragonelli; Steve and Lizzie Framingham; and Vickie and Rory MacKenzie.

In the back row sat Chumpy, no fishing pole, and his large soft-sculpture family, assorted dolls, and stuffed animals. Standing behind them, the hat rack family. The girls must have planned that.

Vivica took the lavender rose and lilac bouquet so Queisha could hold each twin by a hand, as if they were marrying Sir Chance, all three.

The carousel music started and drifted their way from the other side of the yard. Then, shock of shock, angels appeared as if from nowhere to line the yellow-brick path curling around the yard. Queisha couldn't believe she could see them.

"Judge," Chance said, "a minute please?" and he walked her toward the small cemetery, their backs to the crowd, where a newborn cherub with tiny rainbow wings and a shock of red hair flew into her arms.

Chance put an arm around her. "Wedding present from the groom." For a blink, her son filled her arms and her heart. He looked up at her, his arms and legs flailing like a healthy newborn, his smile entirely for her, his green eyes bright and happy.

Since she'd lost him, she'd yearned to hold Connor for just a minute. One minute. And this, this was it, magick, love at its purest, hers as a mother, Chance's as a husband, Connor's as a son—a memory for eternity. She raised him in her arms and kissed his tiny brow, his heart-shaped mouth. "I love you, Connor. I always will."

"The whole family," Chance said. "Ready to begin the ceremony?"

"I guess I've had my minute and more," Queisha said, loathe to let go, but she did, and they watched Connor fly over to hover beside the angels on the path.

"He was born for that role," she whispered, touching Chance's cheek. "Thank you."

"I love you with all my heart," Chance whispered, and, hand in hand, they returned to face their guests and proceed with the ceremony.

Queisha's eyes filled when she had to say, "Till death do us part." But she loved Chance and marrying him was worth everything.

She also loved the whimsy of the day, the angels, their magick, the eternal feel of Connor in her arms.

Despite the fact that her groom was technically dead, this marriage was real, and forever, however long that lasted, their union based on more love than she could have hoped for herself.

"I now pronounce you man and wife."

Their kiss was interrupted by honking horns and a possible fender bender, which seemed to culminate near the circular drive.

Jaydun ran toward the commotion, trying to hold people back. But three couples fighting among themselves, shouting about custody and rights, had apparently arrived with lawyers in tow.

Angels stood protectively before her and the twins, the angels led by Auntie Mom, her birth mother—she'd know her anywhere—and her adoptive mother, the woman who raised her.

Mothers protecting daughters and granddaughters.

Queisha guessed the old adage was true. Family was always there for you. Always.

"Why can I see the angels?" Queisha asked Chance, awed by their show of protection. "Am I still alive?"

"Wondrously so. They must want you to see them."

"Motherless most of my life," she whispered, "and suddenly I have two, though they're as dead as my husband."

"I like being your husband. And I knew helping you wasn't going to be a walk in the park."

"No, it's more like a walk in loony land. Can the girls see them?"

"Judging by their lack of reaction, no."

The angels on the path disappeared, including Connor, leaving only her maternal protectors, and their presence changed her. She didn't know how, but they'd given her strength.

Jaydun, Vivica's bodyguard, swore and moved Vivica to stand beside them. "The journalist who's been stalking you is here," he told her.

Queisha saw the popular television journalist at the corner of the property.

Vivica whispered something in her cat's ear, and the cat loped toward the carousel.

"Queisha," Chance said, "take the girls inside and tell them what we've been trying to protect them from, before one of these greedy fools does. I'll deal with the intruders."

A girl on each hand, she ran straight to the house, ignoring paths, but every time they had to cross the grass, her heart jumped.

Skye talked her over every patch. "Good job, Mama." And Lace comforted her, too. "It'll be okay, Mummy."

Big steps for her, big step for her girls.

Queisha rushed them inside and up to the attic, locking doors behind her, and they cuddled in the middle of the bed beneath the tree of life quilt from the back of the chair.

"Are we on our honeymoon?" Skye asked.

Queisha laughed. "No," she said, "we're hiding from those people who, I think, came to the wrong wedding."

She hadn't wanted them to think they were hiding from the law, or lawyers, as the case may be. She wanted them to respect the law, and she couldn't call the other couples greedy, because one of them could, conceivably, end up caring for the girls.

If she and Chance didn't become their parents, she wanted them to love whoever did.

Meanwhile, she needed to tell them what happened to the Fitzpatricks. Instead, she got up from the bed to look out the window.

She looked down on the drive and saw a woman emerge from the front door of the carousel. Her hair a white blond, she wore a white dress with black spots and a diamond choker, an exact replica of the one worn by Vivica's cat, Isis. The strange woman had the journalist in her sights while Queisha opened the attic window.

"And who might you be?" the journalist asked.

"Savannah," the woman purred. Like a Savannah cat? Nah. Well, she'd just married an angel, and could still feel the silk of her son's red hair on her arm, so why not?

The journalist talked Savannah into an interview, and Savannah sweet-talked him into a ride, and just like that, Vivica's stalker was removed from the premises.

Queisha saw Chance talking to Vivica and the judge while the intruders were nowhere to be seen. Maybe she should wait for Chance. He and Vivica seemed to be inching their guests toward their cars. There'd been amazing hors d'oeuvres and champagne before the ceremony, because there was no reception afterward, and everyone knew it. Whimsical informality had been the theme of the day.

Eventually, Jaydun and Vivica pulled away in the DeLorean and she heard Chance calling her.

Queisha went to the top of the attic stairs. "Chance. We're up here."

He took the stairs two at a time, caught her in his arms, and danced her around the room. The twins applauded.

"Appointment with all parties concerned," Chance whispered, pretending to kiss her ear. "And Judge Harcourt, here, day after tomorrow."

Queisha shivered. "You're just in time for the big reveal."

"Thanks for waiting," Chance said, "I think." He took her hand and led her to the bed, sat, and took Lace on his lap.

Queisha got in on the other side, taking Skye, who willingly curled into her arms, that small head on her breast.

"First," Chance said, "Lace and Skye, do you know any of the people who came screaming into the yard at the end of our wedding?"

Both girls shook their heads. "Nope."

Chance looked over at her.

Queisha had to swallow the lump in her throat. Was she supposed to give her girls up to strangers?

Chance rolled his eyes. "They said *close* relatives."

"Invisibly close," Queisha added.

THIRTY-SEVEN

"It's time," Chance said. Before the vultures try to claim them.

"I know," Queisha replied, crossing her arms. "Can you do it, Papa Bear?"

"Girls," Chance asked, "did anybody tell you why you were taken from boarding school and sent here to Mama Bear?"

Skye crossed her arms, set her mouth, her bottom lip coming up over the top one, in a pout that was assuredly much practiced but making its first appearance in this house. In that way, she shook her head in a good demonstration of Queisha's stubbornness. "No one knows where Mother and Father are."

Queisha bit her lip. A sign of guilt or amusement?

Chance wasn't quite sure what Skye's negative display stood for, but he'd never seen either girl pout like that before. "Do you know where your parents were while you were in boarding school?"

One hard nod from Lace. "Mountain climbing."

Skye raised both her arms as if to punctuate her sister's point. "Always mountains for them and always boarding school for us, 'cept now."

Queisha combed her fingers through Skye's curls and away from her face. "But babies don't go to boarding school."

Lace, the independent one, swiped the hair from her own eyes. "We had Nanny Bee."

"Nanny," Skye said. "No hugs, no kisses, no smiles. Pulleeeeze."

Lace giggled. "Father said Nanny Bee talked like a wind-up doll."

Well, Chance thought, scratching his chin. It seemed as though they had some kind of relationship with their father, but back to the point. "Girls, do you know what's dangerous about climbing mountains?"

Skye raised her hand. "Falling off?"

Chance cleared his throat. "Did you know that your parents left directions that, if they ever fell off a mountain or anything like that, they wanted Queisha—"

"Mama," Lace said, interrupting him. "We voted."

Chance met Queisha's gaze. "Whoa. When did that happen?"

She pulled Skye in for a quick hug. "Don't know for sure. They called me Mama Bear after the birthday party and Mama and Mummy when I crossed the grass getting them in here, just now."

"Oh," Chance said. "Well— Wait! You crossed the grass?"

Queisha looked proud enough to have swum from Salem.

Chance reached for her hand on the attic cabin quilt and covered it with his.

"I think you should be kept in the loop, Papa Bear."

"Yes, please," he said, giving the twins a look of appreciation and love.

They cheered and tackled him, turning the three of them into a pig pile, their squeals not conducive to being told their parents had died.

Lace and Skye sat up suddenly. "Mother and Father are dead?" Lace asked, Skye's eyes filling, her bottom lip trembling.

Blessed saints, they'd hovered in that place between life and death, too. Around them, he needed to close his mind, not bare his thoughts.

Lace fisted her hands, her eyes nearly as bright as her sister's, her lips hard set. "If they fell off, I hope they fell from the top. They *hate* it when they don't reach the top." She hid her face against Queisha's gown.

Queisha rubbed Lace's back and Chance followed her lead with Skye, who patted his chest. "You're a good Papa Bear."

Chance looked at Queisha.

"I know psychic when I see it," she said. "I have a bit of it myself. One of us thought it, and they caught it."

"I figured," Chance said. "Got it at the same time as you, at their birth while getting life breathed back into them."

"Down deep, they probably knew before we did."

Skye nodded, still leaning against him.

Lace reached blindly but unerringly for her sister's hand. "Mother said it wasn't polite to read people's minds, mostly because we could read Father's, and his thoughts she said were X-rated, which we didn't understand, anyway."

That'll teach me to keep my mind shut, Chance thought.

"What we don't understand," Lace said, "is, well, you promised, member, that you wouldn't give us away? So why were those people arguing about keeping us when we're yours?"

"I remember what I promised," Queisha responded. "And I plan to fight for you."

"Lace, don't say it," Skye said. "We *don't* want them to know."

Queisha moved Skye so she could see her face.

Skye gave a deep body shudder. "It's our fault Mother and Father died."

"No!" Chance said. "Not possible. Talk to us."

Lace raised her shoulders, almost to her ears, released her breath, and lowered her shoulders to a pose of utter despair. "We shut them from our minds 'cause we were mad they left us at boarding school."

Skye sighed. "Two days before the school sent us here, we knew something was bad wrong, but being here is good, and we know you belong to us."

Lace agreed with a nod. "We like it better here than boarding school, better than—well, we don't like climbing or skiing or any of those things, and that made Mother mad."

"You play with us," Skye added. "You hug us. You kiss us. You read to us. It's like—" Skye stopped as if she couldn't give voice to her thoughts. "We divorced them in our minds and then they fell."

"What do you know about divorce?" Chance asked, sitting straighter.

Skye laced her fingers with his. "Parents get divorced. It happened to lots of our friends."

"Cecily divorced her parents, so we divorced ours."

"They died that day," Lace said. "The day the school sent us here."

"No." Chance pulled them both into his lap. "You didn't cause it. According to the report, your mother and father actually died when their thoughts stopped reaching you."

"It's not our fault, then?" Lace fake fainted against him.

"Are they in Heaven now with the angels?"

"Yes, and they want you to be happy. So stop feeling guilty."

"You're allowed to be sad and miss them," Queisha said.

Skye huffed. "We always missed them. We were always with Nanny, or the maids, or in boarding school."

Lace went over to touch a rocker. "Our favorite times, Father rocked us."

Queisha kissed both of them. "Glad to hear it. You talk about them all you want, but especially if you start thinking you caused their accident, 'kay?"

Chance picked Lace up and sat in the rocker with her. "Mountain climbers are a thousand times more likely to fall off mountains than non-climbers," he said as he started rocking.

Queisha sat in the other with Skye.

In his navy tux, holding hands with his fairy princess, in a matching rocker, they celebrated their honeymoon wiping tears, rubbing backs, and hearing Fitzpatrick family stories, until yawns replaced words and exhaustion claimed them all.

THIRTY-EIGHT

He and Queisha lingered, trying not to disturb the peace that came with sleep and obliterated the loss of a parent.

Eventually, after they put the girls, who never woke, to bed, Chance escorted Queisha down to the safari den expecting warm champagne and a cold supper, but he was mistaken. "Vivica's a peach," he said. "She must have realized we'd be with the girls, after the invasion, so she had our champagne iced and our lobster dinner put in covered warming pans."

Determined to make theirs as normal a wedding night as possible, despite the circumstances, they sipped champagne and fed each other lobster. Then he slow danced her to "You Needed Me," singing to her the first stanzas, the words so appropriate to their situation. Then "Hawaiian Wedding Song," corny and old-fashioned, maybe, but the "leaving me never" was tempered by "loving each other longer than forever," quite appropriate.

He'd simply asked Vivica to find them a compilation without "Could I Have This Dance" given his short-lived circumstances.

"I can't believe I married my guardian angel."

"You married him to give your children a father."

"Chance, they're not mine."

"Tell them that."

"I'm as likely to lose them as I am you. I'm brimming over with love that can get snatched away at any moment."

"Imagine a life of never experiencing a minute of this. I don't know about you, but I'll be grateful for my time with you, and the girls, for eternity."

She shook her head, her eyes overflowing, her frustration dissolving. "So will I."

He traced her high cheekbones, kissed her lashes, nipped a lobe, took to kiss-nipping her neck, down toward her breasts, lower, undoing each crystal button, part of his grand design, and bared her breasts to bury his face between them.

Still slow waltzing, he worked a knee between her legs, dipped her, and loved the way her breathing changed, her long luscious lashes lowering, her thick, dark, amazing hair flowing behind her in wondrous waves.

"I want to take my wife to bed and make passionate love to her."

"Mmm."

Chance unplugged the warming table, turned off the lights, and with his arm around Queisha's waist, he let the wedding music follow them up the main stairs, until it faded in the distance.

Vivica had decorated her room, turning it into a bridal

suite, with another bucket of champagne and several vases of lavender roses. The bed was turned down on both sides, his and hers terry cloth robes at the foot.

One thing Vivica didn't figure on: two six-year-olds sleeping in the center of their nuptial bed.

Chance and Queisha took the robes, went to Chance's former bedroom, locked the bathroom door, and undressed each other—sweet, quiet—and showered together, a calm lovemaking, slow and sensual. A first. New experiences, adventurous strokes, orgasmically enhanced, each of them in turn, her coming pinned to a marble wall, him where his *whomp* couldn't get him into trouble.

Good thing her auntie mom had believed in huge showers with no doors.

They muffled their moans, and their amusement, with kisses.

"You know," she said, walking around him, "your wings are looking brighter every day."

"I know, since I got here, and especially since we started making love, two rows—the gold at the top for love, and the lavender for hope—have grown thicker and brighter."

"Glad to hear it. Gives me a little thrill."

He wiggled his brows. "What kind of thrill?"

They took advantage of the Jacuzzi jets on low, lots of bubbles, to rest in each others' arms. More strokes while floating to earth, then when they could hardly keep their eyes open, they found wholesome pajamas inside those robes, variations on the red plaid and solid red theme, of the his and hers variety. "Vivica was more perceptive than I thought," Queisha said.

Tonight of all nights, the girls would need the comfort of having them there, so no question of where they'd sleep.

They climbed into separate sides of Queisha's bed, the girls sandwiched between them.

When Chance turned out the lights, Queisha reached for his hand across the girls and he wondered, on this his wedding night, if an angel bridegroom had ever run away from home.

What felt like a minute later, his foot twitched.

"Try again," one of the twins whispered.

"Okay."

Righteous folly, he was being tortured, tickled to death on the bottom of his foot with one of his own feathers. "It's not working," the other twin whispered.

The muffled laughter belonged to neither of the girls.

He turned to see the twinkle in Queisha's eyes across the mattress. She lay on her side, head in her hand.

"Is he awake?" Skye asked when he moved, so she climbed up the middle of the bed to sit between them on the pillow. "We're hungry, Papa Bear." She frowned. "You forgot to feed us last night."

"We just fell asleep." Chance covered his face with his pillow.

"I believe my husband asked me to wake him early so he could read my surrogacy contract for an appointment with a judge and three couples who shall remain nameless." She hit him with her pillow.

He retaliated, and so did the girls.

An uproarious pillow fight was a good way to wake up in the morning . . . if you couldn't wake up making love to the woman you loved.

After breakfast, Queisha and the girls went to the

miniature golf course in the basement so she could teach them to play.

Chance went to the study to look over the surrogacy contract in preparation for their meeting with the girls' relatives and their lawyers the following day.

Queisha brought him a cup of African Redbush tea. "To calm you," she said, kissing the top of his head.

He curled an arm around her neck and brought her mouth down to his. "That's better. How are the girls?"

"Some laughter, then they remember their parents, so there are tears, too. But Skye had an idea, and that gave them something to focus on."

The girls came to stand in the doorway. "We miss you, Papa Bear," Lace said, a big admission for her.

Chance called them over with a curled finger and pulled them on his lap. "What are you two doing that requires focus?"

"We like Chumpy the fisherman—he's like sorta real, and always there," Skye said, playing with one of his shirt buttons, "so we asked Mama if she would help us make Mother and Father soft-sculpture mountain climbers."

"That's a great idea. Too bad we don't have a mountain to put them on."

Queisha ran a loving hand through his hair. "Oh, ye of little faith," she snipped. "Don't you know that I have a miniature golf course in the basement?"

"With a madhorn," Lace said. "Mama says we can put the climbers on that and make it a morial to Mother and Father."

"*Matter*horn and *me*morial," Queisha clarified.

"That." Lace nodded. "We're going to put Mother and Father on *top*. So they will always have reached the top."

"We'll plant their flag," Skye added. "And like them, no matter what we try to do, we won't give up, ever, like Mother and Father never gave up. Mama said that was a good thing."

"Go, Queisha." Chance kissed her hand. "I knew you'd figure it all out. Gee, your wedding band looks plain. Whaddya think, girls? Don't you think that every wife and mother should have an engagement ring?"

The girls cheered. "Can we go shopping with you, Papa? We like jewelry." Right after Lace called him Papa, she clapped a hand to her mouth, making her sister giggle.

"Shopping is not necessary," Queisha said. "Just go up to Auntie Mom's bedroom, top drawer, and pick one out that you'd like to give me. Your choice. She loved jewelry, too."

Chance raised a brow. "How romantic. Not."

"You'll have done the choosing. That's what counts."

"I'll do it later, so you can be surprised. Hah. Go ahead, help the girls with the soft sculpture, so I can get back to this contract."

"It might sound silly," Queisha said, "but it's giving them closure and something respectful to do for their parents, a way to stop shutting them out. How's the contract? Any loopholes?"

"Pretty standard so far. Vivica's getting a copy of the will so I can read the wording in the guardian clause. Don't forget that I'm an unremarkable lawyer."

"You're remarkable in other ways."

As he went back to reading, Chance hoped that whomping topped his remarkable list in her estimation.

Queisha split her time between the girls creating their soft-sculpture parents and half pacing beside him.

"There's no way this issue can be settled tomorrow, can it?" she asked.

"I don't see how."

"Good."

He sat straighter. "Why? Don't you want the girls' futures to be settled?"

She threw herself into his arms and buried her face in his neck. "You'll disappear in a puff of smoke when they're settled, and I can't stand the suspense of looking for you around every corner, knowing that one day, you won't be there."

A lump formed in his throat. Empathy. Sorrow. He held her tighter, found her mouth, and devoured it. Went back for more.

She cupped his face between her hands the way he liked, combing her fingers from his hair to his cheeks as if trying to bring him closer and closer to her.

She wound her legs around his waist and the back of the chair. "Ready for liftoff," she whispered.

"All you need to do is grab the gear shift and put it in drive," he said

They sighed, went brow to brow, cheek to cheek, a nuzzling cuddle, but no more with the girls awake downstairs.

His arousal aside, she reminded him of the spider monkey he tried to get up that escape tunnel. It was the agoraphobia, he knew now. She'd felt safer buried with him than taking a step back into the world.

How *could* he leave her? *Angus,* he called, telepathically, *does Everlasting have a legal department?*

Angus appeared, hovering behind Queisha. "No, you randy Irishman. They don't, and you might want to keep your husbandly attentions to the bedroom with me in and out."

"Hi, Angus," Queisha said, as Chance turned the chair on its casters, and she rested her head on his shoulder, still clinging like a monkey.

"Has anyone ever tried to sue God?" Chance asked his friend. "Got any good lawyers up there?"

Angus grinned. "Anybody who could pull it off is too hot a property."

Chance chuckled.

Angus saluted and disappeared.

Queisha picked up the contract and tapped it on the desk. "Well?"

He pinched the top of his nose to ease his stress headache.

She massaged his temples. "Give it to me straight."

"With you in that position, I couldn't give it to you any other way."

Her grin doubled his readiness to do just that.

"The contract?" she prodded . . . while he prodded.

"Oh right. Good news and bad: the Fitzpatricks did indeed leave the twins to you, but their relatives can fight the will."

"Can we play the guardian ace in court?"

"I can't go to court. I'm no longer a member of the bar."

"Why not?"

"I'm dead. They might find my appearance suspicious."

"But Vivica got you your Social Security number."

"Serendipitous fluke. The bar's a bit trickier. Even Vivica doesn't have that kind of pull."

"What will we do? Hire another lawyer?"

"We could do that. Or we could do exactly what we're

doing, acting like we've got the upper hand and laying our cards on the table with Judge Harcourt. Think about it. I'm gonna take a break and go look at the rings. Where did you say I'd find them?"

"Same place you found the surrogacy contract. Top drawer in Auntie Mom's second-floor bedroom, not the attic bedroom."

His mother-in-law's room held more of a nod to her Kenyan roots than the safari den with her giraffe drapes and spread in bright earth tones. He particularly liked her elephant nightstands, which Queisha had told him were carved from a rare and therefore expensive black wood. On the walls, Auntie Mom had hung Kenyan landscapes and assorted ritual drums and masks.

As he went to open the drawer where he'd found the surrogacy contract, he was stopped by what he found on top of the bureau, something that hadn't been there yesterday.

He saw the very ax handle he'd held while its blade had revealed the keys to the locked tower attic. He considered the handle a calling card from his mother-in-law, and what he found beneath it a message. Or a sign.

Picking up the folded paper, he saw a staple mark in the corner, as if it had been separated from another document. Opening it, he looked it over and found an addendum to the surrogacy contract.

It didn't take much reading to understand the implications of what he'd found.

THIRTY-NINE

Judge Harcourt arrived promptly at two, but the cou-
ples fighting Queisha's guardianship arrived a half hour
later, livid because Queisha refused to give them access
to the girls.

Skye and Lace were upset at the thought of seeing
their mother's relatives, afraid they should be wearing
uniforms, afraid to say the wrong thing.

He and Queisha agreed to let Vivica and Jaydun take
them to Salem for the day to ride the trolley and stop at a
few haunts, stopping at the Dragon's Lair for lunch and to
play with Wyatt and Whitney and the four babies there.
Lace said she liked that they would each have a baby to
hold.

Chance set up Queisha's office so that Judge Harcourt
could sit behind the desk with all parties across from
him.

The old man loved it and sat before the relatives arrived. "Chance, Queisha," the judge said, "if you'd put this desk on a pedestal, I'd feel right at home." He folded his hands in front of himself, then took his gavel from his briefcase and smacked it to test its resonance. "Understand that this will be an informal hearing and doesn't count where the law's concerned. We're doing it here for your sake, Queisha, and to hopefully nip a long court battle in the bud.

"Oh, I'll give my recommendation to the courts, should the contesting families go that far. Huge inheritance involved. Always suspicious." The judge raised a cautioning finger. "You didn't hear that from me. Vivica and I have been friends for years. I forget myself when she asks a favor. Great judge of character, that woman."

"Understood," Chance said, liking the guy.

"Let the vultures in," the judge whispered.

Chance opened the door. Barely inside, the three couples began bickering with one another at once.

The judge banged his gavel. "I *like* doing that. Silence! I like hearing myself talk, too. I'll let you know when I want to hear *you* talk, if ever.

"The way I understand it, Queisha Saint-Denis has legal custody of the girls, according to the Fitzpatricks' wishes, as stated in their will, and the couples present, the Connollys, the Molloys, and the O'Rourks, all relatives of Mrs. Fitzpatrick, are challenging the guardianship portion of the will. Is that correct?"

They, and their individual lawyers, started to speak together.

The judge raised the gavel but didn't need to lower it. Everyone went silent.

"Too bad. I was looking forward to using it again.

Time for a quiz." The judge opened his briefcase. "Here you go. Four couples, four pads of paper, and eight pencils. Write your names at the top and jot down everything you know about Skye and Lace Fitzpatrick." The judge set a time clock. "You have two minutes."

When the clock went off, he collected the pads of paper, read the answers, tore the quizzes off the pads, put them in his briefcase, and handed the blank notebooks back to each of the four couples. "Will each couple note the estimated monetary size of the girls' fortune. The one who comes closest wins," he said and laughed.

He took those papers back immediately.

Chance hoped he was joking. He and Queisha had written a dollar sign with a question mark.

Judge Harcourt looked over the answers. "Just kidding about coming closest, by the way. Bit of courtroom humor. Before I make a *guestimation* as to who should get the girls, because I have no jurisdiction at all—though I can give you a good bet as to your chances—do any of you have an argument as to why you *should* be their guardian?"

"Yes, Your Honor," one lawyer said, and he and a second high-powered attorney made a run-on speech that never mentioned love or caring for the girls.

The third attorney, the one representing the O'Rourks, cleared his throat. "Mrs. Chance Godricson is unfit to be a mother. She became pregnant at the age of sixteen, was thrown out by her parents, and became a ward of the state."

Chance shot to his feet. "That's not a case for you being the twins' parents, it's a case against their guardian."

"That's the least of it," the attorney said. "This woman is agoraphobic and unable to run a normal household."

The first two lawyers looked surprised as did their clients, but they submitted the same objection on the basis of Queisha's agoraphobia.

Chance could see Queisha paling and trembling beside him, and he remembered why and how much he hated the law.

The judge used his gavel. "Do any of you have children?"

"We do, Your Honor," Mrs. Molloy said, with pride and a raised chin toward the other contesters. "A son, nineteen years old."

"Ah," Judge Harcourt said. "Freshman in college? Grade A student? Works in a soup kitchen on weekends when he's not studying?"

The woman paled.

"Don't think I didn't do my homework," the judge said. "You raised a pretty good boy, normal and not perfect. No one is. And you know, anybody can have children. Greedy relatives *and* agoraphobics. You, by the way, got the girls' fortune right to the nearest dollar.

"Mrs. Godricson's agoraphobia *could* tip the scales in court, but her therapist would be willing to testify as to her progress. That's, as I see it, the biggest problem with the Godricsons getting custody of Skye and Lace Fitzpatrick. Mr. Godricson, would you like to plead your case?"

Chance hated to let go of Queisha's hand, but he did so he could stand. "First, Your Honor," he said, "The Fitzpatricks left the girls to Queisha in their will. She's their choice as guardian. Second, she carried the babies for the Fitzpatricks. Third, I'd like to offer a copy of this addendum to the surrogacy contract for you to peruse, Your Honor. In view of that, I humbly avow that Skye and

Lace Fitzpatrick belong to Queisha Saint-Denis without question."

Judge Harcourt took and read the addendum, twice, clicking his tongue as he did.

He slapped his hands on the desk. "Before I go any further, I'd like to mention that your quizzes will go to court, if this custody case goes to court. The Fitzpatrick relatives wrote lists similar to one another about the twins, but they jotted down impersonal facts that could be found on the Internet about the daughters of famous sports figures, jet-setters, and millionaires. Facts in the public domain."

"But, Your Honor—"

"It's not your turn to talk, Counselor."

"Mr. and Mrs. Godricson, however, say that Lace asks endless questions, is a talented artist, right-handed, super tidy, won't color with a broken crayon, likes her clothes to match, especially her shoes, is bossy, and has to change outfits if she gets dirty."

He looked at the relatives. "Did you know that? Any of you? I didn't think so."

Chance hid his smirk. The judge was just toying with them now.

"Skye likes to dance," Harcourt said. "She makes everything into a game, is left-handed, doesn't like her earrings to match, likes rainbow-colored clothes, bare feet, rock-and-roll music, spontaneity, is a rebel and a nurturer." He put down the quizzes. "I *like* these kids."

"So do we," Queisha said.

"That has nothing to do with raising them," another woman said.

The judge cleared his throat. "Not if they're in boarding

school. I should note a further comment by the Godricsons: 'They don't belong in boarding school.' Who among
you didn't intend to send them to boarding school?"

One woman raised her hand, ignoring a sister and
cousin, according to the paperwork, as if they were in-
sects in her crème brûlée.

"You're trying to get on the judge's good side," one
said. "You wouldn't keep them underfoot, either."

Lawyers cautioned both to be quiet.

The judge shrugged. "As for their fortune, you all estimated between nine and twelve million dollars. The
Godricsons have no idea."

"I doubt that," a lawyer muttered.

"Doesn't matter," the judge packed his briefcase.
"Other than the Godricsons, you are all related to *Mrs.*
Fitzpatrick, is that correct?"

The three couples nodded.

"I have an undeniable fact for you, which I believe will
hold up in any court. Meanwhile, Queisha, I'm surprised
you let us go through this."

"Why?"

"This addendum says it all."

Chance thought Queisha looked confused. He hadn't
shared it with her, and now he knew why she hadn't mentioned it. She hadn't seen its importance to the case.

"May I see it?" she asked the judge.

She read it. "Oh, at the last minute, we learned that
Mrs. Fitzpatrick didn't have any viable eggs. Mr. Fitzpatrick confided in me that his wife would be brokenhearted
to learn that she couldn't provide an egg, much less a hos-
pitable environment for the babies to grow. So I let the
fertility specialist harvest some of my eggs to fertilize. I

was trying to pay it forward, as the cliché goes. I thought of it as a blip in the proceedings, nowhere near as big a deal as the pregnancy and birth, never mind giving up the babies. Besides, I signed a confidentiality agreement. I hope I'm not breaking any laws by discussing it?"

The judge nodded. "That's called ethics. You're not breaking any laws, given the case before us. And you didn't present the information to us. Your husband did, without your knowledge, I take it?"

"Correct. Without my knowledge."

"What's the point?" one of the women snapped.

The judge shook his head. "You're related to Mrs. Fitzpatrick, who had no eggs. She wasn't the twins' biological mother. Mrs. Chance Godricson is."

One of the lawyers stood. "The twins are not up for grabs, ladies and gentlemen, especially not by the relatives of a non-parent."

"Wait a minute," one of the husbands said. "If the girls aren't related to Mrs. Fitzpatrick, then we're Mrs. Fitzpatrick's closest relatives, so we inherit her money, right?"

Judge Harcourt chuckled. "If Mrs. Fitzpatrick had a separate will saying she was leaving her money to her family, sure, but I have in my hands a joint will. And according to these death certificates, the missus passed first, about six hours before her husband, which made him her legal heir, and the girls are his only heir. It's all right here."

Chance wondered if the echoing sound of their collective groan might not be loud enough to be floating across Salem Cove right now.

FORTY

She guessed that hiding was a waste of time.

"Queisha, are you up there?" Chance called.

She hated for him to find her curled up on the attic bed, crying, but that's where she needed to be.

"Ah, sweetheart, what's this?" He kissed her eyelids, first one, then the other. "Tears and a safe place because you've got your babies back? Why didn't you tell me you provided the eggs?"

"It was a secret and I signed a contract to keep it a secret. They weren't mine."

"But when they came back to you?"

"There was still a confidentiality contract."

"But when you found out their parents were dead?"

"I think I was too worried about whether an agoraphobic would make a good parent. For the longest time, I didn't think I was good enough to keep them. It was a nonissue. Then we slept together, your wings whomped,

I found out you were a dead angel, you made me go outside, then you *married* me. Life got crazy for a while."

"Does your decision stand about the girls?"

She wiped her eyes. "I finished my mother's old journals while you read the contract and the girls worked on their soft sculptures. Giving me up was her greatest regret and she outlined all the reasons why. Yes, Chance, I, Queisha Saint-Denis Godricson, am the best guardian— no, the best *mother*—for Lace and Skye Fitzpatrick. I won't let the agoraphobia hurt my daughters, I promise."

"Yes! That's my girl!" He pulled her into his arms.

She burst into tears. "I'm so happy."

He hid his smile in her hair. "I can tell."

"I'll love them forever."

"So these are happy tears?"

"No, now that the girls' guardianship is pretty much settled, I'm afraid you'll disappear. Unless you get to stay until after the paperwork is done. That could take years, right?"

"The paperwork won't take years."

She got on her knees and threw her arms around him. "Months?" She couldn't stop her heart from racing, her stomach from churning. "Please say it'll take months."

"Angus met me downstairs. He said the triumvirate has given me three days to settle everything before I go back."

The floodgates opened. She knew she was out of control and couldn't do a thing about it. He seemed as shaken. They made love with a rush of mutual solace and panic, unable to get enough of each other, trying to store love for a lifetime.

Impossible of course, so they tried harder.

Each touch aroused a deeper, keener thrill. Each orgasm lasted and lasted, the rush to release heady and outrageous. Thrice, she came near to passing out, and Chance broke a record by whomping twice himself.

They made love on the bed, the floor, in the tower attic surrounded by her heritage, in the sunroom with sunshine blessing them from two directions, in the center of the carousel with music and joy all around them.

When they were on their way to play strip billiards, Vivica called and asked if the girls could do a sleepover at the Dragon's Lair with Whitney. "They can use Whitney's things. Jaydun and I would spend the night as well. Frankly," she said, "the girls told me they slept with you two last night, and I thought you could use a honeymoon. Oh, and I talked to the judge. Congrats. Here, Skye wants to talk to you."

"Pulleeeeze, Mama. This place is awesome and the Framinghams have triplets. Can we have triplets? And they live on a farm with kittens and the cutest baby pigs."

Queisha sighed. "Then you'll be wanting a sleepover of your own," she said, having trouble concentrating with Chance nibbling his way up her arm.

"Yes, please. Can we, Mama? Lace thinks it should be a costume sleepover."

"Good idea. Maybe for Halloween. You can be lobsters."

"Oh, yuck."

"Vivica, here. Can we? Can we, huh? Please?"

"Thanks, Viv. I owe you one."

Queisha hung up. "Viv is giving us a honeymoon night. She and the girls are doing a sleepover."

"Well, what are we waiting for?" Chance rolled all the billiard balls into their pockets and lifted her to the edge of the table. "I have a new game for us to play. Sex billiards."

She tilted her head. "And we don't need balls to play, we need a submarine?"

"Uh, we need balls, too." Chance wiggled his brows. "Mine." He kissed his way up her legs, pushed her back on the table, and lifted her skirt. "Hey, where did you lose your panties?"

"I have no idea."

He chuckled and began to make a feast of her.

"Chance, don't."

He sat up. "Remember when I said 'live life for both of us' and how well you did?"

She swallowed her tears and nodded, thinking she'd be doing that again soon.

"Well, here's a new sign for the top of your closet. Paint these words: 'Try new things' . . . starting with this."

He went back to giving her wondrous pleasure with his tongue, and though she tried to push him away at first, she was getting all floaty. And before long she held him in place and begged for more. She laughed, she came, she cried out, and she was loved. Then she loved him in return.

And for his final performance, he entered her from above and he gave her a triple whomping orgasm incredible enough to last a lifetime.

A long time later, she gave a sated sigh, her head on Chance's shoulder, his arm around her, as they wandered into another room. "I will never look at that billiard table the same way again." He pulled in his wings while she checked the clock. "You know, I have a terrible inclination to count hours, rather than days."

"It'll come down to that. Do you want to talk for a bit?"

"Are we going to tell the girls? They just lost one father, now they're going to lose another."

"Angus got the triumvirate to listen to my idea about how I go."

"Did they agree?"

"They listened, but listen is not 'do.' "

"So what's your idea?"

"It's a possibility I've been thinking about for a while."

"I can't imagine one satisfactory way for you to leave us, but I'm listening. I'm not liking it, but go ahead." She went for the tissue box.

"The mural. Skye said that was their angel. You take them to the playroom; I come down wearing my dream coat and wings, looking the way I look in the painting. If they don't make the connection, I make it. I'll explain that I was needed during this transition and came down to help you all."

"Sure," she said, blowing her nose. "That'll be easy. We'll give you a going-away party."

"Less brutal than watching somebody—"

"Get buried?"

He shook his head. "Vanish. Unless you want a body for a funeral. Think about it. Burying your husband would be easier, if you wanted to marry again."

"You sonofabitch!"

"Queisha, I asked Vivica for divorce and annulment papers, which I'll sign before I go, and you can file whichever, if and when you choose."

She charged him, pummeled his shoulders with her fists, and he let her, and when she ran out of energy, slowed her movements, and stopped, she looked up at him and saw the tears on his face.

FORTY-ONE

He lifted her in his arms, sat in a big overstuffed chair in the safari den with her on his lap, and they held each other for a long quiet time. She closed her eyes and tried to memorize the beat of his heart for after he—for later.

He surprised her then by slipping on her finger a two-tiered ruby, wedding cake–style ring, set in gold, with a diamond in the center. "It reminds me of you at your most whimsical. Love everlasting," he said. "That's what I want you to think of when you look at this."

"You. I'm going to think of you making love to me when I look at this. How lucky I was to have you, even for so short a time."

"I'm hungry. There's some cold lobster left from yesterday. Let's grab some and go sit on a blanket by the water." He stood with her in his arms.

Her panic knew no bounds. Nausea rose up in her.

She hadn't had a real panic attack in months. The closest she'd come was the day she walked the yellow-brick path for the first time.

"Let's sit by the rose garden where we got married," she suggested. "Not by the water."

Chance shrugged. "Fine by me. But eventually, you will have to try new things, and going in the water should be one of them."

Her panic receded. She grabbed an old quilt from the hall closet and followed him outside. He laid the quilt in the grass and she rolled her eyes but joined him. Before long, they were on their backs, arms and legs tangled, an empty dish of lobster beside them.

She didn't like her horrific fear that this might be the last time. She wasn't being psychic, she told herself, but paranoid.

He watched her watch him, and her love rushed forth, shocking her with its intensity. She sighed and got closer, and he closed his eyes, both of them savoring.

She fiddled with the hair on his bare chest. "Chance?"

"Yes, Queisha"

"In my whole life, nobody ever held me the way you do."

He kissed a tear as it trickled down her cheek. "Want to talk about her?"

"You mean Auntie Mom?"

"Stop making jokes. Want to talk about forgiving her for giving you up for adoption?"

"No." Queisha raised her mouth, inviting another kiss.

The rhythm of his heart made Chance light-headed, as if within him beat the wings of a thousand angels making their way from a scene of chaos to the welcome bosom of Everlasting, charges in tow.

The sound echoed in his head and broke his heart as he slanted his lips over Queisha's.

He was drowning and she was air. He was parched and she was water.

A heaviness weighed down his heart. Chance shook it off and lost himself in his wife.

"It's all right," she said on a sob. "I think I know that our time is coming to an end."

"Neither of us could possibly know for sure." Then he really kissed her, the touch of their lips sparking fire and memory, as if they'd kissed a thousand times before. Except it had only happened since he got here, like a homecoming.

Mouth to mouth. Heart to heart. Body to body.

A reunion of souls.

Pleasure surged again, fast and shocking, pounding through his body, everywhere.

"Chance, hold me tight. Please," she said, as if trying to climb inside of him. "Don't let me go."

"Glory," he said. "As if I could. As if I could ever let you go."

He kissed her with ten years' worth of longing and the desperation of a man finding then losing his love nearly as fast.

After they made love again, he tried to look into her eyes.

"Just hold me. I need to be closer. I'm afraid, Chance. Don't let go."

"I never will," he said, trying to think of a way to keep the impossible promise.

She adjusted her position, every part of her touching every part of him.

"Am I hurting you?" he asked.

"I need to get closer," she said, afraid she was being psychic, afraid to confirm their fears.

"Closer? I don't think that's possible. We're still connected. My wings are bent." He was trying to lighten the mood, failed, and slipped them back into their muscle sacs.

Her breasts were soft and bronze, her nipples a ruddy rose and swollen. Delectable and calling for a taste.

There would be no calming for him.

God help him, he needed her as much as she needed him, especially with his departure on the horizon.

Within the safety of his embrace, she slipped from her dress and reached for him once more. In the open air, she was making a naked declaration of love and possession, but she didn't seem to care.

He closed his arms around her, but couldn't get enough air. Or enough Queisha.

The flare of her hips under his hand beckoned. He couldn't help but explore. And when he did, the air became thinner; he became harder. "Queisha, sweet." He used his most serious voice to bring her to her senses, yet it sounded more a plea to continue than an appeal to stop.

She rubbed her cheek against his, parted her lips, brushed his ear, and combed her fingers through his hair.

Righteous folly, he found this more sexually arousing than anything he'd ever experienced.

As far as Queisha was concerned, they were making the slowest, sweetest love of her life. Under heaven, for God, the angels, and all the world to see. "He's mine," she shouted, just to be contrary. "Mine forever."

And when he came, *whomp, whomp, whomp,*

whomp . . . whomp, they enjoyed the moment, the rebellious moment. His wings shot out every time, without fail, but he'd only ever sprained them that one time. And it had become their personal ritual, the sound and picture of satisfaction, so he put them away again.

After this last amazing union, exhaustion won, the sun lowering in the sky, her lover's wings wrapped softly and gently around her.

How blessed. How perfect.

Queisha opened her eyes, shivered, and reached for Chance. He wasn't there.

She sat up, looked around, and saw him swimming not far from the dock. "No!" she shouted, throwing on her dress. "No, Chance. Not the water."

He waved. "Come on in. We never whomped in the water."

"Come out. Please," she called as she ran toward him. Why did she know this was terrible?

She wanted to pass out just looking at the water but wouldn't let herself. If she didn't get her hands on Chance, this was the end. She had to touch him, hold him in her arms. This was no time to be phobic, it was life or death.

She walked into the water, hating the way it cloyed at her, as if holding her back when she needed to reach him.

He stood to wait for her, applauding her bravery with no idea of her fear.

She saw shadow angels behind him. Hundreds of them coming closer.

They brought a wave. She saw it take Chance under, knew she had to get to him, but it took her down, too, carried her far from shore, from Chance.

She saw nothing but water above her, a few curious fish, and swimming cherubs with their little legs and tiny wings. She looked for Connor or Angus but saw neither.

The water weighed heavy on her chest then she was floating, looking down at herself, watching her body fall backward toward the bottom of the cove, her hair in long waves flowing with the current, her body tossed by the undertow.

She never expected to see Chance swimming toward her, his wings huge, bigger than ever, his dream coat flashing colors like a neon sign beneath the water.

From another direction came an angel bigger than Chance, his wing colors darker but glowing brighter, his dream coat alive with light.

An archangel?

She guessed they needed the big guns to get someone like Chance back.

He and the archangel had a frenzied discussion, Chance furious, his hands animated, an argument of gargantuan proportions, but she heard nothing.

Finally, the archangel nodded and Chance looked her way.

Yearning she read on his face. Love. The forever kind. Was she drowning or was he leaving, or both?

"The girls," she tried to communicate, "someone has to take care of the girls."

He nodded, touched his lips to hers, breathed air into her lungs. "You'll take care of them while I'll be loving you all every day of your lives."

Angels surrounded Chance and carried him away with the current, but before they disappeared, his eyes closed and his body went limp.

At the same time, she felt her spirit reunite with her body, life surging through her. An angel radiating love helped her to the surface and accompanied her to shore.

There she collapsed and cried in the angel's embrace until there were no tears left. When she looked up, Queisha recognized the consoling presence. "No more being afraid, my little mouse, and I called you that because you squeaked." Then her birth mother was gone.

They searched Salem Cove for two days and never found Chance Godricson's body.

Queisha mourned inwardly to the depths of her soul but she tried to be strong for the girls. A week later, she held a graveside service at the family cemetery where a headstone for Chance was erected.

The twins missed him something fierce and cried often. Queisha couldn't shed a tear. She was too mad at God for stealing their three days. She would have been just as mad three days later, but that wasn't the point.

Another quarrel she had with the She of Life: the feathers were missing, bags of them. She and the girls, however, found a gold one in each of their beds. Gold for love. She had a feeling Chance put them there, that he knew he'd leave sooner than expected.

Every time she was alone outside, she'd look up and throw him a kiss, and more often than not, a rainbow appeared. She knew they'd taken him back to Everlasting, under protest.

FORTY-TWO

"Michael," Raphael *said. "Angus, fourth class, has* just snuck into Chance, Son of Godric's, domain to give him news of his wife."

Gabriel sat straighter. "It's been nearly two months. Son of Godric has been an exemplary guardian angel. His charges sing his praises."

Raphael agreed. "Exemplary despite no news of his wife or children. And after being banned from the cherub nursery, which he always loved, but he'd love more now since he knows his wife has a son there."

Gabriel shook his head. "The man is in deep mourning but doesn't let it affect his work."

Michael hit the floor with his staff. "He stretched the rules by marrying, but he was honest with her, I'll give him that. She knew he would return to us."

"Michael," Raphael said. "Son of Godric practically performed a miracle with Queisha of Saint-Denis. She's raising those girls and going out into the world every day."

"Your point?" Michael asked.

Raphael lifted a thick, heavy tome from the shelf of life and flipped it open to the proper page. "I'd like to cite the ancient law of death cheating."

Michael considered it. "We haven't needed to consider that for five or six millennia. Let's look and see how Queisha's doing first."

"She's sitting in her yard reading to her girls about angels," Raphael said. "She harbors no ill will against us. I like a girl who doesn't hold a grudge."

"Throw her a rainbow," Michael said. "She sees them as a wave from Chance."

Raphael cleared his throat. "Generous of you."

"Keep your opinions to yourself," Michael thundered. "Gabriel, bring Chance here. Now."

"It's too bright here," Chance said, a few minutes later, taking in his surroundings. Not many angels ever saw this high holy place.

The archangel dome shimmered with a veneer of effervescent gold, purely ornamental, of course. True riches were left to the living. Value was counted in the love of one's fellow man in Everlasting, not in currency.

Michael dimmed the lights with the snap of his fingers. "You've been in seclusion too long."

Chance looked far beyond them, to the recesses of his memories at the reason for his seclusion. "I'm in mourning for my family. Do you have a quarrel with that? Do you feel it affects my work?"

Gabriel shook his head. "On the contrary."

"May I ask why I've been summoned?"

Michael got up to pace, hands behind his back, his dream coat, almost too bright to look at, his train yards long. "Queisha Saint-Denis was scheduled to die on July twelfth, in the year of our Lord 2000. Instead, you saved her life and died in her place."

"I remember."

"To right the discrepancy, we arranged for Queisha to die with her twins at their birth," Raphael said, "and you got in destiny's way, again."

Chance paled. "You're not going to take her now that I can't get to her? *Please* don't take her from our girls."

"Relax, Son of Godric, you've closed that door. We tried again, on the day we took you home. We tried to take her with you. You would have been together. But you breathed life into her. Three fateful times, they say, invokes the law of death cheating. That's not just a cliché, it's a rule of Everlasting."

"I beg your pardon?"

"This rule is rarely, if ever, enforced."

Chance looked from one to the other. "What does it mean?"

Gabriel raised his brows. "If you cheat death three times, you get to live out your life and die of natural causes at an indecently advanced age."

Elation shot through Chance. Disbelief. "Then Queisha is safe? She can live a full life and raise the girls to adulthood?"

"Your Queisha will see her great-great-grandchildren."

She'll likely have someone else's children, too, Chance thought, glad he wouldn't have to see it. From elation to sadness in a blink.

"So I saved Queisha three times and now she's safe. As

her guardian angel, I guess I did my job." He whistled as he slipped his hands into his dream coat pocket and turned to leave. "Thank you. I'll be able to guard my charges with a great deal more enthusiasm from now on."

"Chance Godricson, come back here."

"Was I not dismissed? I apologize."

Raphael and Gabriel took him each by an arm and escorted him back to Michael.

"I repeat," Michael said. "Listen well: if you cheat death three times, you get to live out your life and die of natural causes at an indecently advanced age."

FORTY-THREE

Queisha had been working hard to make peace with water. Salem Cove, swimming pools, oceans, lakes, cranberry bogs. For one thing, she realized that her psychic instincts had been telling her for years that something terrible would someday happen around water. And it did. She lost Chance, the love of her life.

Now, she and the girls were taking swimming lessons every Tuesday and Thursday.

On alternating days, weather permitting, they sat near the water to play in the sand.

"Mama," Skye said. "My castle is way bigger than Lace's."

Lace raised her chin and gave her sister a superior smirk. "But mine is neater."

"Mama, what's that?" Skye pointed.

Queisha shaded her eyes. "A waterspout, maybe? Come here. Now." Queisha stood, took the girls' hands and backed toward the house. The water curl headed toward shore as they watched. It came so close, it covered the dock, and when it receded, an angel appeared.

Queisha blinked to clear her vision. Wide colored wings and a Technicolor dream coat.

"Our angel!" Skye said.

"Papa!" Lace screamed.

The girls started running.

Chance said they'd recognize him as their angel.

"Chance?"

Another wave followed, just as big, bigger, and engulfed him, and Queisha screamed and screamed, because she knew—she knew—he'd be gone when it receded, and he *was* gone . . . in a way.

In his place stood a man. Minus the wings, in white slacks, a white shirt, and bare feet. At his feet, not feathers, but . . . puppies. Two of them.

Behind him, in the water, hundreds of colored feathers floated farther and farther to sea, a dream coat floating among them.

The girls got to him first, and he lifted them in his arms at the same time, getting hugged and kissed to within an inch of his life, giving as much as he got.

When Queisha reached them, he put the girls down and jumped off the dock.

They went to play with the tiny red dachshunds.

Chance caught her in his strong, capable arms. "I wouldn't believe it until I got here."

Fast, hungry kisses they shared, hands everywhere, his, hers.

"You feel so good, taste so sweet," he whispered against her mouth.

She kept making sure he was really there. "You're not going to vaporize, are you?"

"I'm alive and here to stay, I promise you."

"I'm afraid to believe it."

"I'd twirl you to prove myself," he whispered kissing her all over her face, "but I don't want to hurt the baby."

"You know."

"Michael told me as he saw me off. A healthy, bouncing baby boy. You can take that to the bank."

"I never thought I'd see you again." She wiped her tears with the back of a hand.

"I'm here to stay, my love." He cupped her cheeks. "I'm mortal. We're going to live to be ancient old codgers. Michael told me himself. 'Queisha is yours,' the archangel thundered, 'as you are hers.'"

"We could have told him that," she said. "I'll miss the whomps though."

"We'll whomp our brains out, make no mistake, without the back strain. Think of the possibilities, the new positions, the locations."

She giggled and ate him up with her gaze. They sat in the sand and the girls climbed into his lap, the doxies in theirs.

In place of an angel, a man. A gorgeous Irishman with thick dark hair, deep-set eyes, sapphire eyes, fire and love in their depths.

"Where did you get the pups?" Queisha asked.

"I stopped at the rainbow bridge on my way down. It's right beside pre-Everlasting. The place where owners meet the pets that went before them. But the tiny ones, like these, died the day they were born, so there was never anybody for them to greet. I knew who they needed and who needed them."

"We love them. Are they girl or boy doxies?"

"Girls."

"Mine's Hannah."

"And mine's Abigail."

Chance scratched the doxies' ears. "They kept me sane the last couple of months."

"So you won't miss Everlasting?" Queisha cupped his face with a hand, eating him up with her gaze.

"We'll go back together when the time comes. There's the Wisdom Brigade for those who live to a ripe old age. I made us a reservation for about ninety years from now."

"You think we'll live to be a hundred and twenty–plus?"

"Michael promised." Chance used a finger to draw a heart in the sand. "I hear you've been out in the world, taking the girls to dance and swim classes, visiting friends. You faced your worst fears. I'm proud of you."

"I discovered there were worse fears than my worst fears. I lost you."

"Yeah, Papa," Skye said, her voice wobbly, "we thought you died."

"That, well. I washed ashore somewhere in . . . Maine, and a family nursed me back to health, but . . . I didn't remember who I was for a long time."

The girls laughed at the joke. "You were our guardian angel. We saw you just now. You're in our mural. God sent you back to us. We know."

"Out of the mouths of babes," he said, hugging them. "Other people won't believe the angel story. You know that right, girls?"

Lace shrugged. "At least we know. We remember that you kissed us when we were borned."

Queisha raised both hands. "They remember."

"You get wise in that place between life and death, and if you come back, you take psychic wisdom with you." He brought Queisha close and hugged her hard. "I'm so proud of you for conquering your agoraphobia and your fear of water."

"I'm telling you, they were nothing compared to losing you."

"I felt the same way. Losing you was the first time I ever *felt* dead."

He pulled the girls closer, the four of them appreciating life.

He picked up Lace's ankle and laughed. "Look at their skin. Those tans are *not* going to fade.

"Our *other* mother," Lace said, "wanted to be as tan as us, and kept matching her arms to ours, then she said something to Father about valuable eggs."

"Viable eggs?" Chance asked.

Lace nodded. "Yes, that. Father got sad and Mother cried."

Skye shrugged. "The next day, they told us they loved us very much, Mother and Father both, but they put us in boarding school."

"That explains so much," Chance said. "A woman who could have anything she wanted wouldn't want to hourly face a failure. I mean, it's shallow as hell, but it explains a lot. Remember, Queisha, when we feared the girls' tans would fade if you kept them inside too long? Wrong. Their other mother figured out they were part Kenyan before we did."

"No fading for us," Lace said, comparing her arm to Queisha's. "We look just like Mama."

Chance stroked Queisha's belly. "So will this little guy."

"Mama, you got a little guy in there?"

"Yes, she does," Chance said. "Your brother. Connor, right, Queisha?"

She stroked Chance's hand on her belly. "Connor Chance Godricson? Is that all right with you?"

"I asked your redhead before I left. He thinks it's fine."

Chance kissed her, Skye and Lace squished and giggling between them.

He swallowed hard. "You know for the longest time, before I came down here the first time, I worried that, because you were agoraphobic, I'd ended your life when I intended to save it. Now I believe that you saved my life."

"Well, I guess I did, since I'm slow baking a mini you."

Skye leaned back to look at them both. "Silly parents. You saved each other."

Keep reading for a special preview of
Annette Blair's next
A Works Like Magick Novel

VAMPIRE DRAGON

Coming soon from Berkley Sensation!

DRAGONS TO MEN AGAIN

A Roman legion the dark Sorceress Killian did change into
    dragons and banish.
To the Island of Stars, on a plane beyond ours, they did vanish.
Wondrous beasts who might well be dead,
But for Andra, their guardian sorceress, from whom hope
    never fled.
At the rise of the moons when all went black,
She turned the first back to a man with scant flak,
So for later spells, her rhyme stayed intact:
"Shed horns, spines, claws, and webbed wings. Shrink scales,
    spade, and tail—"
Killian countered with a fiery bolt; Darkwyn writhed as he
    took the jolt,
While Andra missed not a beat nor a mote:
"Warrior to beast, now back again. Send this man to the plane
    he began."
Darkwyn twisted to shift from dragon to man. In the steam
    from the rift,
An elder stood by to share the gift.

ONE

*Darkwyn Dragonelli rolled naked into a damp, pun-*gent alley and jumped to his feet, heeding Andra's warning to control his leap. The scent of fermented grapes filled his nostrils. A centuries-old memory. Civilization, Andra might say. Earth, he hoped.

A man once more, he needed to find a heart mate and assume responsibility for said mate's life quest. He must also defeat the sorceress Killian, Crone of Chaos, to regain the magick Andra depleted to send him here. Without her magick, Andra couldn't send his brother dragons after him. If that happened, they'd perish on an island currently being swallowed by a boiling lava sea.

Infused with determination, Darkwyn straightened. Without scales to protect or clothe him, he appreciated the half wall topped by a flat plank that separated his alley from the humans on the opposite side. With spirits being drunk from glass rather than pottery, he presumed this to be a wealthy pub, and extraordinary, as well, in that it allowed females inside. Women who drank spirits. Another world, indeed. Where half-dressed strumpets and camp followers lived equal to men . . . and birds squawked in the distance.

His guardian dragon—an elder, miniaturized to extend his life and allow him to accompany Darkwyn on this journey—flew about smoke-testing the area, yellow smoke signaling security. The pocket dragon surprised him by changing colors to match the walls, people, or objects behind him, while emitting a faint air-shivering whistle.

Darkwyn opened his thoughts to the elder. "Jagidy, methinks we stand in Rome no more."

The humans had begun to stare, though none could see Jagidy but him.

"What's this, naked entertainment?" asked the man entering the alley beside him, a barrel on his shoulder. "Only the bartender—that's me—belongs on *this* side of the bar, though I'm not sure you want to step around it advertising that fancy johnson of yours. The ladies of Salem will follow you like rats to the sea."

"What? He's *entirely* naked?" a half-dressed female asked. "I want one of *him*, to go."

"Or *come*," another said, while a third moved in. The three leaned over the bar, all but baring their bosoms as they eyed his misshapen organ, their greedy attention making the broken thing misbehave.

"Will ya look at that," one said, her gaze pinned to his rising soldier. "I gotta get me one of those."

Unsure of his next move, Darkwyn backed into a line of flasks, knocking them against one another, their colorful contents swishing like banes and toxicants. He searched his mind and found one of the few phrases he'd learned from Andra. "What *is* this place?"

A huge bird appeared and headed straight for him. "It's Drak's Place, Peckerhead," the bird squawked. "Drak's Place at the fricken Phoenix." It landed on Darkwyn's head, its talons closing to get a foothold, causing no small amount of pain.

Unexpectedly, the blue and gold bird leaned down and stared upside down into Darkwyn's eyes. "Ride in a coffin, drink some blood. It's Drak's Place at the fricken Phoenix. Run for your life!" *Squawk*.

The bartender kicked open the door behind him and tried to slap the bird with a cloth. "Get lost, Nimrod."

Darkwyn backed away to protect the bird, the first friend he'd made on this daft plane, sharp talons or not.

"Wanna buy him? Puck's a prime macaw. Valuable," the bartender said. "He's brilliant, if a little jaded. Quotes Ambrose Bierce and cusses like a sailor. I'll give you a great price."

Puck squawked, "Hypocrite: One who, professing virtues that he does not respect, secures the advantages of seeming to be what he despises."

Darkwyn understood neither of them.

A woman swept into the pub, her dotted cloak flying behind her, the tall feline at her side dotted to match, while tiny, fast-flapping birds and black pinging creatures flitted about her head. "My name is Vivica," the woman said telepathically as she came right to him, cloaking him with a covering as black as his hair and as long as his overtall body. "Follow me, Dragonelli. Your brothers are on their way."

"But my heart mate?"

"Is she here?" Vivica asked.

He would know the woman whose heart belonged to him when he found her, Andra had said, so Darkwyn looked from one female to the other. Their hearts varied as much as they. Hearts for money, he saw in several. Hearts for lust. No kindness, no softness; one closed heart, one dark, one clouded, two as empty as the cloth-flicking bartender who'd as soon destroy his talking bird as keep it. "No heart mate here," Darkwyn admitted.

Vivica nodded. "Fine, then. Give the man the bird."

"No," the man said. "I'll give *him* the bird."

"Well, Puck me," the bird said.

Keep reading for a special preview of

CRUEL ENCHANTMENT

by Anya Bast

Coming September 2010
from Berkley Sensation!

Emmaline Siobhan Keara Gallagher.

Clang. Clang. Clang. The shock of hammer to hot iron reverberated up his arm and through his shoulders. As Aeric shaped the hunk of iron into a charmed blade, Emmaline's name beat a staccato rhythm in his mind.

He glanced up at the portrait of Aileen, the one he kept in his forge as a reminder, and his hammer came down harder. It wasn't every night the fire of vengeance burned so hot and so hard in him. Over three hundred and sixty years had passed since the Summer Queen's assassin had murdered his love, Aileen.

Emmaline Siobhan Keara Gallagher.

He'd had plenty of time to move past his loss. Yet his rage burned bright tonight, as if it had happened three days ago instead of three hundred years. It was almost as if the object of his vengeance were close by, or thinking about him. Perhaps, as he'd imagined for so many years, he shared a psychic connection with her.

One born of cruel and violent intention.

He was certain that if the power of his thoughts truly did penetrate her mind, she had nightmares about him. If she ever thought his name, it was with a shudder and a chill.

If Aeric knew what she really looked like, he would envision her face with every downward impact of his hammer. Instead he only brought her essence to mind while forging weapons others would wield to kill, maim, and bring misery. If he could name them all, he would name them *Emmaline*.

It was the least he could do, but he wanted to do so much more. Maybe one day he would get the chance, though odds were against him. He was stuck in Pieffer-burg while she roamed free outside its barriers. Aileen was far from him, too, lost to the shadowy Netherworld.

He tossed the hammer aside. Sweat trickling down his bare chest and into his belly button, he turned with the red-hot length of charmed iron held in a pair of tongs and dunked it into a tub of cold water, making the iron spit and steam. As he worked the metal, his magick pulled out of him in a long, thin thread, imbuing the weapon with the ability to extract a fae's power and cause illness.

Aeric O'Malley was the Blacksmith, the only fae in the world who could create weapons of charmed iron. His father had once also possessed the same magick, but he'd been badly affected by Watt syndrome at the time of the Great Sweep. These days he wasn't fit for the forge, leaving the family tradition to Aeric.

Making these weapons every night was his ritual, one

he had kept secret from all who knew him. His forge was hidden in the back of his apartment, deep at the base of the Black Tower. The former Shadow King, Aodh Críostóir Ruadhán O'Dubhuir, had been the only one who'd known about his illicit work; he'd been the one to set him up in it.

Now the Unseelie had a Shadow Queen instead of a king. She was a good queen, but one who was still finding her footing in the Black Tower. Queen Aislinn might not look kindly on the fact the Blacksmith was still producing weapons that could be used on his own people. Queen Aislinn wasn't as . . . *practical* as her foul biological father had been.

He pulled off his thick gloves and wiped the back of his arm across his sweat-soaked forehead with a groan of fatigue. The iron called to him at all hours of the day and night. Even after he had done his sacred duty riding in the Wild Hunt every night, the forge summoned him before dawn. He spent most nights fulfilling orders for illegal weaponry or sometimes just making it because he had to, because his fae blood called him to do it. As long as his magick held out, he created.

The walls of his iron world glinted silver and deadly with the products of his labor and in the middle of it all hung Aileen's portrait, the one he'd painted with his own hands so he would never forget what she looked like.

So he never forgot.

Despite the heat and grime of the room, her portrait was still pristine, even as old as it was. Angel pale and golden beautiful, she hung on the wall and gazed down at him with eyes of green, green as the grass of the country she'd died in.

His fingers curled, remembering the softness of her skin and how her silky hair had slipped over his palms and mouth. His gaze caught and lingered on the shape of her mouth. Not that he needed to commit the way she looked to memory. He remembered Aileen Arabella Edmé McIlvernock. His fiancée had looked like an angel, walked like one, thought like one . . . and made love like one. Maybe she hadn't been an angel in all ways—no, definitely not—but his memory never snagged on those jagged places. There was no point in remembering the dark, only the light. And there was no forgetting her. He never would.

Nor would he ever forget her murderer.

Emmaline had managed to escape the Great Sweep and probably Watt syndrome, too. He couldn't know for sure; he just suspected. His gut simply told him she was out there in the world somewhere and he lived for the day he would find her. She'd taken his soul apart the day she'd killed Aileen and he'd never been able to put it completely back together again.

It was only fair he should be able to take Emmaline's soul apart in return. Slowly. Piece by bloody piece.

The chances she'd walk through the gates of Piefferburg and into the web of pain that awaited her was infinitesimal, but tonight, as Aeric gazed at the portrait of Aileen, he hoped for a miracle.

Danu help Emmaline if she ever did cross that threshold into Piefferburg.

He'd be waiting.

ABOUT THE AUTHOR

Annette Blair admits to having fallen *accidentally* into the enchanting world of her characters in visiting the Witch City of Salem, but these days, witches, dragons, and angels are only a small part of the magickal, supernatural ancients inhabiting her high-spirited imagination. She's solving mysteries in one series, and making way for time travelers and werecritters in another, not to mention the return of the old friends you've been asking to see in their own stories. She loves sharing her zany, whimsical worlds and hopes you enjoy them as much.

Please visit her website at www.annetteblair.com.

Enter the tantalizing world
of
paranormal romance

MaryJanice Davidson

Laurell K. Hamilton

Christine Feehan

Emma Holly

Angela Knight

Rebecca York

Eileen Wilks

Berkley authors
take you to a whole new realm

penguin.com

M4G0907

Discover Romance

berkleyjoveauthors.com

See what's coming up next from your favorite romance authors and explore all the latest Berkley, Jove, and Sensation selections.

Fall in love

- See what's new
- Find author appearances
- Win fantastic prizes
- Get reading recommendations
- Chat with authors and other fans
- Read interviews with authors you love

berkleyjoveauthors.com

M1G0907

Enter the rich world of historical romance with Berkley Books.

Lynn Kurland

Patricia Potter

Betina Krahn

Jodi Thomas

Anne Gracie

Love is timeless.
penguin.com

M9G0907